Digby Sherwood

Anthea Ingham

Bright Pen

A Bright Pen Book

British Library Cataloguing Publication Data.
A catalogue record for this book is available from the British Library

ISBN 978-0-7552-1555-3

Authors OnLine Ltd
19 The Cinques
Gamlingay, Sandy
Bedfordshire SG19 3NU
England

This book is also available in e-book format, details of which are available at www.authorsonline.co.uk

Chapter 1

"We believe in our aspirations and we aspire to our beliefs," said Digby Sherwood, Headmaster of Mowberry School, in his beautiful voice. "We succeed because we believe we can," he paused, but only imperceptibly, "one hundred per cent pass rate at Advanced Level, one hundred per cent pass rate at GCSE, an unbeaten first eleven record, six Oxbridge places, five award-winning school plays, the list is endless – but my speech is not, you will be pleased to hear," (this for the boys). May I leave you with our school motto for I believe it says more eloquently than I, all that lies in our hearts, 'Quia posse videntur', 'because the potential is theirs'? Thank you, ladies and gentlemen."

He sat down amidst loud applause, and some members of the first eleven cheered. It was over. It had gone well, just as Martin had said it would when he ran through it with him the previous night.

"Great stuff," he had said reaching for the whisky bottle. "It's the goods, Digs."

"Really, Martin? Are you sure?"

"Of course I'm sure," Martin had replied smiling from behind his glasses, "when have you ever got it wrong?"

And now, Digby thought, as he cast his eyes over the School Hall from his position on the platform, he could relax, for a seemingly endless queue of worthy teenage boys, hair combed and ties straightened, were waiting to receive their prizes.

1

"Lower School Geography Prize, Jason Hawkins," Martin was announcing in his flat midland tones. "Simon Thompson, Middle School History Prize; Prize for exemplary conduct, James Whitman ..." He was assisted by Harold Avonmore, Senior Classics Master, clad in an extraordinary suit, but nevertheless, conveying the prizes to Lord Fawcett, the presenter, in orderly and faultless succession.

After staring straight ahead of him in a suitably impartial headmasterly fashion, Digby moved his head imperceptibly to glance at his young and beautiful wife who sat at his side. Why, oh, why had Elizabeth not worn a longer skirt? Half the school would be able to see her knickers; old Colonel Haslett for one, had his eyeglass in, Digby noticed, and heaven knows what the sixth form would be thinking. Her long, straight, golden hair, which he had insisted she wore up as befitted a headmaster's wife, was already falling about her face in careless profusion. Oh, Elizabeth, why can't you learn?

Elizabeth had forgotten how the skirt rode up when she sat down and, of course, she was on the platform, too, which meant everybody could see everything. She had tried uncrossing her legs to pull it down, but it seemed to go up even further. And Digby would be so cross. He would put that horribly superior look on his face. "Elizabeth," he would say (he always called her by her proper name when he wanted to tell her off), "you must realise that I have a position to keep up. You must behave with some dignity." She had once replied that she knew better than anyone what he liked to keep up, but he had not found it funny at all, and had been sterner than ever. He was always cross with her nowadays, although she did try to be a good wife to him, and a good mother to Ronnie, of course. And the Prize Giving was all so terribly tedious; she looked at the programme and could see there were dozens of boys yet to get prizes, and then there would be the boring old speaker, and the Chairman of the Governors, and then the School Hymn, and all sorts of things going on and on before they could all go off to the marquee and have their strawberries and cream. How stern and important Digby had looked giving his speech! How amazed all those stuffy governors and people would be if they could see Digby in bed with her, panting and groaning. It was silly of him to pretend that wasn't the real Diggy. Of course, he had to have his job and be a Headmaster and things, but what really mattered was the two of them having fun, like they had on the honeymoon. Why had he married her if he hadn't wanted fun?

"Upper School Natural Sciences Prize, Rayvin Chuck Wing Xi," announced Martin Wood, Second Master darting a look of triumph at Digby who had bet him a fiver he would get it wrong.

"Black lace," whispered St John Davies, who was at the back of the queue waiting for the Captain of Cricket Prize. But his friend Simon Stewart made no reply because he could see his mother in the next row, anxiously watching for him to go up on to the platform. Nevertheless, he could see that they *were* black lace. Very transparent black lace, and he could swear he saw blonde hair beneath. If he was the headman he would make his wife wear a longer skirt.

Gowinder Singh, standing next in the prize-winners queue, was distressed by the black lace knickers; he was anxious not to entertain lewd thoughts of any nature, and particularly not in relation to the Headmaster's wife, for did he not owe his whole education to Mr Sherwood, not to mention all the other kindnesses he had done for him?

The audience were getting restless. There were too many prizes altogether, Digby thought. He would talk to Martin about them. Was the school really best served by clever boys getting prizes for being clever? It needed some thought. Still it was good that Gowinder had won three.

"It seems our colonial friend has taken all the prizes," muttered

Lord Jenkins to his disagreeable wife. She, however, merely frowned, she was longing to get out to the tea and talk to everyone about the length of Elizabeth's skirt. She felt a pleasant glow of righteous indignation. A marvellous headmaster like Digby Sherwood married to a woman like that! He really could have done better for himself. Of course, he had been divorced from the first wife and she knew (nobody more so) that men had appetites. Well, they had to learn to sublimate them; it was as simple as that. After all, her husband had managed!

And now the endless queue of prize-winners was finished, and Martin had sat down thankfully behind the lectern with Harold Avonmore next to him. Once the speaker was under way Martin saw Digby fleetingly glance at his watch. Nobody but Martin knew and understood everything Digby did. Ever since they were young house-masters together at Stanstead, they had had a bet on the length of the speech. Was it '73 or '74 when a boy had fainted and the speaker had stopped while he was taken out? Digby and Martin had argued amicably for years afterwards as to whether the five minute break should be added into the speech-time (in which case Martin had won), or if it should be ignored, giving the victory to Digby.

The speaker was every bit as tedious as Digby had known he would be, but it had been necessary to ask him (Martin had agreed), due to the ten thousand he had donated towards the new technology centre.

Digby looked into the heart of the school hall and felt great happiness. In less than three years he had brought the school back into the top league from a run-down, third rate establishment, and he had done it by flair and hard work. He gazed upon the wood panelling and portraits round the walls, the great oak doors at the back, and at the balcony full of boys of all shapes and sizes, who might at any moment do something unexpected, maybe horrible, or even delightful. You never knew with adolescents. Still, he loved to think of them growing up here amidst the beauty of the eighteenth century buildings and the hundred acres of grounds.

His eyes swept the great sloping green lawns that led past the first eleven cricket pitch, and down to the fast moving (and strictly out of bounds) river below, and his heart swelled.

Most of his life had been spent in public schools, as boy, housemaster, headmaster of a minor public school, and finally as Headmaster of Mowberry. He loved the whole public school thing: the bonhomie that existed between staff and boys, the house system, the work ethic, the emphasis on sport, the development of the timid thirteen year old into the Captain of the First XI and, finally, the emotional farewells. It was magic, but it was also extremely hard work, and he could not have done it without Martin.

He thought he could detect his two grown-up daughters at the back, but he could not be sure; it would be good if they came. For a split second he looked for Belinda too. How often he had sat on a platform making a speech, or handing over a house trophy, and seen his first wife suitably, if unfashionably, dressed, looking on with quiet approval. Belinda would have enjoyed today. She would never have worn a skirt like Elizabeth's, but then nor had she satisfied his terrible sexual hunger as Elizabeth did. And even now, as he looked covertly at his second wife's long lovely legs (why had she not put tights on?), he felt the familiar stirring of desire. Thank God Lord Fawcett was coming to an end. Martin had won the bet, of course; Digby was five minutes out.

Harold Avonmore, large, stout and sixty-two, Head of Classics for twenty-five years, was beating time to the music of the school orchestra, on his thigh. His suit, bought some decades earlier, struck a bizarre note on the platform, so that it almost vied for people's attention with Elizabeth's skirt; the trousers were very tight and narrow, and as he sat with his legs crossed, it could be seen that he was wearing immensely thick purple socks, favoured perhaps by alpine walkers, and also, that his flies were held securely in place with a large safety pin. From his position on the platform he could not see Elizabeth, but he could see a number of "nicely-rounded young mothers" in the audience; there was one in particular, wearing something with a sheen to it. Hrrm. The music was tolerable, tolerable, and Sherwood's speech had been excellent – the other chap's execrable. Of course, Digby should never have done away with the Classical Oration, Greek one year, Latin the next. That was in the days when people were properly educated, and not the ignorant young whippersnappers brought up on a diet of pop music and television, such as he saw now. It had been pleasing, however, to hand the prizes to Wood for the speaker to present, since each book contained a hand-written book-plate inscribed by himself. This was an arduous task, his magnum opus, particularly difficult when you had a Chinese like Raynor Chuck Wing Xi, he had been hard put to it to get all the letters in. He could see St John Davies there at the back whispering to that stupid boy, Stewart. He would have to have a word, especially since it was rumoured that Davies was to be the next head boy.

As Martin listened to the music he thought it a pity about Elizabeth's skirt, but not a matter of great importance, Digby was strong enough to carry her through. She was undoubtedly a blemish on his otherwise spotless record, but only a blemish and, after all, she gave Digby what he needed, he supposed. Of course, Belinda would have been better at a function like this, well-turned out and looking every inch a headmaster's wife, but Belinda had not been right for Digby, either. Mostly, however, he wished Jean, his wife, now five years dead, were here. She would have loved to have seen Digby as Headmaster of Mowberry. How nervous she would have been before his speech, and how delighted at its success! Dear Jean.

"In this year of nineteen eighty-two ..." Colonel Haslett, ninety seven, original new boy in 1918 and now Senior Member of the governors, was winding up proceedings. Digby was almost as nervous of this part of the afternoon as he had been of his own speech, for Colonel Haslett was forgetful, often muddling dates and names. In the great long pauses between his words, Digby could sense the growing boredom of the audience. The boys had been good on the whole, but you could not expect too much of them.

"In this year of .." he was starting off again. Would he get the year right this time? An immensely long pause ensued into which the noise was heard of Elizabeth's hair comb slithering out of her silky hair onto the platform floor. There! If only Digby hadn't made her put her hair up, it wouldn't have happened, and now she couldn't bend down and pick it up because of the skirt. She could see everyone staring at her. Perhaps she could edge it under the chair with her foot. The afternoon had gone on so long, and now she thought of it, the tea wouldn't be much fun either, because Digby had said she was to collect Ronnie from Marie-Louise and bring him in his push chair. And she could never work out how to put the brake on properly, and then Ronnie would scream and want to get out, and she wouldn't know what to do, and Diggy would look cross and pick him up, and Ronnie would stop crying immediately.

"This year that takes us from ..." Digby met Martin's eyes. He saw laughter glinting behind the glasses. But mercifully Colonel Haslett had come to an end at last, and boys were nudging each other and dropping programmes and squeaking their chairs in the way boys do when they see release in sight.

St John Davies, Captain of the First XI and potentially the next Head Boy, reckoned he would get out of the back quickly. There might be a couple of bottles of wine left over from the governors' lunch hanging around in the dining room.

Everybody had sung the National Anthem really much too loudly, but Digby knew it was just the boys' way of getting rid of the boredom of the last half an hour. And now the school orchestra was playing them out, and the Headmaster, his wife, Mr Martin Wood, Mr Harold Avonmore, Lord and Lady Jenkins, Colonel Haslett and Lord Fawcett, donator of the ten thousand pounds, were walking out down the central aisle.

"Well done, Digs," mouthed Martin, as they proceeded out of the oak doors at the back of the hall and came out into the sunshine. Digby smiled at him and Elizabeth shook back her hair, as if she didn't care. It was as if there was some secret that belonged just to the two of them that she would never be allowed to share in. Just because Digs and Martin had known each other for hundreds of years, and their stupid old wives had been best mates, there was no need to leave her out. Why couldn't Martin go and get a job somewhere else and leave Digs to her? How gorgeous he looked, standing at the bottom of the steps, smiling at Martin – with that smile he never gave to her, even after she did the best blow job in the world on him.

Chapter 2

"You will observe," said Harold Avonmore, "Pericles' use of the word 'aei'. Perhaps in this word, more than any other – and I trust you remember the positioning of the breathing in the Greek, it is not on the diphthong – is encapsulated Pericles' beliefs about, and aspirations for, the Athenian Empire." He paused and dared them to doubt him. They were a poor lot really, only three A level candidates. Why, he could remember the days when there had been a dozen; there was that glorious year of '59 when he had ten Oxbridge entrants, and five of them scholars. No scholarships now, of course, levelling down, levelling down. Three candidates and one of them a wog, not that he had anything against Indians, certainly not, but there was always the difference of culture ... Still, Singh was the best of the three. Look at Davies; hair all over his face, not concentrating properly, and Steward, a so-called dyslexic. Dyslexic! Hah!

Davies, from his position in the back row, looked surreptitiously at his watch; it was less obvious than looking at the clock in front of Hazzer. Christ! Only ten minutes gone, it was incredible how slowly time went in Greek lessons, if you compared it to other activities. Davies treated himself to a mental view of another, more fulfilling activity.

"And what, Davies, would you say is the main burden of

this speech, which you are privileged, so deeply and, I trust, not unworthily, privileged ..."

The door burst open and a small boy of not more than two or three years entered and surveyed the company. He clasped a large purple rabbit in his arms, which he held out at the big old man by the blackboard. "Rabbit", remarked the small boy conversationally.

Mr Avonmore stood transfixed; it was outside the realm of his experience in all his forty years of teaching (twenty of them in this very room), he had never encountered anything so improper. A Greek verb came into his mind: "aporeo," he said to himself, "I am at a loss".

The small boy might well have been abashed at the sight that lay before him, for it was not a room which many children would have found appealing. In the first place, it smelt, not strongly but still unmistakably, of adolescent boy and chalk and some disinfecting agent which was presumably in use to dispel the pungency of the first two odours. Secondly, the room itself was forbidding, being oak- panelled and hung about with maps of places it seemed unlikely anyone would want to visit. And lastly, Mr Avonmore, large, stout, be-whiskered, clad in an old tweed jacket and voluminous trousers, a fierce and unpleasant look on his face, was the personification of hostility.

Perhaps the child's fearlessness had something to do with the fact that there was welcome on the part of the boys. True, Singh still conned his text diligently, but Davies smiled and Stewart stood up in welcome. However, the more likely reason for the child's continued stance at the door with his hands clutching the rabbit, was due to the fact that schools held no terror for him; he was, after all, the Headmaster's son and the world of Mowberry (pronounced Mawbry by the initiated), was the only world he knew. It was a good world. People were usually very nice to him. He wondered whether this funny fat man would be nice to him, too.

"I ... er... hrrm." Given a class of thirteen - year old boys, or even eighteen- year old boys, Harold Avonmore had no problems,he could crush them, demolish the troublemakers, deal with them almost unthinkingly, but this infant was out of his ken and, furthermore, it belonged to the Headmaster.

Davies held his hands out.

"What's your rabbit called?"

"Ronnie", the child replied.

There was something distressing to Avonmore about Davies' levity. He was finding it difficult to bring himself back from fifth century Athens, and there was Davies carrying on, as if he was positively welcoming the distraction. Stewart, too, was grinning inanely, but then he was a stupid boy. Only Singh was behaving in a sensible and scholarly fashion.

The small boy advanced further into the stronghold and tugged at a map that was hanging uncertainly.

"Wot's that?" he asked.

"Mind! Mind!" Exclaimed Avonmore. "It's a most valuable map showing the relative positions of Pylos and Sphacteria." Suddenly inspiration dawned. "Where is your mother?" he demanded sternly. But his words were lost as the child explored the possibilities of a desk-lid. He raised it high and let the lid bang to. It made a pleasing sound.

"Shall I go and look for Mrs Sherwood, Sir?" asked Davies eagerly. What a bit of luck, this kid turning up!

"I'll go, Sir," said the stupid Stewart, standing up and knocking his copy of Thurcydides off the desk in his haste.

"If I can be any help, Sir?" ventured Singh from his texts.

Mr Avonmore felt a sensation akin to fear; he could see a situation where he was left alone with this demon, who was even now walking along the row of desks at the back, lifting the lids and allowing them to fall, with increasing vehemence.

In the event, nobody needed to go, for Mrs Sherwood appeared, a true *dea ex machina*, in the doorway. She was not unaware of three pairs of adolescent eyes upon her. Perhaps she was more interested in them, than she was in her son, and she certainly noticed them before she noticed Mr Avonmore.

"Good morning, Elizabeth," said Davies, for the Headmaster was progressive and liked the boys to call his wife by her Christian name.

"Mummy, Mummy!" The child threw the rabbit on the floor and ran to his mother. She picked him up and smiled at them all. She was fully aware of her appearance, and knew that her son with his head buried in her well-shaped breast made an attractive accessory.

Davies went on smiling politely. His eyes noted that three buttons of her shirt were undone and, as she struggled to hold her son, another was about to pop. He noted too the tightness of the jeans, and wondered how the Head Man had any time left to run the school after servicing her. She looked as though she'd like to be at it all the time. But then, who wouldn't?

Singh cast his eyes toward Pericles' Funeral Oration, and tried to concentrate on what Mr Avonmore had said before the interruption. He saw Davies nudge Stewart and felt a sense of shame; Davies was foul, the antithesis of everything Mr Sherwood stood for. It was not right to make disrespectful insinuations about such a good man's wife. Davies slid his hand under the desk and had a quick feel. Mmm. Perhaps he would ask old Hazzer if he could go to the bog when she'd gone.

Elizabeth liked standing there with four men looking at her and smiled happily. She looked even prettier when she smiled. She wished, though, that Ronnie would stop kicking her. She was only five years older than these boys, nearer in age to them, than she was to her husband, by twenty-five years. Mornings were often long and boring, and she thought how amusing it would be to show how old and silly the Classics teacher looked, standing at the blackboard with a lot of boring old Latin on it. Fancy spending your life doing that!

"Oh Mr Avonhirst," she said, opening her large blue eyes very wide, (had she got his name right?). "Ronnie and I have disturbed your Latin lesson." She tossed back the long straight blond hair, and waited for him to say something nice to her. She put Ronnie down because he was hurting her.

"Greek," he said.

"Sorry?" Elizabeth was thrown. What on earth did he mean?

Seeing her confusion he continued, "this is ah …" he indicated the blackboard which was covered in Greek sentences, "this is.. ah … a Greek lesson."

"Oh!" said Elizabeth, managing to suggest by the "oh", that if you thought that mattered, there must be something wrong with you.

"Rabbit," said Ronnie.

"Here it is", said Davies, picking it up and using the opportunity of returning it for a clearer inspection of Elizabeth's tits. Yes, he'd definitely have to go to the bog afterwards.

Nor was Harold Avonmore averse to female beauty, and it struck him forcefully what a very attractive woman Elizabeth Sherwood was. It was a pity she was an ignorant one, but a lack of Latin and Greek might be pardoned in a woman of beauty. He felt inclined to make a pleasant gesture, now that she was about to depart. After all, they had only lost a few minutes, and he could make it up at the end of the morning. He wouldn't begrudge ten minutes of his lunch-hour. What should he say? Perhaps a humorous remark would be the best: something amusing with a Classical allusion. The child had shown a great deal of strength in banging the desk lids down.

"I'm afraid we have no snakes here for the young Hercules to strangle," he smiled gallantly.

"His name's Ronnie, actually," said Elizabeth, seeming puzzled, "and why should there be any snakes?"

Singh looked up and sighed inwardly that such an erudite man as Mr Sherwood, should be married to such a young and ignorant woman. Mr Avonmore felt acute embarrassment.

"I'm Ronnie," cried the child.

"A literary Classical reference," said Mr Avonmore faintly.

Suddenly Elizabeth Sherwood felt bored. Anyway, she remembered now there were some parents coming to lunch. She would sit next to the husband and be terribly nice to him, because Diggy said she must make an effort with parents, and the husbands were more fun than the wives, who often looked at her quite nastily. Well, she wouldn't bother with the wife, though it might be fun to try making her jealous.

"Come on, Ronnie," she said. "We mustn't disturb Mr Avebury's Latin lesson." She shot a furtive look at the good-looking blond boy with all the hair, she could see he fancied her rotten.

"Come on, Ronnie," she said again more urgently, and picked him up, because she knew he would most certainly not do what she told him otherwise. He was never good for her in the way he was with his father.

"Pericles' funeral oration," began Harold Avonmore sternly as the door closed. There would be no further wasting of time.

"Excuse me, Sir?" It was Davies again.

"Yes!"

"Sir, I have to go to the lavatory."

"Can't it wait?"

"Not really, Sir"

"Oh, very well!"

"Wanker" mouthed Stewart as Davies made for the door.

"And what, Singh, are the main claims of Pericles in this speech that we are all so privileged to hear?"

As Gowinder held forth and Avonmore nodded his head, Stewart reflected that Davies was certainly taking his time. Mentally he compared the size of Elizabeth's tits with those of his girlfriend, Melissa. Melissa, he reflected contentedly, won hands down.

Davies returned to the classroom just as the bell went.

"I trust you will catch up what you have missed, Davies."

"Sir."

"I should advise consulting Singh, as it is no use asking Stewart, I'm afraid."

"Certainly, Sir." He watched Avonmore depart and saw that Singh was determined to do his duty.

"Davies, I could tell you now what Mr Avonmore ..."

"Sod off, Singh," was St John's only response. "I want to talk to Stewart. White men's talk."

Gowinder made no reply, but put his books methodically into his case. He was used to Davies. He was just one of the many things he had learned to ignore in order to pursue this superior education.

Stewart paused in his search for the board rubber and struck an Avonmore pose in front of the blackboard. "Enjoy your wank, Davies?" he asked sonorously.

Davies nodded dismissively, for a new thought had occurred to him on his way back from the lavatories. "Would be better to do the real thing."

"Oh yes, like you could."

"I bet I could."

"How much?"

"Well," said St John thoughtfully. "There could be a sort of sliding scale."

"What?"

"So much for snogging – say a fiver. Then so much for tits – a tenner – and call it fifty quid for a fuck."

"And how am I supposed to know you've done it?"

"I'll get proof," said Davies casually.

Stewart laughed as he rubbed the Greek off the board. What a bull-shitter Davies was.

Chapter 3

Digby Sherwood lay in bed, pondering the question of his wife. It was now two in the morning and he felt as wakeful as he had at eleven when he had gone to bed, made love to Elizabeth, and immediately dressed again and gone to his study to do a couple of hours work. This was his usual practice; he was a man who had much to do and who needed little sleep.

He regarded the naked figure of his sleeping wife and asked himself the question that he often asked: was she worth it? Nowadays, he doubted it. That she was lovely, very lovely, was undeniable; that she could please him, delight him, give him exquisite pleasure was irrefutable, but sadly, that seemed to have been the only skill he had been successful in teaching her. He doubted now that she would learn much else from him, even if he had the time to teach her. Poor Elizabeth! She was not a bad woman, he reflected, merely shallow and very limited.

"Running a public school is a twenty-four hour job," he had told her when he first tried to explain what marriage to the Headmaster of such a school would involve. "I shall be able to spend very little time with you."

"Even in bed?" she asked in her silly way.

"Even in bed," he said.

"Darling Diggy ..."

"Do you understand?"

"Diggy?"

"Yes or no?"

"Yes, Diggy."

On the other hand, he had explained, she would have money to spend, and little to do but entertain. He felt she would be capable of that, not at first, perhaps, but she would learn and become a perfectly acceptable wife for the Headmaster of Mowberry. Of course, she would never be as good as Belinda who had been the perfect headmaster's wife, and whom everyone had respected, boys, parents, colleagues, everyone. She was such a lady – perhaps too much of a lady, and not enough of a woman, that was the trouble: sex was of no interest to her, it was even distasteful. And he wanted more than physical satisfaction; he wanted a woman who would excite him with her own sensuality, and who would demand and take, as avidly as he.

Belinda and he had been childhood sweethearts, and they had continued going out all the time he was at Oxford and she at Leicester, and when they both graduated, they married.

It hadn't really mattered at the beginning that Belinda wasn't interested in sex, for they were very fond of each other, and that was almost enough. And there was so much else in their lives, with the school and running the Boys' House. And Belinda was a wonderful housemaster's wife. Later, when Digby became Headmaster of Brooks, a minor public school, she had become an equally splendid Headmaster's wife, for Belinda was firm and kind, efficient and sensible; and Belinda, like Digby, came from an old county family, a thing which went down well with the parents. They enjoyed the same company, too, and the Woods were close friends, since Martin, too, had been a housemaster and his wife, Jean, as good a housemaster's wife, as Belinda was, but in a different way; she was less formal. Their children grew up together, and they spent holidays together too, and it was on one such holiday where they were sharing a cottage in Wales that Digby, lying late one night with Belinda asleep by his side, heard Jean in bed with Martin, and it was brought home to him that there were women who enjoyed sex, and that Jean was one of them. After the birth of Richenda, Belinda became more difficult about sex. Whereas previously she had treated the subject as rather a bore, her attitude changed to one of distaste. Digby was courteous and reasonable.

"Please, Belinda," he would say. "I can't manage without it, I can't concentrate on things."

"I'm sorry, darling?" she said, "it's just not me really." Then she stopped taking the pill too, so the whole thing became as difficult as possible.

When Digby was offered a lectureship at Granchester, it had seemed a good sideways move; he had been housemaster, headmaster of a minor public school and now with a little academic kudos, he might aim still higher.

Belinda was quite happy with the idea. She had recently gone back to teaching at the local Girls' School; she enjoyed her job and didn't want to give it up; furthermore, they both felt it was important to see Richenda through her last year at school without uprooting her. There seemed no reason why Digby should not have rooms on campus and return home most week-ends, and university terms were short, anyway. Belinda knew Digby was ambitious and she supported him all the way, but she also knew it was important to develop herself intellectually, so she became a more worthy partner to him. Digby admired intelligence in a woman and believed in the value of fulfilled potential.

Perhaps his motives were not quite so pure. The possibility of extra-marital sex passed through his mind, and he did not entirely dismiss the possibility. His youth had been passed before the pill was widely available; he remembered girls being extremely apprehensive about full intercourse, and had permitted little more than what he had known as 'heavy petting'. But times had moved on and the old fears long gone. Girls, he now discovered, were as eager as he, for sex.

Nevertheless, he was astounded at the ease with which it came his way, for Digby, courteous, sympathetic, good-looking and affluent, was an extremely desirable commodity. And, beset as he was by temptation, he yielded. He was amazed at what women were prepared to do for his pleasure, and astounded by what he discovered.

And yet he was racked with guilt; he knew what a good wife Belinda had been to him, he was very fond of her and he loathed deceit. When he returned home after his first term, he confessed to her that he had made love to more than one other woman, and he told her without trying to make excuses.

"I wanted it, Belinda," he said, "and I did it. I cannot tell you it will not happen again."

Belinda, whom he had only known to have cried once, and that at Jean's funeral, wept unrestrainedly, and he was unable to comfort her. He had always been honest with Belinda; he had too much respect for her to fob her off with half-truths now, and yet he knew that she would not accept infidelity. They both knew there was no solution, he would not change, and she could not live with his behaviour. In the end she asked for a divorce.

It was a dreadful Christmas, with Dolores siding with her mother, and Richenda full of anger, with Digby, her mother and herself, for she could not accept that any of them should fall below the high standards expected in the Sherwood household. Rather than subject his wife and daughters to further displays of domestic strife, he agreed to the divorce and returned to university life. He lost count of the number of girls he had gone to bed with. He was not proud of himself, but confused as to where his life was tending. Perhaps Martin could have helped him through this patch, but he was learning to cope with Jean's recent death, and Digby did not wish to burden him with his own problems.

And then the Headship of Mowberry came up. It was so exactly what Digby had always wanted, a major public school that had seen better days and needed someone with authority, to pull it together.

There was a strong field, but Digby was chosen. He had been afraid that the divorce would go against him, but he had an otherwise blameless record, and he was a man who commanded the governors' immediate respect. His name, too, was well known in the Headmasters' Conference as an up- and -coming man. And there was an additional piece of good luck, the Chairman of the Governors had been at school with his father.

He was happier than he had been for years. But he reflected that all the sex he had become so used to over the last year or so, would be no longer available once he was Headmaster. Besides, a Headmaster needed a wife (so much had been hinted to him), and he decided he must remarry. Two weeks later he invited some students to his flat for drinks. One of them brought Elizabeth. She was just twenty.

He knew she was not ideal; he also knew the governor of Mowberry would be unpleasantly surprised when he suddenly produced a wife half his age, but he decided to do it, anyway. She satisfied his desires, and he had fallen prey to his weaknesses – impetuosity, arrogance and a constant need for sexual satisfaction.

He had spent many years of his life as a housemaster, and was used to getting the best out of young people; developing character was one of the qualities that people associated with Digby, and he believed Elizabeth had potential.

He knew she was not bright, but he was prepared to attribute her lack of academic success to the early break-up of her parents' marriage, and more recently to the uninspiring nature of her college course. If Elizabeth was guided into the right channels, she would lose any silliness she had, and develop into a fine young woman.

As he looked back he realised with remorse that her beauty had blinded him to exactly how limited she was. Elizabeth was not unwilling to learn; it was simply that she had no capacity to do so.

He had not pressured her and had spelt out, as far as he could judge, what her life would be like as the wife of a headmaster, but he had not been able to envisage what a huge amount of work Mowberry would entail. Elizabeth didn't listen anyway. She hated the college, she liked Digby, and was thrilled by the idea of being a Headmaster's wife. She imagined five hundred boys all looking at her, and thought what fun it would all be.

Nevertheless, Digby knew that all would not run smoothly unless he made concrete plans for the future. Elizabeth must be kept busy and not allowed to sit about doing nothing – something she did far too much of, in Digby's opinion. So he arranged for her to embark on a new course at the Art School in the nearby town of Hopton. He decided that she should regard the course as a nine-to-five job, and in the evenings she would enjoy gong to school functions with him, and take a full part in the activities of the school.

However, it didn't work like that because Elizabeth lost her supply of the pill on the island of Cos and didn't dare tell Digby. The result was that she came back from her honeymoon pregnant.

As soon as Digby took up his duties at Mowberry, she started on the Art course, but was dreadfully sick in the mornings and didn't feel like driving six miles into Hopton, and gave up the course, without consulting Digby. He, for his part, was enormously busy, working all day and half the night. To be honest, in those early days he didn't much mind what Elizabeth did, so long as he could get on with his job.

She didn't mind too much either, because she was generally happy doing nothing, and she was still enjoying the novelty value of marriage and her position in the school.

Digby thought things would improve once she had had the baby. Belinda and Jean had both been excellent mothers, and he had a vague feeling that all women must be so, by nature. But Elizabeth had been terrified of the baby and couldn't manage to breastfeed. Digby was up half the night with bottles. He could see that this would not do, and a series of au pairs ensued, but Elizabeth couldn't get on with them, and they didn't stay long. When it came to the fifth au pair, Digby said that Elizabeth must see to it that this one did stay, as there would be no one else. He hated his son being brought up in this way and determined there should be no more children so he had a vasectomy in the Easter holiday, for he could not trust Elizabeth to remember to take the pill.

As time went on, he began to see how hopeless she was. In fact, everything that everyone had said, seemed to be true, Martin, his mother, practically everyone. She was completely unsuitable.

Today, for instance, he had had two prospective parents to lunch. Elizabeth should have been there to hand out the sherry, but she was late, and he had to do it himself. She had almost totally ignored the wife and she had got the husband's name wrong. In fact, one of the few constants about Elizabeth was that she seemed almost totally incapable of remembering names. But these were customers, for God's sake! You were talking five times twelve thousand for the five years the boy would be at Mowberry, plus all the extras: money for music lessons, the Buttery, and heaven only knows what; when all was said and done, you weren't far off a hundred K. And she hadn't sold it to them. OK, they weren't much cop, didn't know what to do with a knife and fork and so on, but you had to take parents as you found them; it was the raw material of their offspring you had to work on, that was what made it all worthwhile. To take a boy at thirteen, shy and homesick, and steer him through adolescence until he finally emerged as a fine young man in the Upper VI with a University place, and heading for the successful future that Mowberry had equipped him to deal with, that was all that mattered; and they had lost the two parents today.

He moved his right hand down over his wife's firm breasts and erect nipples, felt her flat stomach (he had feared she would lose that after Ronnie), and down to the nub of it all, hot and moist and sticky. He inserted his fingers. He'd wake her up, and make love to her in a minute. What was it the boys said about girls nowadays? Fit,. that was it.

Well, Elizabeth was certainly fit, but 'fitness' was inappropriate to a headmaster's wife – or at least, it should be disguised beneath elegant, well-cut clothes; after all, he gave her enough money, but she preferred jeans and tiny shirts, such as the girlfriends of his sixth formers might wear. But it wasn't just a question of clothes, it was her whole style; she had no idea how to behave, and he shuddered as she made one faux pas after another.

On the other hand, although in most respects Digby was a modest man with no personal vanity with regard to his good looks, keen brain and successful career, he did have a naive and almost childish liking for status symbols. He was proud of his daughters' beauty and academic success. He drove an XJ6, and shamefacedly gained an immense and secret pleasure from the fact that Elizabeth was a desirable woman, and was seen to belong to him. He found it immensely pleasing, for example, when she came to fetch him from external meetings. Take the HMC, the Headmaster's Conference, for instance, she had turned up in the new XJ6 at the end of the conference, it had been one of those hot summer days – in a pair of tiny denim shorts and a bare midriff. Half of them thought she was his daughter.

"I don't think you've met my wife Elizabeth," he said to Graham Sutherland, HM of Mapleton, who'd always tried to patronise him, and who had opposed him on the matter of GCSE starred A's. He had placed his arm lightly, but proprietarily on Elizabeth's shoulder.

"Elizabeth, I should like you to meet my colleague, Graham Sutherland." And Elizabeth had run her hands through her golden mane and smiled her sexy smile. He knew that Graham would swap him any amount of GCSE's or, probably, Mapleton itself, for a night with his wife.

No, perhaps he wasn't being fair to Elizabeth in the matter of the lost parents; what was the name? Cockburn – and Elizabeth kept calling them Cox. No, he shouldn't have let Davies show them round, well, Davies was all right – staff thought well of him, should make Oxbridge, but because the boy was doing Classics, it had seemed natural to take the parents to Avonmore's domain. He played idly with Elizabeth as he went over events in his mind.

"Well, Mr Sherwood," Mr Cockburn had said, "I can see you've got the new Technology Centre and all that, but what I say is, what are you doing with those rubbish subjects? That boy of yours took us to some room where there was this old geezer going on about Latin verse. I mean, what's the point of Latin verse in this day and age? And it wouldn't have been so bad if the kids were interested, but they weren't. They looked bored off their arses!"

"Ssshh", the wife had said.

"Well, they were, Trace. You said so yourself."

No, he extracted his fingers and rolled over to bite a nipple. It was a shame about Avonmore. He had intended to keep him on to retirement, but he would have to go. Put something in, instead of

Classics, something to pull a few into the sixth form: Psychology, Business Studies.... He'd have to look into it.

"Want to fuck, Liz," he said, moving very agilely for a man of forty-eight. It was a statement, not a question. Anyway, Elizabeth always wanted to; she never minded being woken up for it."

"Dig deep, Diggy," she muttered sleepily, in her stupid way. He was, however, happy to ignore the naive phraseology, and to deal with the request in a thoroughly efficient manner. He was, in every sense, a high flyer.

Chapter 4

Digby Sherwood was not the only person to be awake at two o'clock in the morning; Harold Avonmore found insomnia an increasing problem of late, but as organised a man in his own way as his Headmaster, he had found various means of dealing with it. Before retiring he filled a vacuum flask with tea and made sure his bedside biscuit barrel was well supplied. He had some excellent biscuits, the very same he had eaten as a child, a mixture of shortbread and oatcake; he had been delighted to discover, through a small advertisements in the Sunday Times, a firm in Dumfries who still made the biscuits. He had placed a regular order, and it was pleasing, nay exciting, to open the parcel once a month and unwrap the contents. Only once had he cause for complaint, when he had received a consignment of plastic mice in error. Apparently the firm was not, as he had imagined, a small family concern, but a large warehouse distributing internationally. He feared that was the way it was all going nowadays.

Also, upon his bedside table lay a selection of Classical texts; these were not for use in the classroom. These were for Avonmore's private consumption. "Ancient Erotica" was perhaps his favourite night-time reading. Harold's interest was really quite innocent, he would no more have considered putting into practice the activities shown in the books, than he would have wished to visit Greece or Rome, but he liked knowing they were there.

It was his habit to retire early after completing various duties around the school: checking the library, collecting lost property, locking the doors and so on. Once he had been a housemaster, but he had given this up some ten years since. He was glad he had, there was nothing but laxity there nowadays.

After retirement he would fall into a deep and dreamless sleep, worn out with the pressures of the day, but his brain, perhaps refreshed by a couple of hours sleep, and a consultation of "Ancient Erotica", began to assert itself, and then he would begin to dream.

Tonight it seemed to him that Mrs Sherwood appeared just as she had that very morning, but here (he subsequently reflected while eating his biscuit), what was so interesting, was the fact that she was wearing no clothes, absolutely nothing, and he could see that her figure was, well, extremely desirable. She was approaching Stewart, that stupid boy, with a provocative expression on her face, "I can cure your dyslexia," she was saying. "Come with me." And then it seemed as if he had become Stewart, or Stewart (God forbid!) had become him, and he was following Mrs Sherwood into the bookroom (where he kept all the copies of the Ancient History texts); then she looked at him sharply.

"You're not Stewart," she said. "You're just a dirty old man. Let me out of this cupboard!"

And here was what was so inexplicable: he found himself saying, "Oh no, Mrs Sherwood, I am going to have sexual intercourse with you." And although he couldn't understand how he could be daring to do it, he had her pinned between the big *Liddell and Scott* Greek Lexicon and the box of old O'level papers (which he had been meaning to sort out), and he was guiding himself into Mrs Sherwood's pudenda and oh and oh and oh, and aah!

Of course, ancient authors had plenty to say about dreams; here Harold Avonmore moved a little to avoid coming into contact with the wet patch in the bed: there was the *Somnium Scipionis*, both Cicero and Pliny were full of references to dreams, and, indeed, you only had to look at Virgil to see how many times Pater Anchises appeared to Aeneas, although possibly, this was not particularly relevant.

It was quite simple really, (perhaps he would boil a kettle and fill a hot water bottle to dry off that slight dampness), he was overworked and overtired. Admittedly, hard work never hurt anyone, but then again, boys weren't as they had been in the heady old days of 1959. Nowadays it was an uphill struggle to get children to learn anything. He put his hand out gingerly to assess the extent of the damp patch. Not too bad really, although his pyjama trousers were a little moist. No, he wouldn't be able to change them, his other pair were in the dirty laundry box. He sniffed at his fingers and took a sip of tea. Take this afternoon: he had been going through Martial's epigrams with the lower fifth, something he always enjoyed. Of course, only a few bits of Martial were suitable for adolescents, but this was "non te amo, Sabine", a masterpiece – it was so succinct and witty it made him laugh out loud. And then he liked to treat them to that famous translation:

> *I do not like thee, Dr Fell*
> *The reason why, I cannot tell*
> *But this I know, and know full well*
> *I do not like thee, Dr Fell.*

A little masterpiece. And he had just got to "cannot tell" when the door opened (the second interruption that day), and there was Davies (hair hanging all over his face, of course), showing parents round.

"Excuse me, Sir. May I introduce Mr and Mrs Cockburn, who are looking round Mowberry as a possible school for their son?"

Harold had smiled and shaken hands, noticing what poor calibre they were – no wonder the boys he taught these days were so weak – no style, no class, no nothing. The wife looked half-witted. Still they had come at the right time. They would be amused by *Dr Fell*, and they would see that Latin still had an important role to play. And he had bade them wait while he read the original Latin, had given a literal translation, and then read *Dr Fell* out. He had waited for their laughter.

His words fell on silence, at least, not quite silence because he could see Fowler whispering to Turner at the back, and showing him something distinctly unclassical. But, apart from that, nobody showed any reaction, except Mannering who was yawning. It was Davies who stepped in.

"Have you seen all you want, Mr Cockburn, Mrs Cockburn?" he asked. "Or would you like to stay a little longer?"

"No, I don't want to stay here," the odious man Cockburn had replied. "I'm more interested in the twentieth century. I haven't got much use for dead stuff." And Davies had shown them out. Only the wife had smiled weakly and said, "Thank you for the Greek" and gone out. Greek!

He had relieved Fowler of an extraordinarily unpleasant magazine called "Viz". He had examined it thoroughly this evening, out of a sense of duty, and had been amazed by its explicit nature.

No wonder he had bad dreams. Perhaps he wouldn't bother with the hot water bottle.

Chapter 5

When Digby awoke around six, as he often did, he was painfully aware of what he privately termed to himself 'his rising call'. For a few seconds he hesitated, torn between the conflicting demands of mind and body. On this occasion, the mind won and he got out of bed straight away to avoid further temptation. He realised that a desire for sexual gratification was gaining a hold on him.

When he had washed, dressed and shaved, he went down the corridor to see Ronnie, who slept in a room adjacent to the au pair's.

He entered the room which Marie-Louise kept in impeccable order, and went to look at his sleeping son. As he gazed on the two-year old child, he was overcome with a sense of guilt, for he felt none of that spontaneous affection that he had felt for his daughters when they were small. Dolores had been sweet and tender and he had loved her incipient femininity. Richenda had drawn him to her by the challenge she had presented, with her fierceness and her tantrums. And then, of course, he and Belinda had worked so hard as a team to bring them up, and the girls, in turn, had gone from strength to strength.

Why could Elizabeth not cope with Ronnie? She had no idea how to bring out the best in a child. Perhaps she did not have enough love for him – or perhaps he himself was to blame, he ought to spend more time with his son, but time was such a precious commodity. Still, something must be done.

His eye fell on a large, purple rabbit lying on the floor; it had been Elizabeth's mother's one and only present to her grandchild. She had made it clear from the start that she had as little wish to be known as a grandmother, as she had had as a mother, having early left Elizabeth's father to go and live in Spain with a succession of husbands and lovers. She had not been seen since their wedding, thank God. She was an awful woman. He picked up the rabbit, which he thought hideous, but because he knew Ronnie adored it, put it carefully into bed with him, and bent down and kissed his forehead. A thought crossed his mind that Ronnie was very like Elizabeth in character.

He went downstairs into the kitchen and made himself coffee in the cafetière (he could not drink instant), and glanced through the newspaper. He liked to make mention of some current event when he held his morning assemblies. Then he went through his diary, checking the meetings and appointments for the day.

Opening the front door, he went down the dozen, broad stone steps which led from the front of the eighteenth century house, down to the rose garden. He stopped and looked over towards the river, the morning was still slightly hazy, and there was dew underfoot.

In the garden (strictly private), Digby picked himself a yellow rose, it lay dewy, with the petals slightly open, and was pale and very soft to the touch, as was the hair that lay about Elizabeth's moist folds. Digby placed it in his button hole.

He liked to be around the school early in the morning, not just for the thrill of its beauty, as the sun hazily rose over the clock tower with the river behind, but so he could see what the boys were up to. Who were the early men? Why were they up so early? Whom were they trying to avoid? What problems racked their adolescent souls, or what nefarious business were they pursuing? There was Davies, for example, coming out of School House. Why did he not trust this boy, with his smiling, friendly ways, whom everyone except Martin and himself, wanted to make Head Boy?

"You're up early, Davies."

"Yes, Sir. Trying to keep fit."

"Is this a regular regime or a one-off venture?"

"Regular, Sir. Everymorning, Sir." Thank God he'd got rid of the Bacardi bottle in the kitchen dustbin before the Headman appeared. Someone would probably be accused of drinking the bloody thing, but at least it wouldn't be St John Davies. After all, that was the secret of success at school, wasn't it; doing what you wanted and making sure the Headman blamed someone else? Elegant sod with the rose in his button-hole! Sherwood thought one hell of a lot of himself. Well, he hadn't forgotten his plans for Elizabeth. How cool would that be!

Digby smiled dismissively. He resolved to keep an eye on Davies.

He strolled down towards the river and wished he had time to walk over to Martin's bungalow on the edge of the village. It was not an attractive building, having been hastily erected in the late forties to provide extra staff accommodation, but was, he reflected, rather like Martin, solid and serviceable, familiar and reassuring. Occasionally he called in early and they made themselves bacon and eggs in Martin's desperately chaotic kitchen. Martin would drop things and burn himself and Digby would then take over because he was better at some things that Martin – which, after all was why he was Headmaster, and Martin his deputy.

And there was Martin now, coming out from the School Hall. What had he been doing? Oh, the start of GCSE's. He would have been checking everything was in order. Martin would allow no one but himself to attend to such jobs.

Digby stood and watched the familiar squat figure moving to and fro in the portico, pinning up notices, taking others down. Martin should not drink so much, he thought. He had put on a hell of a lot of weight since Jean had died, but perhaps it suited him, along with his scanty hair and heavy glasses. It gave him a comfortable mother-hen air. And now Martin had seen him, but Digby knew he would not come down to the river to join him, for Martin always let Digby make the first move, whether in connection with ideas for a new trust-fund or just arranging a meeting.

"Martin!" Digby set off up the path towards him, and Martin felt the surge of pleasure that he always experienced on seeing Digby unexpectedly. As he waited, he saw a yellow rose fall from his button hole. But although Digby must have seen it go, he did not stop to pick it up, but allowed it to remain on the gravel of the path as he walked on towards Martin on the steps of the portico. Martin reflected that he would have picked the flower up and probably put it in water. Not so, Digby, he was concerned with greater things, the details he left to Martin.

Chapter 6

Harold knew there was something up when Sherwood made a fuss about the coffee. Since when ... (always a difficult construction to put into Latin, easier in Greek) ... Since when had Digby bothered about the quality of coffee offered to staff? But perhaps he was being unfair, for he must admit that Digby was always a conscientious host.

"Ah Harold," Digby had said, "do sit down. Make yourself comfortable."

And his secretary, Felicity, staid, matronly and unpleasant, had sailed into view, bearing a Wedgwood cup, saucer, sugar bowl, tongs and plate, and there were to be biscuits too, biscuits with thick rich dark chocolate over them, such as were offered to prospective parents.

"Take a couple, Harold," Digby had said. He ate none himself. "I'm told they're excellent."

Harold told him that the only biscuits he ate came from Dumfries, and he explained about the special order, and (because he felt a sense of well-being, sitting on the HM's chintz sofa in his extremely elegant drawing room), even about the consignment of plastic mice.

"How extraordinary!" Sherwood had said, and Harold immediately regretted telling him, although he could not exactly say why. And then Sherwood had evinced his concern about the coffee.

"Is this coffee strong enough for you, Harold?" He asked, his brow furrowed with concern, "and I'm not convinced it's frightfully hot. Felicity!" (for the unpleasant secretary was almost at the door), "please bring us some more coffee. This is undrinkable."

"Oh, it's quite all right!" said Harold, "I seldom drink coffee nowadays. With advancing years I find I prefer tea."

"Tea! Felicity, could I trouble you for a pot of tea for Mr Avonmore?" And they had waited until Felicity returned with a second Wedgwood cup, but he noticed she had not brought in a pot as she had been asked, the tea was ready-made in the cup (probably with a bag.) And this time Digby did not ask him if it was all right. In fact, he sensed an unaccustomed sense of nervousness on Sherwood's part. He felt it incumbent on him to make things pleasant.

"Is it about the book-plates, Headmaster?" he asked, although he knew it couldn't be, with Prize Giving only just over.

"No, no, nothing like that," said Digby. That was something else, of course. It was all going to be done on computer next year. Another way in which poor old Harold would become redundant.

And even now, Digby was loath to make a start on it. He did not like making people suffer, but it was an unfortunate fact of life, that in his position, he was often forced to do so. There had been the distressing expulsion of three normally quite law-abiding boys last year (one of them Oxbridge material too), but an uncompromising line must be taken where drugs were concerned. Anyway, a frightful business with the boys crying and one of the fathers trying to bribe him to let his son stay. And now this Avonmore business, better get it over with.

"I'm afraid this is going to come as a bit of a shock to you, Harold," he said, putting the tips of his fingers together, 'steepling' Martin and he called it. He wished fervently that it was still politically correct to smoke. He would have dearly liked a cigarette, and offering Harold one would have eased the tension.

And although Harold knew something unpleasant was going to come, he still had no notion how unpleasant, as he gazed around the drawing room.

It was a truly beautiful room. Most of Mowberry was eighteenth century, and the Headmaster's house was a little gem with its high-moulded ceilings and Adam fireplaces. And then, of course, the interior design of the drawing room had been done by one of the most expensive firms in London. The great curtains hung in high festooned cascades of flowers, each flower hand printed on silk from an eighteenth century botanical book. The walls, too, were covered in the finest watered silk and were of a particularly pure green, putting one in mind of a lagoon or picture by Monet. It was as if the river Mow itself had taken a slow meander around the walls before returning to the turbulent waters which flowed alongside the school boundaries. For the room offered a fine view of the water, out beyond the rose garden – both of which were, naturally, out of bounds to the boys. The furniture (Adam again), cost four figures every year, just to insure, (no wonder Ronnie wasn't allowed in here). The mantelpiece contained an ornate clock and a Dresden shepherdess, who marshalled not sheep, but invitations to various events, easily recognisable to prospective parents: the words 'Henley' and 'Burlington House' appearing. The carpet on which Harold Avonmore's large feet and purple socks now rested, had been woven in some faraway village in Iran, where entire families might well have lost their eyesight in its manufacture. An exquisite barley-sugar legged table stood between the two men, it held a photograph of Digby's wife and son. The photo of Elizabeth contained only her top third which seemed to be virtually unclothed, and which reminded Harold unpleasantly of the previous night's dream. A portrait of Digby's two daughters hung over the grand piano, and every time Harold looked up he could see Digby's reflection in the huge gilt mirror hanging over the fireplace.

And, of course, the very fact that he had been invited by Sherwood into this Aladdin's palace, and not into the more mundane study, boded some extraordinary intent on Digby's part. Quite possibly, he was minded to dismiss Wood and appoint a senior man in his stead; now he might well be intending to sound him out on such a subject. "What we need, Mr Avonmore, may I call you Harold…?" He might say, "is a man versed in Classical learning."

"I have to tell you, Harold, that I have taken the decision to phase out Classics."

The blow was so tremendous that Harold nearly dropped the Wedgwood cup and its sour contents, only recovering just in time, to put it down next to the semi-naked Elizabeth. It was a tremendous shock, so tremendous that he could not immediately take it in. He was as much a part of Mowberry as … as the School Hall. Digby's words made no sort of sense.

"I hardly understand you, Headmaster."

"It's something I've been thinking about for some time." This was not entirely untrue. He had had it in the back of his mind for a while, and had been meaning to discuss it with Martin, but it had come to him with extraordinary clarity last night, prior to making love to Elizabeth. Since his marriage, he had observed as a sound principle, that if a decision under consideration ante-fuck was still tending the same way post-fuck, it was probably the right one.

"I feel, Harold," he said, (Mr Cockburn's words ringing in his ears), "we have to move into the twenty-first century. And sadly, and I do say 'sadly', Harold, with the constraints of the curriculum, and the plethora of new subjects abounding, we cannot …" and here he held up his hand to stop any interruption, "we cannot, I say, afford the time given to the Classics."

"You surely don't mean to abolish Latin and Greek?"

"I'm afraid I do, Harold."

And now he would allow Avonmore to talk on and on, as he knew he would, because while he talked, his subconscious would be getting used to the idea that the end of the subject meant the end of the man, the end, at any rate, at Mowberry.

As Harold poured forth his amazement, his indignation and his horror, Digby caught sight of his wife, sitting with the au-pair and Ronnie down by the river. They really shouldn't let him play there. But more forcibly, it struck him how sexually attractive she was.

"Quite, Harold. I am absolutely with you. Absolutely. It's merely a question of curriculum feasibility. And I can show you the figures, Harold – we have to fit ninety-seven subjects into fifty hours." She was twenty-four and looked no older than his daughters. He felt a surge of the familiar desire, and momentarily lost track of his words.

"And where does that leave me, Headmaster?" He had got there at last.

"You'll have to talk to the Bursar, of course. It's not my pigeon, but I would have said you could more or less name your own terms, Harold. Redundancy nowadays is often a matter of four figures. And after your years of service ..."

"It's not a question of money." There was something dignified in Avonmore's remark that compelled Digby's respect.

"What is it a question of?" Avonmore's eyes suddenly filled with tears.

"I had expected to go on teaching Classics at Mowberry until I retired."

Digby loathed what he was doing, loathed himself for doing it.

For two pins he'd say, "all right, Harold, stay on." But there was Mowberry to consider. It was from such decisions, such chopping down of dead wood that he had rebuilt the school. But he should have discussed this with Martin. Martin would have known the right way to do it; he was not handling it well.

"I've explained, Harold. It is no reflection on you or your undeniable abilities. It simply isn't feasible. Let's face it, you're sixty-two!"

"Sixty-three."

"Sixty-three. You would only have had another two or three years, at most. Teaching is becoming more and more stressful for us all. Do you not find it so? Now you can enjoy your leisure. Travel to Athens, visit Rome!"

But Harold Avonmore did not want to travel to Greece or Italy. In fact, he had never had any inclination to go to either place; Blackpool suited him very well. All that he needed to know about the Classical world was contained in the walls of the class room, and in the book cupboard behind it.

"I am very upset, Headmaster, deeply, deeply .."

"Of course, I understand that. In some ways ... I am as upset as you." As he spoke, he realised it was true, he hated to see this old man suffer. "But you will not be leaving us yet. You will, of course, see the GCSE classes and A level classes through next term. It will simply be a question of running things down."

"Running things down!" exclaimed Harold with heavy sarcasm. Yes, it had not been a well-chosen phrase. Nevertheless, it had been done. Harold had been told. Glancing up, he saw his wife walking past the window, tossing her hair at him. He could see she wasn't wearing a bra. He cast his eye covertly at his diary on the side-table. Nothing until the governors' meeting at four. Ronnie would be with the au-pair. Elizabeth wouldn't mind, she never minded. He, however, minded; he disliked being at the beck and call of his body, and wished to God he wasn't bothered by it.

"Well, Harold, food for thought, eh? I mustn't keep you from your duties. I know as well as you, that it's all a great shame the way education is going ..." He would drive him to the door with the force of drivel. And as he succeeded in his aim, and Harold went silently out, he did feel something close to compunction, but not for long. He was convinced that this was the right thing and, anyway, he had only twenty minutes in which to fuck his wife, shower and regain his urbanity for the governors' meeting.

Chapter 7

After leaving the Headmaster's drawing room, Harold Avonmore went straight to his class room to teach Lower Sixth Latin prose. It would not have occurred to him that he would be justified in setting his class work, and going back to his flat to deal with the immense blow that had befallen him, in whatever way might be most easeful. His timetable was like his clothes, something that one used by day, something that it would be unthinkable to omit. Once outside the Headmaster's office, Digby's words seemed strange and unreal, for here was Mowberry School going about its afternoon business, the shouts of the Sergeant of the CCF, the Second Eleven climbing aboard a minibus, some junior school boys with clipboards, picking leaves of different sorts from the trees lining the edge of the cricket pitch. It was all so extraordinarily familiar to him, and he so much part of the scene, that it seemed inconceivable that it should exist without him.

"Good afternoon, Sir."

"Good afternoon Massey. Where's your tie, Langley? Hurry up, Forward, you'll be late ..."

"Sir, Sir! I've left my Latin Unseen back at the house. Can I go and get it, Sir?"

It was all so ordinary that it seemed almost impossible to him that he should be separated from it, or it from him. He had been at Mowberry for thirty years, and its life and his, were firmly intertwined. He was, he reflected, like a prominent cliff top in a landscape: a geographer might tell you that in time such a landmark might be eroded away under the influence of storm and time, and although you would not disbelieve the geographer, you would not completely believe him either, for the evidence of your senses lay before you.

And so it was with Harold Avonmore. Now, dealing with the Lower V prose class, he was like a tired man driving a car, so well did he know the route between subjunctive and ablative absolute, that no one would have guessed there was anything wrong. Indeed, Adams said to Handsworth, "Hazzer was on good form today, wasn't he?"

"If you're into Latin prose," his friend replied.

And it wasn't until he had returned to his flat (an annexe of Humbert House, with his own side entrance), and picked up his post, made himself a pot of tea (proper tea, no bags), and filled the flask for the night, that he suddenly felt immensely tired, so tired that he sat down in his chair and slept for an hour, finally waking up with a jolt.

He was assailed with all sorts of emotion, hatred for Sherwood, sorrow, anger, a desire for revenge, a desire to creep and crawl to get his job back and, oddly superimposed on all these feelings, were the hundred plastic mice which had been sent to him by the firm in Dumfries that wasn't actually a firm, but a warehouse, and an ardent wish that he had not told Digby Sherwood about them.

He was not a drinking man, but his flat did contain a single bottle of brandy (he had bought it back in '81 when there was the heavy fall of snow, and he had slipped and his ankle pained him because he preferred not to go to the hospital, and have the sprain treated). And now it occurred to him that it would be beneficial to try this remedy again.

He pulled open the sash window and let the sound of the boys float up from the quad below, then he sat down in his leather arm chair and drank his brandy, and a great sadness came upon him. He saw himself like a figure out of Greek tragedy. Full of good intent, he had been like Oedipus searching out the cause of plague in Thebes; but perhaps he too, had been full of hubris, thinking with too much pride of 1959 when he had twelve Oxbridge Classics candidates (five of them scholars); and then had come peripeteia, the reversal of fortune; he had given up being housemaster, the numbers for Classics had dwindled and dwindled, and he had gradually been ousted in favour of people teaching such subjects as Theatre Studies and Psychology. And now, his final downfall, the loss of his job.

"I do like your dress, Elizabeth." It was the ubiquitous Davies passing by below the window, and although he could only hear him from the depth of the leather armchair, doubtless, if he could see him, his hair would be hanging over his face.

"Oh, do you?" A tinkly laugh. "My husband thinks it's much too short."

"Oh no, Elizabeth, it really suits you." Another tinkly laugh. That woman! She was like a bad omen. First, she had come bursting into the class room in search of her horrible brat of a child; and then when he had tried to be pleasant and made an amusing jest, she had deliberately misunderstood him, and treated him rudely. And then she had had the temerity to insert herself into his dreams causing him to ... and then this afternoon, this dreadful, dreadful afternoon, she had walked like a creature of doom, a Sibyl or a Cassandra, across outside the window with her golden hair hanging down her neck, and her breasts unrestrained by a brassière. And now she stood beneath his very window, allowing impertinences from a sixth form boy. He felt his anger and hurt fasten upon her. Perhaps, it was she who had said to her husband with her silly laugh, "why don't you get rid of old Avonmore. He made some idiotic remark to me in the classroom, and thought Ronnie was called Hercules. Perhaps, he's got Alzheimers." But Sherwood wasn't stupid, he wouldn't have taken any notice of that. Harold sipped some more brandy and unbuttoned the cardigan that he wore winter and summer under his sports jacket, for normally he felt the cold. But now he was hot and oppressed, and his brow felt sweaty. He closed his eyes and saw Elizabeth Sherwood.

"Diggy," she was saying; for it was common knowledge that such was her pet name for her husband. "Diggy, get rid of Harold Avonmore". She was pulling the straps of her short dress down and the unrestrained breasts swelled out, she let the tiny dress slide down, and he could see she was wearing no knickers. "Diggy," she was saying. And he could see Sherwood, undoing his flies. Now he could see his membrum virile ... "Diggy", she was saying, "get rid of Avonmore". And as he nodded his head, Elizabeth knelt at his feet and took it into her mouth, and her long straight blonde hair waved gently, as her face moved to and from between Digby's legs.

He had to move quickly to get to the lavatory in time. He hadn't vomited in years, he supposed it was the brandy on an empty stomach. When it had all passed, he felt very much better; and, as he pulled the lavatory chain, it seemed to him that something very unpleasant was gone from him, and that, perhaps, he would, after all, be able to face the future.

Chapter 8

Dear Headmaster,

It is with deep sadness that I received your news yesterday. I shall not, however, endeavour to make you change your mind, as I understand your decision is irrevocable.

I do not, however, intend to spend my remaining time at Mowberry in a caretaker role; this would hardly, I am sure you agree, be tolerable for a man who has been both Housemaster here and Head of Classics.

I have (in spite of what I regard as shabby treatment), a highly developed sense of responsibility to the school and would not wish to jeopardise the future of my pupils, in particular, those who may wish to become Oxbridge candidates. I, therefore, suggest you appoint another man as soon as possible, and I will remain, as long as need be, to ease him into his caretaker role. When he appears to be cognisant of his responsibilities, I will take my departure.

I must repeat that I did not look to leave Mowberry under such sad circumstances, rather, I had intended to complete my fifty years here.

I remain
Yours
Harold Avonmore

My dear Harold

I am delighted that you have adopted so positive an approach to what is understandably, a disappointing situation for you.

I fully concur with your idea for appointing a temporary staff member to lead out the Classics Department. I have to say, however, that this person will not necessarily be a master. I am sure you will agree, that in these days of political correctness, the post must be equally available to a man or woman. Your opinion will, of course, be most valuable in making the appointment, and I trust you will sit on the selection board with me.

I have placed an advertisement in the TES, making it clear that the job is for a limited period of time only, and have indicated a fairly short application period, in order to expedite this business as quickly as possible.

I would envisage your remaining on the staff of Mowberry during next term. I am sure this will allow the new appointee ample time to settle in. You will, of course, wish to discuss the timetable for next term with Mr Wood. Your salary, needless to say, will be unaffected.

We shall, of course, wish to organise a small leaving ceremony for you, with a suitable presentation. You must let me know if you have any ideas on the format of this.

It remains merely to thank you on behalf of boys past and present, colleagues and, of course, myself. Your contribution has been an invaluable one. I wish you a full and happy retirement.

Yours,

Digby Sherwood

Digby Sherwood placed Harold's letter in the tray for filing, and sealed his own hand-written letter to put in the out- tray, a hand-written letter was, he felt, more suitable. It was a horrid business, and he lightly massaged his neck as though to reassure himself. He got up abruptly, switched the light off and went into his dressing room to take off his clothes. Unlike Avonmore, he did not wear pyjamas in bed.

As he got into bed he found his wife sprawled over on his side. He pushed her over with no great gentleness.

"Diggy," she muttered sleepily, "want to fuck".

"No," he replied. "I'm absolutely knackered." He had it in mind to go straight to sleep, but when he felt the warmth of his wife's body next to him he experienced, almost angrily, the familiarity of desire. "Elizabeth!" he commanded tensely, and Elizabeth, a model wife in this respect (unlike Belinda), did as she was bid.

Whether it was due to tiredness, lateness of the hour or, indeed, to his wife's lengthy and exquisite attention to his cock, Digby experienced an orgasm of such intensity that the experience was more akin to pain than pleasure, and he found himself crying out, something that he seldom did, in the throes of intercourse. Elizabeth, encouraged by what she attributed to her skill, said, brightly,

"My turn now."

"Sorry Liz," he said, turned over and fell heavily asleep.

Accordingly, the following morning, Elizabeth felt she was owed some form of reparation, but he was having none of it.

"I have Assembly to do, the Curriculum Council Meeting, the Assessment Committee – I told you Liz, a headmaster's job is a twenty-four hour one." This was only part of the truth, the rest lay in the fact that his penis was amazingly sore from the previous night.

"It's all right for you," said Elizabeth crossly, as he got out of bed. "I gave you a lovely time last night – you were moaning and groaning and shouting ..."

He went off to his dressing room, showered and dressed, but when he came back for his cuff-links, he found she was still complaining.

"I mean, I know you're busy and everything, but it's not fair when I suck you off, and you won't do anything for me. I love it when ..."

He turned back from the mirror where he was straightening his tie, and had seen he did not look in particularly good shape. His penis still hurt and he was conscious of an enormously heavy day ahead.

"Don't you ever think about anything other than sex?" he asked, knowing full well that he was accusing Elizabeth of the very thing that worried him about himself, and spoke, for that reason, all the more angrily.

"Yes, of course I do," said Elizabeth.

"What *do* you think about then?"

"I think about lots of things."

"Such as?"

"Such as ..." Elizabeth racked her brains. It was so difficult being married to a clever man, then a thought occurred to her.

"I think about Ronnie."

"Why don't you spend more time with him, then?"

"I do! I spend lots of time with him – all the time Marie-Louise goes to her English classes ..."

"Twice a week – two hours. It doesn't seem an excessive amount of time to spend with your son!" Digby, usually a reasonable man, felt his fury rising.

"He's your son as well!"

"That is not the subject under discussion. Try and discipline your mind a little. Are you doing your language tapes? Are you speaking French to Marie-Louise?"

"Sometimes."

"There's no earthly point in our having the house in France, if you can't speak a word of French. You have the perfect opportunity to get your French up with Marie-Louise, who seems a very pleasant, willing person."

"It's so boring."

He was taking excess change out of the pocket of his suit jacket so the line would fall better. He stopped in this activity and stared at his wife. Her hair looked rather greasy, and there were streaks of mascara under her eyes. What a mess she appeared, and without her looks, what was she? His penis throbbed, and he felt a surge of intense irritation.

"Things cannot, by definition, be boring. Only people are boring."

"Are you saying I'm boring?"

"Quite frankly, at the moment, yes. You need to get yourself up out of that bed, wash your hair, go and see your son, take him out. Talk some French, do some charity work ..."

"Anything else?"

"Yes, about five hundred other things. Make me a list!" He was nearly at the door.

"Don't talk to me, as if I was one of your boys."

"I shall talk to you exactly as I please. And remember, truly sexy women are intelligent women, not women who lie about in bed all day wanking."

"I don't ...." But he was gone. Off to this silly Curriculum Thingummy or whatever. She thought she would like to have a cigarette. He didn't like her to smoke and she was meant to have given up. Furthermore, she was expressly forbidden to smoke in the bedroom. She got out of bed and took her cigarettes out of the drawer where she kept her knickers. It made her feel better to be disobeying him.

He was so unfair. Look how hard she had worked on him last night! And she hadn't complained when he hadn't done it back for her – and she naturally wanted something this morning. Her nipples were all tingly, and she felt she would have liked to spend the day, just having sex. It wasn't much to ask, was it? She wasn't exactly ugly. She got out of bed again and surveyed herself in the mirror. Nobody would think she'd had a baby. And she did love Ronnie, she loved him lots. It was just that ... he was so difficult to manage, always having tantrums and pooing and stuff. Anyway, Marie-Louise was better at looking after him than she was. And it was all very well for him to talk about doing French with her. She had tried, but Marie-Louise came from the South, and her accent was all different from the tapes. And he talked about doing charity work! What, go out and stand in some old Oxfam shop? And, anyway, there were always people to lunch and things, and he liked her to be there. She'd been really nice to that couple the other day, Cox or something, and he'd just been cross because she'd got their names wrong – and she'd been sure that it was Cox.

Thinking these thoughts, Elizabeth stubbed out her cigarette (she didn't really feel like it, anyway), and went to have a shower. She'd go and say hello to Ronnie before Marie-Louise took him off to Leicester for the day. She wasn't cross any more, and she did love Diggy. Only he was so difficult to understand sometimes. But she would try, really she would.

Chapter 9

The two men were sitting in Digby's 'den', Martin very upright in a hard-backed chair by the window, Digby sprawled out on a sofa whose springs touched the ground. They often met in the den, where they could not be disturbed. It was located at the back of the main school building, kept locked and available to no one but themselves. It was, in marked contrast to the drawing room of Digby's house, more akin to Martin's bungalow: the walls badly needed painting, the sofas upholstering, and the curtains renewing. They both loved it because it offered pure escapism from the respectability that surrounded them.

"You shouldn't have acted so quickly, Digs. You were always impetuous – but then, I suppose, in some ways, that's your strength." Martin Wood smiled at his friend. He found it impossible to be angry, they had known each other too long. They had been friends from young men when they were both new housemasters together at Stanstead Park; and when Digby had got the Headship of Mowberry, he had appointed Martin in as his Second Master, as soon as the post became vacant.

There was no apparent reason why the two men should be friends, they could hardly have been more different; whereas Digby, tall, handsome and urbane, would be noticed wherever he went, Martin was distinctly plain. He was rather short and had a decided beer paunch. Bespectacled, the remains of his greying hair brushed forward, he presented a kindly, but insignificant presence. Their voices, too, reflected their intrinsic differences: whereas Digby's voice was mellifluous with overtones suggesting generations of wealth and privilege, Martin spoke in the flat tones that took their origin from a Midland grammar school education. Whereas Digby moved like some exotic fish, here and there, glinting as he went, Martin remained relatively static, like a carp of immense age.

Perhaps the bond between them lay in their early years of housemastering; they had made their mistakes together, although their very mistakes illuminated the difference in character between the two men. Digby's mistakes, (there were not many) sprung from trying to innovate too many things too quickly, from a lack of tolerance for the less than perfect, from a kind of arrogance which sometimes made him feared or disliked. Martin's mistakes sprung from over-caution, a desire to think the best of a man or boy, and offer a second chance, even when such attempts were unrealistic, an over-attention to detail, a lack of imagination, even perhaps, a pedestrianism.

Their qualities,too, were very different: Martin was conscientious and meticulous and, more importantly, utterly trustworthy, loyal and kind. The smallest boy would tell Mr Wood about the death of his hamster, and rest assured that Mr Wood would find him a replacement. As a referee in a rugby match, he was totally without bias. Anything could be said to him, and its speaker be confident that it would never be repeated.

But Digby had flair, authority and gravitas. No small boy would bother Mr Sherwood with the death of a hamster, but Gowinder Singh had been flown at the school's expense to and from the Punjab every term. The scheme had, only partly, been prompted by altruism. The fact of the matter was, that Digby had got tired of hearing the sanctimonious voice of Sutherland at the Headmaster's Conference expounding on the benevolence of his school, with regard to assisted places. Digby heard himself saying that not only did Mowberry offer assisted places and bursaries for likely, working-class boys, but Mowberry's policy was further- reaching. He had plans in hand to bring in boys from deprived areas overseas. It was another of his typically impulsive reactions.

When he had come to Mowberry three years ago (four weeks after his second marriage), he had found a run-down, third-rate institution. He had tackled it from every direction, expelled the drug-takers, sacked the inefficient, raised half a million for the new technology centre, updated the uniform and built a new sixth form centre; and behind all his ideas, had been Martin's meticulous planning. Together they had hacked their way through a jungle of inefficiency, hypocrisy and indolence: the face of Mr Rolfe the art teacher had been a picture of amazement when Digby demanded courses in IT and an artist in residence. He left before Digby had been there a term. Martin had instituted a complicated computer network, and Mr Thring, who had done little for years, had been forced, much against his will, to spend his holidays on numerous courses.

A bond had been forged between them in their earlier years through their wives and children; Martin had boys roughly the same age as Digby's girls, and they had grown up together, Digby's wife had been a great friend of Martin's wife, Jean. Together they had enhanced and complemented their husband's qualities. Belinda had something of Digby's calm authority, to which she added sympathy and compassion. Jean had the qualities which Martin lacked, vivacity and audacity. The four of them made a splendid team, and Digby often wondered whether Jean's sudden death from cancer, had somehow hastened the breakdown of his marriage to Belinda.

Martin and Digby saw in the other what each lacked in himself, and both men were intelligent enough to convert envy to advantage. Martin owed his job to Digby and Digby owed his success to Martin. And yet it was more than a sense of mutual advantage, for Martin was not an ambitious man and would have been quite happy to remain where he was; and Digby, reliant as he was on Martin's planning, liked the man for himself. Indeed, he more than liked Martin, he loved his friend, perhaps, because he was the only person with whom he felt totally at ease, and to whom he could say what was on his mind, without fear of reproach, without having to pretend or impress. Certainly, he loved him more than he loved his wife. Timid himself, Martin loved Digby for his very unpredictability. Digby satisfied vicariously any need for danger within his friend.

And now Digby leant back in his chair, and he massaged the back of his neck in the way he would never have done in the presence of anyone else.

"I know. I should have broken it to him more gently, thought it through. But Mart…" and here he straightened up again and leant forward, "I am right, Mart. Classics is a dinosaur and Avonmore a Brontosaurus. Think what that freed time can produce. You know I have a great yen to do the Baccalaureate …"

"And you want me to do a feasibility study?" asked Martin amiably. "Of course I will, Digs, on one condition."

"I don't like conditions."

"On condition that you give Avonmore a jolly good send-off."

"Oh fine! I thought you were going for something frightful like central feeding! Yes, of course, we will: Latin orations, a Greek play maybe."

"We'd need a decent theatre."

"We could always build one. We could raise some more money for 'The Avonmore Greek Theatre'. He'd like that."

"Are you serious?"

"Don't know. Maybe. Yes. You're right, we'll send him off happy. Now I want to talk appraisals ..."

And they talked over school business for a couple of hours, much to the satisfaction of both, after which Digby got out the bottle of brandy, kept at the back of the shelves containing 1908 volumes of *The Encyclopaedia Britannica*, a secret vice dating many years back. They relaxed.

"Actually," said Martin, putting the confidential papers in his briefcase, and taking a sip of the brandy, "you don't look well, Digs."

"The fact is," said Digby, and it was a measure of the absolute trust he had in Martin, "my prick hurts like hell."

"Seen the doc?"

"No, no; it's only since last night."

"Well," said Martin.

"I know what you're thinking, and yes, you're right. Three fucks and blow job all in the course of a few hours is too much for a man of my age."

"Don't show off."

"I'm not. It's true! I don't show off to you."

"No, I know you don't. I could manage a drop more, Digs."

Digby, pouring out some more for Martin but none for himself, regarded Martin quizzically. "How do you manage, Mart? I mean, Jean's been gone six years. What do you do? Wank all the time? I mean, you can't risk anything spicy, can you?"

A look of hurt surprise passed across Martin's face. His enduring love for his dead wife was a very sacred thing, and Digby was filled with contrition.

"Sorry. I spoke out of turn."

"No, you didn't. You don't tend to speak out of turn to me, any more than you show off. Yes, I wank a bit. Not a lot. You see ... you'll find this hard maybe. You know how I loved Jean, and I liked making love to her, I suppose, because I loved her – and because it made her happy. I suppose that's what gave me the buzz. I'm not really that bothered about sex now."

Digby opened the desk drawer and took out his secret supply of cigarettes. He offered one to Martin, who shook his head, and Digby lit up in silence.

"But it's not like that for you, is it?" said Martin softly, watching Digby in concern.

"No," said Digby sadly, and he looked up at Martin with his blue eyes flashing at the unfairness of it all. "You know, Mart, I read some article other day by some feminist saying 'gosh, how frightful, men think about sex twice every hour'. Well, I think about it twice every minute ..." Martin was going to say something but Digby stopped him.

"I'm not like you, Martin. In all those years with Belinda, I didn't care whether I satisfied her or not. Well, I couldn't. Belinda couldn't come to save her life. I used to toss up whether to go to the bog and wank, or fuck her. Do I shock you?"

"No. I just appreciate how difficult your life is. I'm sorry, I ..."

"And yet they were happy years, in many ways, weren't they Mart?"

"They were for me, certainly."

"The kids and the picnics, and getting a grip on teaching and understanding the whole public school thing."

"But it wasn't enough for you."

"No!" Digby brought his fist down on the table, so his untouched brandy slopped over the side of the glass. "I stayed with Belinda for twenty years, for Chrissake; but it wasn't enough ... I wanted ..."

"And is Elizabeth enough?"

"Elizabeth? Oh, Elizabeth! Elizabeth will give you a blow job any time of the day or night."

"That's not what I meant."

"No, no. I know exactly what you meant, and the answer is, no, of course she's not."

"What you want is Belinda in Elizabeth's body."

"Maybe. Oh, she's so stupid, Mart."

"Well, you knew that before you married her," said Martin brutally, and then added gently, "but she's very young, you know."

"And very pretty. I get a hard-on just thinking about her. I need to have her satisfy me a great deal."

"And do you satisfy her?"

"When I bother."

"I think you should. Not that it's my business."

"In case she has it off with anyone else? No opportunity, poor love."

"Digs, you have a problem."

"But it's not just that – and thanks for not criticising me – it's the biological thing. I suppose some people need it a hell of a lot more than others. You say you don't. Well, I believe you, but I don't understand it. I can't function without it, a lot of it. And there it is." Digby looked at Martin helplessly, of all men, only Martin could be shown his Achilles' heel.

Most men, most friends would have made some conciliatory gesture, offered some weak sop, some palliative, but Martin would not do that; he and Digby knew each other so well that Digby would understand what he was doing, and think the lesser of him for it, and Martin would know that he had failed the man he loved most in the world.

"You made a bargain, Digby." He chose his words carefully.

"Yes, like Dr Faustus."

"No, not like Faustus because his fate was sealed, the clock would strike twelve and he would be carried off. But you only chose between Psyche and Cupid, and you chose Cupid. Cupid is an easier chap to live with than Psyche.

Digby sighed and averted his glance from Martin. He wished he had not broached the subject, but Martin continued.

"You have to educate her, Digs. You were good with Richenda and Dolores. They adored you before you left Belinda – they probably still do, particularly Richenda. You have a great knack of inspiring love ..." Martin was conscious of treading on dangerous ground, and lightened the tone: "After all, look what I do for you, the bloody Baccalaureate now!"

"You can have a salary rise."

"You have to educate her; she's very fond of you, and there's Ronnie. You like doing family things."

"Not now, Martin. I'm too old. It sounds terrible, but I have little real interest in Ronnie, he's not bright."

"Digby! He's two!"

"I can tell ... what chance does he have, brought up by au-pairs. That's another thing.... Elizabeth is hopeless with him."

"Then you must teach her."

"I'm too busy, Martin. You know that."

"You have time in the holidays. And when you've done your good father act, you might manage more than three fucks and a blow job."

It wasn't like Martin to use such language, and Digby knew he was doing it in his anxiety to win him over to his point of view, to help him reach some sort of solution to a problem they both knew to be insoluble. He was immensely touched, so much so, that he, the epitome of self-control, felt dangerously close to tears, and he turned his back on Martin to hide them.

"I haven't offended you?"

"No," said Digby, turning round to allow his friend to see the tears. "I didn't want you to see me bloody crying."

"A drink, please, Digs" said Martin.

"Another one?"

"Please."

"Are you doing this to humour me or are you drinking too much?"

"Bit of both, I'd say."

Digby sat down at the desk again. "We ought to go sailing again, you know, like we did in '78. Do you remember how drunk we were all fortnight, and how disapproving Jean and Belinda were? Belinda made us take all the children on a five mile walk to that awful butterfly place, and Jean poured a whole bottle of brandy down the sink!"

"Course I remember. Oddly enough, I was looking through some old photos only the other day."

"Looking for Jean?"

"As you say. And I came across a whole batch of them."

"Why don't we do it again in the summer, just the two of us?"

Their eyes met across the table, these two men whose characters and aspirations were so different, but who had known each other far too long for either to hide anything from the other. Martin moved in his chair, and Digby thought Martin would get up and come over to him, but he merely leant back in his chair, instead. The moment passed and they were both conscious of something having been averted.

"You have Elizabeth now", said Martin, and his voice was oddly stern.

"Why, so I have!" said Digby lightly. He gathered up some papers and politely held the door for Martin to pass through, as the senior for the junior. Martin smiled ruefully, after all, it was not his job to be Digby's mentor.

"Don't forget to look into that Baccalaureate business, will you, Martin. By Wednesday, if possible."

Chapter 10

Elizabeth didn't manage to see Ronnie before Marie-Louise took him off for the day. She did, actually, look out of the window and see her au-pair with the pushchair, walking purposefully down the school drive to the bus stop, and she toyed with the idea of getting the XJ6 out and giving them a lift into Hopton, but then she thought that perhaps she wouldn't because Ronnie would only start crying as soon as she arrived, and it would be difficult to get away again.

She decided instead to wash and curl her hair, she was bored with it straight, and anxious to try all those curly-whirly things she had bought from Boots the other day.

It took a good deal of effort, but she had to admit, when she looked in the mirror after an hour or so of winding and unwinding, that the effect was pretty good. It was a pity there was nobody coming to lunch today. She was wearing her new jeans as well, with a little, skinny top. It seemed such a waste to be looking so good, and all for nothing. Digby wasn't coming home today because he said he had all sorts of boring meetings and things. It was his day, too, for the weekly meeting with Martin. Bloody Martin! They probably sat and talked about Belinda and the good old days.

But what to do now? How to fill in a great, long, empty day? She could always go and have lunch at one of the Boarding houses – she was looking so good, it could be fun. She had done that a lot when she first married, sat at the lunch table and watched them lust after her. But then she'd got pregnant and they began to snigger at her instead, and she had stopped going. And after she had Ronnie, everybody asked about him all the time, and she got the feeling that people thought she should be looking after him, and not be there at all.

Perhaps she would make a cake for Diggy's tea. She had done Home Economics for A Level and nearly passed. Yes, she'd make a cake. But when she got to the kitchen and looked in the cupboard for ingredients, she found there was almost nothing there. Mrs Handley mainly cooked their meals or, more often than not, Diggy had dinner in one of the Houses with the boys, or a working meal with a governor or a parent and then Marie-Louise cooked the food for Ronnie and her. She hardly ever needed to cook herself because she didn't eat much. She had put on ten pounds after having Ronnie, and it had been a fight to lose it. Of course, she could get the car out and go down to the village and get some things, but it didn't seem worth the effort really because it might all go wrong. She wasn't a very good cook and, anyway, now she thought of it, Diggy was never home for tea anyway, and he didn't like cake.

And then the bell went. It was usually someone boring like Martin, dropping great files of stuff in for Diggy, so he would sit up half the night working and not come to bed with her. But it wasn't Martin. It was Davies, that boy who had been in Mr Avonworth's class with lots of nice hair. He appeared to be surprised.

"Oh, Elizabeth! I was looking for Mr Sherwood; I've got some proofs for the school magazine." He looked towards her smiling, not simply because of the effect it would have on Elizabeth, but because he was thinking of Stewart's amazed admiration – always provided the plan worked, of course Well, the timing was right: he had seen the Headman walking off to lunch with Mr Wood in the direction of Humbert House.

"Oh," said Elizabeth. She thought how nice it was to have someone smile at her. Diggy had been so nasty this morning. Before she was married boys had smiled at her all the time.

"What do you think I had better do with the papers?" He had large blue eyes rather like her own.

"You could come in and wait," said Elizabeth slowly. "He might come back." Only she knew he wouldn't, because it was Thursday.

"Are you sure I won't be in the way?" He was across the threshold.

"No," said Elizabeth, "come into the kitchen. I was just going to make a cake."

"Gosh," said Davies. "That's jolly domesticated. I hope Mr Sherwood knows what a lucky man he is."

"Would you like some coffee?" asked Elizabeth, leading the way.

Davies regarded the tightly fitting jeans as he followed her into the kitchen which didn't show any signs of cake-making. "I haven't introduced myself," he said, "my name is St John Davies."

"Sinjin? That's a funny name – I've never heard it before."

"I suppose it is – it's spelt Saint John."

"Why's it called Sinjin, then?" asked Elizabeth, puzzled. She was trying to work out if she needed to fill up the kettle.

"I've no idea," laughed Davies. It was a friendly, warm, open laugh. Elizabeth looked up and smiled.

"It was great fun, your little boy coming into our Greek lesson the other day. How did it happen?" St John Davies sat down on one of the beautifully carved mahogany benches that faced the Aga. "I say, if you're going to put the kettle on the Aga, I'd unplug it first."

"Oh yes." Elizabeth took the kettle off the Aga and switched it on. "Ronnie ran away from me, you see. He's very naughty and he won't do anything I say. He's much better with Marie-Louise."

"Who's she?"

"She's the au-pair. She's French."

"Do you speak French, then?"

"No," said Elizabeth, "but I'm trying to learn."

"It's easy for me," said St John, "because my mother lives in Paris."

"Oh, does she?" said Elizabeth. "My mother lives in Spain, but I don't really see her."

"I don't see my mother much either," said Davies. "I live with my father in London mostly, and some of the time in Scotland. We've got an island on a lake."

"Really?" Elizabeth opened her eyes wide, partly because she knew it made her look very pretty, and partly because she really was impressed.

"I don't know where the sugar's kept," she said. "You don't want any, do you?"

"Oh no, thank you." said Davies, regarding his mug of coffee. It didn't look very hot and there were lumps of brown grains floating in it.

"I say. It must be awfully lonely for you, all alone all day in this big house?" He opened his eyes almost as wide as Elizabeth had opened hers, and shook his head slightly, so that his hair fell over his face.

"Oh yes," burst out Elizabeth, "I get terribly bored. Marie–Louise looks after Ronnie most of the time and I don't really have any friends – I mean, all Diggy's, I mean all the Headmaster's friends are old, well, I don't mean old, but not ..."

"Not your age." His eyelashes moved up and down; they were long and lustrous.

"And Diggy ..." she abandoned calling him the Headmaster, it seemed silly somehow, "and Diggy's always so busy."

"He's a very good Headmaster," said St John. A bit of flattery would do no harm.

"Yes, I expect he is," said Elizabeth, and then, in one of her rare

64

moments of insight, she added, "He's probably a better headmaster than he is a husband."

"You have a very hard time, don't you?" said St John Davies. If the Headman had just gone into lunch, he'd have about half an hour to make Elizabeth. Would she have any cleaning women or anything around? And, come to think of it, where was the au-pair? Well, it all sounded pretty quiet.

"Yes, I do really. I mean, I'm sure people think I'm really lucky. I mean, being a Headmaster's wife and everything ..." St John stretched out a sympathetic hand across the table. It met with no resistance.

"Elizabeth", he took away his hand and moved round the bench next to her. "May I ask you a big favour?" Elizabeth nodded. She hadn't had such an interesting time since she lay in bed after having Ronnie, and everybody brought her flowers and chocolate and things.

"Elizabeth," the blond locks moved forward, "may I kiss you?"

He had not known what to expect really, but five pounds was his immediately. Ten and fifteen didn't take long, and twenty looked to be soon available.

"Shall we go upstairs?" asked Elizabeth, at last. She had her hand inside his flies.

"There's no one about?"

"No. Come on. I want you."

"I want you too, gorgeous. Where are we going?"

Davies' life at Mowberry was pleasant. He generally expected to succeed in what he did, but even he had not expected to be led into the Headman's bed with so little resistance. He smiled as he thought of his last encounter with Mr Sherwood, the man had stood there looking superior with a rose in his button-hole, asking questions. Well, he hadn't found out about that bottle of Bacardi, and he wouldn't find out about Elizabeth, either. Not so very clever, after all. Who was smarter when it came down to it, then? St John Davies, or Digby bloody Sherwood?

As he followed her upstairs and watched her undress, he had a momentary stab of fear: was he jeopardising his Oxbridge career? What about his Head Boy prospects? More immediately, how much time had he got? Not more than ten minutes, all done. OK. Wow! The bedroom was quite something. Bit different from Mum and Dad's.

Elizabeth could not resist putting on a little show for Davies, cupping her breasts in her hands and putting her hand between her legs; it had really got Digs going – in the early days.

"You drive me crazy, baby," Davies said as he climbed on top of her.

But it wasn't much fun at all. He'd hardly got inside her before he came, and then he didn't bother about her any more than Diggy had.

"I'm awfully sorry, Elizabeth," said Davies, straightening his prefect's tie, "I have to belt off – I've got a Greek lesson, and Mr Avonmore's a stickler for punctuality. It was absolutely super. You have an unbelievable body ..."

"Will you come and see me another day?"

"'Course I will. Don't bother coming down. You lie there and look beautiful. Ciaou!" And he was gone. She played with herself until she came, but it wasn't any fun on her own, and it hadn't been any fun with St John. She only really wanted Diggy. She wished she had never done it now.

For a while she lay and wondered why things never went right. Nobody ever cared about her: her father had left when she was only three, she couldn't even remember him, her mother had always been busy chasing after other men; her sister had been mean to her because she wasn't pretty like she was, and anyway she was six years older and had never had any time for her; and now her son seemed to hate her, and even Digby didn't bother about her any more. St John hadn't really cared either, just fancied her. Why was it when she was so pretty and fun, nobody in the world had any time for her?

Eventually she got up, had a shower and went to get dressed. It was funny, but she couldn't find her knickers anywhere. Not that it mattered, she'd find them later, and anyway, knickers were one thing she had plenty of.

As she went downstairs a really nasty thought occurred to her: she was exactly half-way through the month, and she hadn't been on the pill since Diggy had had the vasectomy.

*****

St John Davies went over to Tudor House to find Stewart, but Stewart wasn't in his study, so he wrote 'Slag' on the back of Stewart's treasured picture of his girlfriend, and went into the Games Room to make enquiries.

"Hi, you," he accosted a small fourth-former with a large bag of crisps, "where's Stewart?"

The small boy looked up importantly; it wasn't often he was spoken to by a really cool sixth former, like St John Davies. And, besides, he had interesting news to impart. He held the bag of crisps out to Davies and announced, "I expect he's dead by now?"

"Dead?" In spite of himself, St John could not maintain an attitude of indifference. "Don't be stupid. What do you mean?"

"Matron took him off to the San before Call-over. He kept on throwing up. I expect it's meningitis."

"Balls," said Davies and took the bag of crisps. What a bugger, just when he wanted to tell him about the fuck! "Singh about?"

"Dunno. Can I have my crisps back, Davies?"

"Say 'please'."

"Please, Davies, give me my crisps back."

"Certainly not, don't you know they're bad for little boys?"

He took a swipe at the boy, and went off to Singh's study. He didn't bother knocking but Singh wasn't there either, so he couldn't even enjoy shocking him. Oh well. He found a piece of paper and wrote '*Blacks go home*', and placed it in a prominent position on the mantelpiece. It was better than nothing.

He stared round at the study. There were no personal possessions and everything was neatly arranged. Its very orderliness struck a chill note; it reminded him of Singh himself, organised and modest, and it occurred to him that Gowinder Singh would make a very good Head Boy – and of course, it would be just the sort of thing the Headman might to do to show how modern Mowberry was. He would have to be very careful if he was to get the job. He removed the notice and put it back in his pocket, along with Elizabeth's knickers, and went out thoughtfully. He had been stupid to take risks and fuck Elizabeth. She wouldn't say anything, would she? Perhaps it would be better not to tell Stewart or anyone about it, after all. If Stewart was in the San anyway, it looked as if the gods had decided it for him.

Chapter 11

"What on earth are you doing?" asked Digby. Martin's office door had been open and he walked straight in.

"Actually," said Martin, "I'm surfing the web."

"Hah!" exclaimed Digby. "I've caught you at last, Mr Europorn himself. Let me see. What on earth is it? I'm pretty inventive, but ..."

"Actually," said Martin, "it's a cross-section of a lizard's tail."

"Oh, Mart! The reptile book, of course."

Martin had been writing a book on reptiles ever since Digby had known him, but because Martin was so meticulous, and probably more importantly, because he was doing it only for himself and deadlines didn't matter – and because he had so much of the daily school business on his shoulders, he never seemed to get beyond the first fifty or so pages.

"In abeyance, Digs, but I've found a marvellous group of men in the States who do nothing but work on lizards. And there's an Italian who doesn't have any English so I'm trying to learn a bit of the language. Look at that tail, Digs. Amazing, isn't it."

"Whatever turns you on, Mart."

Martin switched the computer off and swivelled round in his leather chair. Digby reflected that it looked a very comfortable chair and that, in his way, Martin was a very wise guy. As he watched his eyes glinting behind his glasses with enthusiasm for the lizard's tail, he wondered if he would like to be Martin, intrigued by simple problems? Well, the question was academic.

Martin's office was altogether quite comfortable and pleasant. There was, of course, the computer and files, and the phone and various office paraphernalia, but there were lots of pictures of Jean and photos of his two sons. On the mantelpiece was a vase of cornflowers and a packet of chocolate digestives, and by the window were two more leather chairs and some cushions, brought back from India by Richenda, Digby's youngest daughter.

"I take it your prick's better."

"What do you take, Mart?" said Digby lightly.

"Stop wasting my time," said Martin amiably, "and tell me what you're here for."

"Two things," said Digby, sitting himself astride one of the arm chairs and fiddling with a yellow cushion patterned with elephants, "interrelated. First, the Head Boy question, and secondly, the candidates for the Classics post."

"Mmm."

"I mean, there's a sort of irony here; the three most obvious candidates for Head Boy are Avonmore's Lower Sixth boys, the ones who are doing Greek..

"Who's that? Davies, Singh and Stewart?"

"And," said Digby, "you'll favour Stewart because he's the underdog. I favour Gowinder because he's my success story, and everyone else in the world will favour Davies."

"In a nutshell."

"They're all panting after Davies," said Digby, "Housemaster, Matron, boys, tutors, first eleven and so on. So why don't we want him, Mart?"

"Because of Singh and Stewart?"

"No."

"No, I agree with you, Digs. There's something that doesn't quite add up about Davies. Something's not quite right."

"And this comes from you, who trust everyone. He looks the part, doesn't he? All that fair hair and blue eyes, the plummy voice, the right phraseology. Go down a treat on Founders' Day.

"Why has he got the plummy voice? The parents aren't anything very posh, are they? Let's run him through the computer. Let's see what we can find out about him. The only significant thing I can think off-hand, is that he is on an assisted place."

"All credit to him, then," said Digby, "he's just like your lizards, Mart. Trying to shed his skin and adopt local colour."

"I'm afraid you can't have Singh," said Martin. "He's not much liked, too much of a loner."

"An asset," said Digby, "splendid impartiality. No giving in to peer pressure. Anyway, you can't have Stewart, he lacks presence. What I'm doing is, letting them show the Classics candidates round tomorrow."

"Well, Davies didn't make much of a success of that before, from what you told me. The Cockburn man wasn't impressed by Davies, or any of us.

"Well, now," said Digby, "that's just where you're wrong – and although I hate to admit it, where I was wrong, where we were all wrong, one person wasn't ... and guess who? Avonmore!"

"Avonmore!"

"Yes, all right Martin, I jumped the gun where Avonmore was concerned, obviously he has his uses. Apparently, he was doing some Latin poem about a doctor when the parents were shown round, and as luck would have it, the name came up the next day in old Cockburn's crossword, so he thought "Bingo! Mowberry for me!"

"No!"

"Well, it wasn't quite like that, but there's a grain of truth in it. The Cockburns went away and are coming back. They like us!"

"Numbers doing well then? There must be one ninety odd for next term?"

"Uhuh. Now tomorrow, Mart, the Classics job: there are four of them arriving at eleven. They'll have coffee, introductory talk, ethos, lunch, then they get shown round, and finally the interviews. God, they'll be shattered. Anyway, I want you and Avonmore in on the interviews and I'm not sure – let the lads have a say?"

"Oh, Digs!"

"No? You think not?"

"Not sure. I think Avonmore ought to decide really."

"Balls! I shall decide, but I shall let Avonmore think he's decided."

"What a twister you are."

"Indeed, but I do have my good side. I'm also going to get those three boys in, give them a talking-to about being nice to him for his last couple of terms, and make suggestions about his send-off. There! Have I redeemed myself?"

"And we're watching Singh, Davies and Stewart? Are they coming to lunch?"

"Mmm."

"See how they cope in an adult situation. Yes?"

"Yes."

"How many candidates did you say?"

"Four. They don't sound brilliant. All right, I know I didn't leave enough time for any decent candidates to apply, but we'll have a look and see. We can always advertise again."

"Do you know what adverts cost?"

"No, but I'm sure you do."

"OK. I'll be there for the sherry."

"Only a couple mind, Mart. There's wine with lunch. Sorry."

"That's all right, Digs."

"Let's find some porn on the Internet."

"You don't like porn."

"No, I don't, really. I like sex straight, first hand, lots of it. Make a good headline though, wouldn't it."

"What?"

"Headmaster and Second Master of famous public school using the web for sex. And it occurs to me now I'm here, Mart. What are we doing about stopping the kids getting access?"

"We've got it blocked at the moment, I think."

"Let me have the paperwork. I want to know exactly how we're stopping it. I don't want the kids involved in sexploits or whatever."

Martin laughed: "Like Dolores and Duncan?"

Five years ago Digby had found his daughter and Martin's son not exactly in flagrante, but not far off. He was absolutely furious and marched Duncan off to his father; and because human nature is never all of a piece, Martin had thought the whole situation rather funny, while Digby had been full of righteous indignation. The two wives had sorted it out.

"God!" Digby unzipped the yellow elephant cushion and peered inside. "Doesn't it seem an age ago?"

"Yes."

"Were we the same people?"

"Oh yes."

"Don't make them like us any more, do they?" Digby zipped up the cushion and put it back. "I'll wager you Singh against Stewart."

"I think we shall both lose," said Martin. "Davies is the winner."

Chapter 12

Harold Avonmore felt extremely well. He could now understand the use of herbs and emetics in the ancient world, (wasn't there a man called Emeticus – where did it occur, was it the *Cena Trimalchionis*?) Ever since the time he had vomited so precipitously and violently into the lavatory, he had felt quite different. With the vomiting he had evacuated much of the horror of his dismissal, his humiliation and his disappointment. Naturally he still felt anger with Sherwood; he reflected on the end of Cicero, whose head and hands were lopped off and placed beside his body on the rostrum. Such a meting out of punishment would be not inappropriate for his headmaster, but nevertheless, it was foolish to dwell on the past. A new era was now opening, as Virgil says: 'A greater story I now unfold', so it would be with him, he would start a greater chapter.

He had had no more dreams. Indeed, he even felt a sense of guilt when he saw Elizabeth Sherwood walking around, for she'd been looking so miserable recently that he wondered whether he had, in some strange telepathic way, subdued her by his shameful dream. There was much that was inexplicable in dreams. Did not the Sibyl point out the tree of dreams to Aeneas in Book Six of the *Aeneid,* and did not false dreams escape from the underworld by the gate of horn? False dreams were what he had been a victim of! "Dreams in the Ancient World"! It might make an interesting study for a paper.

For now he would have time to write papers, and he would also have time for the telescope.

It occurred to him, gradually, that there were many, many, unpleasant duties in his life that he would no longer have to fulfil. He would not have to stay up until eleven and lock all the doors of Humbert House; he would not have to daily bag and list lost property; he would not have to write out in longhand all fifty-eight of the prize-winners' bookplates; he would not have to teach Classics to stupid and unresponsive children. It also occurred to him that he would be gone when next year's GCSE and A Level results came out. He would not, of course, neglect the boys sitting these exams, (that was not in his nature), but he would not feel inclined to slog away for the sake of getting them a few more marks. He would concentrate on what interested him.

There were other benefits too. When the news broke in the Common Room, he was an object of interest and concern. Men who had not spoken to him for two years or more, or some who had never spoken to him at all, became most solicitous. Yes, even the woman in the Buttery had asked him about his plans. He was under no illusions, he knew that a great deal of sympathy was directed at him because people were glad it was he that was going and not themselves. He observed that in their very sympathy, they tried to elicit the details and the stages of his demotion so, he supposed, they might develop some form of protection for themselves. Nevertheless, it was pleasant to be, as it were, centre stage and the object of courteous attention.

Take, for example, Roger Coles, the rugby coach. He had for months sat sideways, with his legs hanging down over the chair which Harold had hitherto regarded as his own in the Staffroom. Since the news, the chair had been vacated and no one sat in it but himself.

Take the matter of free periods and cover: because his teaching load was not an unduly heavy one, Martin Wood had placed him high on the list of staff to do 'cover' when a colleague was ill. And now, although there were three staff absent, his name did not appear on the list.

The third window pane in the second window from the end in his classroom had been broken for as long as he could remember. He had given up asking Mr Sunas, the handyman, to see to it, but now, inexplicably, it had been mended – although this might, of course, have something to do with the four candidates who were coming for the Classics post. Sherwood always liked outsiders to see the school at its best.

"Sorry to hear the news," said a young man who had joined the staff last term, and whom he had once overheard making derogatory remarks about the safety pin in his trousers. He had smiled graciously.

"It's a great shame," said Filbert, who taught Physics, and was himself approaching retiring age. "I remember when you had twelve Oxbridge candidates."

"Five of them scholars, too," he had concurred, he trusted Filbert would not find him unduly hubristic.

But the person who had been most genuinely concerned and practical, had been Martin Wood, a decent chap, Avonmore had always thought. Perhaps too hand-in-glove with the Head, but fair-minded for all that.

"This is a sorry business, Harold," he had said one day, coming into the Changing Rooms as he was collecting up the Lost Property.

"Res moventur," acknowledged Harold.

"Quite!" said Martin, who had no Latin, (not that Harold held this against him). "What we all want to know, Harold, is what sort of a send-off you'd like next term."

"Hah!" said Harold, "a triumphum!" And he thought how he

would like to ride along the school drive in a Roman chariot, with Digby Sherwood tied to the wheels and a few other unhelpful people walking along behind, in chains. Perhaps Elizabeth could grace the procession, dressed in a torn stola with her hair hanging loose."

"I'm only an ignorant scientist, I'm afraid," said Martin. "You'll have to give me some ideas."

"Most kind." said Harold. "I shall put my mind to it."

"The Head and I were talking," continued Martin, as Harold lined up three cricket boots, "he is particularly anxious that it should be something special."

"Ah," said Harold, as he carefully removed the laces from a boot ready to list separately. "Something special?" Once Digby Sherwood had been castrated, he might wait on him at cena, while he himself dallied with Elizabeth on a purple couch.

"Do you have any thoughts?"

As Elizabeth removed the wreath of laurel leaves from his brow, he placed a hand beneath her stola and felt for her pudenda; they were very moist ...'

"That boot's soaking," said Martin. "I should put it on the radiator – do say, if you think of anything you'd like or need."

Harold nodded his head. "I shall give it my full consideration," he said. "Thank you Martin, I know from whom the thought emanated."

"If you mean me, I'm afraid you're wrong," said Martin. "It was solely the Head. He is very concerned about the whole matter." He got up to go. He wondered why on earth Avonmore should be sitting with his hand inside a wet cricket boot. Perhaps Digby had been right after all. He usually was.

Harold watched him leave and continued his train of thought: there was all the business connected with the interviews. Again, he was to be man of the moment. He would, of course, have liked to have composed the advertisement. It would have been a courtesy to him, he would have thought. As it was, he was only permitted to approve it; he had said he thought the application period too short, but, of course, this was ignored. He had to admit, however, that the wording was satisfactory. When the advertisement had appeared in the TES, he had cut it out very neatly, and stuck it in his scrapbook, the one he kept for matters that appertained to himself. He had been keeping the scrap-book for fifteen years now. And whenever he took it out, he wished it had not got pictures of the Mr Men on the front. But now he would have time to cover it with something suitable. The most recent cutting showed a picture of quite a youthful man in a gown, surrounded by twelve worthy-looking boys. "Oxbridge Bound!" it was entitled. The article itself unfortunately made disappointing reading, being full of errata.He measured an interval of five centimetres from the top and drew lines with his BB pencil so he would get it in absolutely straight.

> *A temporary vacancy exists in the Classics Department at Mowberry School. The successful applicant will aid the present distinguished Head of Classics, Mr Harold Avonmore, to successfully bring to completion the Advanced and GCSE courses ...*

Harold took out a red, highlighting pen and underlined "Present distinguished Head of Classics, Mr Harold Avonmore." He was not displeased with the result.

Chapter 13

May passed into June. She had never known days go so slowly. She wasn't worried really. After all, she was only one day late and that wasn't much, really. Only she was often early – but one day was nothing. She would probably start during this lunch and get her dress all messed up. Perhaps she would go for a walk or something this afternoon, do some exercise. It might start things off. She wouldn't worry anyway, or Diggy would get suspicious. He'd already said how quiet she'd been over the last few weeks and she hadn't even felt much like sex. Anyway, she mustn't do anything that might make him suspicious. Even if the curse hadn't come, she might have to pretend that it had, because he would know when it was meant to be, but then, suppose she pretended it had come, and then if it really did come he'd know she'd been lying. It was all so complicated.

"You look pretty, Liz," Digby had come up to their room to change his shirt and to fetch her so they could go into lunch together.

In fact, he did not think she did look at her best facially. It seemed to him that she looked rather white and listless and she had a spot on her chin; but for various reasons he was following a policy of being nice to her and trying to say things that would make her happy. He paused a minute from running a comb through his hair (which he wore rather long). "I like that dress".

"It's my new Laura Ashley; you said wear something long."

It was an amazingly light and filmy dress, made of white chiffon with flowers all over it, and it seemed to float about Elizabeth as she stood with her long straight golden hair hanging down her back; she looked almost ethereal, other-worldly, and yet, at the same time, sensual. Another thing about the dress was that it was low in the front and very, very tight over Elizabeth's rather full breasts.

Ever since the night of the extraordinary intense and painful orgasm, he had felt peculiar in regard to Elizabeth. When he had been married to Belinda, he had felt a constant desire for sex which he had partially satisfied by a sort of automatic plunging into Belinda's dry depths. It had not been good, but it had kept things under control. Elizabeth, on the other hand, with her beauty and her inexhaustible appetite for sex, had seemed to provide the answer, and certainly almost until Ronnie's birth, and even since, he had been relieved of the constraints put on the rest of his life, by the relief he obtained from her body.

But recently, since that night in fact, he had been consumed by a sort of hunger, and he wasn't sure that it was a healthy sort of hunger; he was aware in himself, not exactly a desire to hurt her physically, but of a need to rid himself of this violent urge as quickly as possible, even if it entailed a lack of gentleness, and then to get back to the business of living, running a school, and behaving in a civilised manner.

In the early days when they had started sleeping together, he had played all sorts of games with her. She had loved it when he cried, "I am crazy with lust and now I shall ravage you." It had been a game that he could initiate when he felt so inclined, something for them both to laugh about afterwards. But, for some reason, it wasn't like that now.

Perhaps, in those early days, he had forgiven her faults, because he had believed that under his guidance she would flourish and improve, for he had always been a talented teacher, achieving amazing results from even the most unpromising boy. There was no reason why Elizabeth, especially when she became a mother, should not lose the naiveté of youth and become sensible, as well as beautiful.

Unfortunately, it had not happened like that. Perhaps, because he was no longer young, he lacked the patience of a man in his twenties or thirties; perhaps, because he had become unused to teaching now, his life being spent in PR work and administration, he no longer possessed the skills he once had.

He thought of these things late at night, lying post- coitally in silence, because Elizabeth tended to fall asleep soon afterwards. And when he thought of them, he was willing to take on board his own shortcomings, but suspected that the real fault lay with Elizabeth: she simply lacked the ability to advance, she had only her looks, and she had allowed herself to become dependent on them. This, of course, Martin (curse him) had foreseen, and tried to warn Digby of, before the marriage, but he had been obstinate, dazzled by the prospect of owning such a desirable object, and seeking the end to being a prey to lust.

Was that now why he in some way wanted to hurt her, because she had disappointed him, and because he could now only see her for what she was, a woman too young and entirely unsuitable?

And, as he looked at her in the filmy dress through which he could almost make out the outlines of her naked body, and out of which her breasts strained as if they longed to be taken and bruised, he felt the all-too familiar hardening and was filled with a great longing to tear at the bodice of her dress, and bite into the breasts of her stupidity. He glanced at his watch.

"Take your dress off," he said harshly, "I have to fuck you." And his voice sounded strange and unfamiliar to him, lacking the habitual civilised overtones.

"Oh, Diggy, there isn't time." She didn't want to do it now, she had just put on all her make-up and done her hair.

"Do as I say." His face was white and had to clench his hands to stop himself from reaching out for the dress and tearing at it. He grabbed hold of her and bit hard into her neck.

Then the door burst open and a small figure ran in. "Dada, Dada!" It shouted gleefully, making for Digby and ignoring his mother.

"Why, Ronnie, where did you spring from?" He felt his whole body relax at the sight of his son. He bent down to pick him up and looked quickly at the door for the au-pair. He could only hope to God she had not been a witness to his behaviour, for which he now felt only shame, as desire faded from him, and he held his son in his arms.

"I am sorry," said Marie-Louise, from outside the door. "He run very quick from me. I am sorry, I regret ..."

"Don't worry about it!" He smiled, his easy manner returning. "Have you had a good morning?"

"Thank you."

"Where have you been, Ronnie?" he asked, still holding him. Elizabeth was re-doing her hair in the mirror and took no notice of her son.

"Dada," he said, reaching for his father's tie, but Digby knew about children and forestalled him by turning him upside down.

"I shan't turn you back up until you tell Daddy." He tickled him and Ronnie started laughing. "Where have you been?"

"Ronnie is not saying much these days," said Marie-Louise.

Digby upturned his son and set him down and looked at the au-pair whom he considered a very sensible girl; it was a pity she was so plain.

"Why do you think that is, Marie-Louise... pourquoi…?"

"I do not know," said Marie-Louise. "I tell Elizabeth, she say that it does not matter. Perhaps..."

"Well, thank you for mentioning this, Marie-Louise. I'd like to talk further with you. Ronnie, leave those things alone! Ronnie!"

"Let's go," said Elizabeth, who had been putting some more scent on, "we don't want to be late."

"Well," he said, smiling at Marie Louise, "we must all have another of our meals together, and then we can talk this problem through, don't you think so, Elizabeth?"

"Oh yes." Perhaps she would wear the other earrings, they made her eyes look bluer.

"Now, Ronnie," said Digby, squatting down next to him. "I want you to promise me you'll be a good boy this afternoon. I shall ask Marie-Louise to tell me if you're a naughty boy, and then I shall look fierce and frown," and Digby frowned. "But if you're a good boy, a really good boy, there might be a little treat. We'll have to see."

Ronnie opened his eyes wide and he looked suddenly very like Elizabeth.

Chapter 14

It was a day Harold Avonmore had been looking forward to immensely; it was the day of all days, for he was to choose the successful Classicist. Hah! The choice was to be solely his. And now, here he was, with all before him, walking across The Green Sward (a privilege only allowed to Senior staff), dressed in his familiar suit, which he had had cleaned specially for the occasion. He did notice that other men's trousers seemed somewhat fuller and reached to the shoe nowadays; not that this in the least mattered, not a thing to worry over when on the way to drinks at the headmaster's house to meet the candidates. Sherwood to give him his due ...

"Langley, tuck your shirt in. We are in England now, not on the beach in Florida."

"I wish we were, Sir."

"Perhaps I shall be, soon, Langley."

"Sir?"

"Nothing, Langley. Hurry along." Yes, Sherwood to give him his due, had said the decision about the new Classicist was to be his. Pleasing that. And next term his farewell ceremony. What form should it take? "Ah Stewart! Are you bound for Mr Sherwood's lunch?"

"Yes, Sir."

"Then we shall walk together, Stewart."

"Sir." He was going to make some excuse, but remembered what the Headman had said about being nice to Hazzer. "Are you looking forward to your retirement, Sir?" Stewart didn't much like old Hazzer Avonmore, mainly because he so often told him that he was stupid, but he was not a boy to harbour a grudge, and now he felt quite sorry for the old chap.

"I shall not be totally displeased to lay down the burden I have carried for so long."

"No, Sir." Probably the Headman had told him to leave because he was so odd. You could never understand what he was on about – and just look at those trousers!

"What would you like us to do for your leaving ceremony, Sir?"

"Everybody asks me that, Stewart. I know it's of great personal concern to Mr Sherwood.

Stewart could see Davies coming round by Humbert House. Avonmore had seen him too. "Ah, Davies, when are you going to get your hair cut?"

"Saturday, Sir."

"I trust so, Davies. I look forward to seeing capillos sectos."

"Sir?"

"You may accompany Stewart and me across the Sward." Harold reflected that others should share in his day of importance.

Stewart suddenly remembered the bet he'd had with Davies - ages ago now, before he'd been in the San with flu; well, it would be interesting to see how far Davies had got with Elizabeth - she was sure to be there. Nowhere, probably. He must remind him about it.

"Sir," acquiesced Davies. It was such a relief to be walking to the Headman's house with impunity. He wished now that the Elizabeth business had never happened. He couldn't stand any more shocks like that one a couple of days ago. He cast his mind back as the three of them walked across The Green Sward together.

Hazzer had been late, he always was nowadays. Singh was doing his Thucydides and he and Stewart were not doing much at all, although Stewart kept going on about his girlfriend, Melissa and he had been sorely tempted to tell him about Elizabeth. Then Felicity, that old cow of a secretary, appeared at the door with a piece of paper in her hand.

"St John Davies, the Headmaster would like to see you." In the seconds that elapsed before she went on to say that the Headmaster would also like to see Gowinder Singh and Simon Stewart, his mind had run the gamut of horrors: suspension, expulsion, Oxbridge gone, parental shame.., a hundred scenarios, each more terrible than the last.

And then, it was all nothing. The Headman had only wanted to talk about Hazzer and the Classics interviews – and a free binge. Brilliant. No worries, after all. Everything OK, as usual. Life was pretty good again, and everybody kept saying he'd be the next Head Boy; well, he didn't want anything getting in the way of that. Best to ignore Elizabeth from now on.

"Ah, here we are!" Hazzer Avonmore was saying, knocking loudly at the door of the Headman's house. "I intend to enjoy this!"

Chapter 15

Martin arrived late because he had been doing the GCSE entries, and now he found everything well underway. As he paused at the door and observed the green silk walls and beautiful proportions of the room, he thought how it suited Digby, but he also thought how sad it was, that he could not be happy here.

A thin, bearded candidate was talking to a large, aggressive looking woman of indeterminate years and a bright red crumpled suit.

"It took me five hours on the train," he was saying.

"I drove," said the Red Suit. "I always drive."

"I prefer to travel by train," said the Thin Beard. "I utilised my time in writing my paper on Theocritus."

"I spend all my spare time in lesson preparation." She turned abruptly away. "Who are you?" she asked Elizabeth.

Elizabeth hadn't known St John was to be there, and she wanted to avoid looking at him, so he shouldn't think she cared about him not coming to see her. Oh, how she wished her period would start.

"I said, who are you?" said the aggressive woman in the red.

"Oh," said Elizabeth, "I'm the Headmaster's wife."

"*Which* is the Headmaster's wife?" said the woman looking round for someone else.

"I am," said Elizabeth. She couldn't imagine a more horrible party; there was no one to talk to, and she had to keep avoiding looking in the direction of St John. There were no dishy young masters, only a man with a silly little beard, an ancient old codger and two women, the great ugly woman who was talking at her now, and a young woman with her black hair in a bob. She supposed that if she dressed properly, she might be quite attractive.

"It took me five hours on the train," the Thin Beard was saying to Digby.

"I am so sorry," said Digby. "I do hope you're not too tired." His handsome face expressed concern.

"No, just a slight migraine," replied the Beard. "I worked on the train, writing my paper on Theocritus."

"How extremely interesting," said Digby, mentally crossing him off the list. "You must let me introduce you to Mr Avonmore, who will, I am sure, want to hear all about it."

Martin helped himself to a schooner of sherry and made his way over to the young, attractive girl. She reminded him a little of Jean, before she had become ill.

"My name's Wood," he said, "Martin Wood. Now, who are you?" and he peered at her name- badge short-sightedly through his thick rimmed spectacles.

"Yvonne Bonnington," she replied, and then she smiled, "I can't help feeling a bit intimidated by all this. I mean the room is so beautiful, and all these people ..."

He considered her unassuming, but confident, and doubted that she was intimidated at all. "Oh, you don't want to worry about us," he said, "we're all quite harmless really. Now tell me, where are you from?"

"Just down the road really," said Yvonne, whose hair, Martin noticed, was extremely glossy-looking, "from Charcester."

"No!" said Martin. "I was brought up there! You didn't go to St Paul's Grammar by any chance?"

"Well, yes, I did actually," said Yvonne, "but I don't remember you."

"That's because you'd have been in your pram," said Martin. "Can I offer you some sherry? Where's your glass?"

"Actually, I don't drink," said Yvonne, "not that I disapprove or anything, I just don't like the taste of alcohol."

"You don't mind if I do, I hope," said Martin, refilling his schooner.

Davies was here, there and everywhere with the canapés. The only person to whom he did not offer them was Elizabeth. He stole a quick glance at her. She was looking quite fit. He had seen Stewart looking at her too. Pity not to tell really, after all, it would do no harm, would it? And it would make him stop going on and on about Melissa. And look at Singh there with his stupid turban. Well, he'd see.

"Mr Sherwood, Sir? No? Mr Wood, would you like a canapé and ..." (he glanced at her name badge), "Miss Bonnington? Would you like a canapé? The ones with the bits of smoked salmon are nice ... a canapé for you, Sir? ..." He moved on with his tray to the large elderly man.

"Would you like a canapé, Sir?"

"I'm afraid I don't hear very well," said the elderly man, "what did you say?"

"I'll have one of those," said the large red woman. "In fact, I'll have two."

"Jolly good," said Davies.

"Has someone got you some orange juice, Gowinder?" asked Martin. He knew the boy was not allowed to drink alcohol.

"Thank you, Sir."

""And these canapés here," Martin prodded one, "are mushroom. You could manage one of those?"

"Thank you, Sir." It struck Martin that Singh would be no good. You couldn't have a Head Boy who didn't drink – and a vegetarian, to boot.

"What A levels did you do?" asked Stewart who found himself next to Elizabeth. What a bull-shitter Davies was! A fat lot of chance he'd have with her! Still, he was surprised Davies hadn't come up with some lie about it all.

"I did Home Economics and Theatre Studies." She concentrated on Stewart, wanting to make it clear to St John that she wasn't looking at him. She had waited in every day for a week, but he'd never come round. She'd even gone to watch a first eleven cricket match, but he hadn't taken any notice of her, at all.

"What grades did you get?" persisted Stewart. He could see her tits through the dress.

"I got an F for Home Economics," said Elizabeth, "And I think I got a D or an E for Theatre Studies."

"Which University did you go to?"

"I didn't go to University. I went to a college, and did Creative Arts."

"Was that interesting?"

"No, it was very boring." Neither wished to speak to the other, but they were wedged in a corner, with no obvious means of escape.

"How did you meet the Headmaster, then?"

"I met him at a party." Elizabeth felt that the standard of conversation was improving and became quite enthusiastic. "I was going out with this boy at Granchester University, and he was doing some subject like ... I think it was some sort of History, and Digby was his tutor, and had asked him to a party at his house. So I went along. And the next day Diggy, the Headmaster, I mean, rang me up and asked me out."

"Didn't your boyfriend mind?"

"I didn't tell him. Anyway, Diggy, I mean, the Headmaster, and I went out, and two months later we were married."

"A whirlwind romance," replied Stewart politely.

"Well, yes, it was really," said Elizabeth. For a moment she forgot about the worry with her period and the fact that St John didn't bother looking at her. And she thought, instead, of that fabulous time that now seemed so long ago, how Digby had bought her lots of things, always sending her flowers and stuff. And the honeymoon in Greece, they'd fucked all the time. Some days they hardly got out of bed. But that had all changed when they'd come back, and he started being Headmaster, and he didn't have any time for her any more. And then she was pregnant, and Digby was cross about that because she'd forgotten the pill, and he said he didn't want any more children because he'd got his two grown-up snooty daughters ...

"Is there a lavatory?" asked the elderly man, prodding Stewart. "Goes right through me, that sherry does."

"Let me show you, Sir," said Stewart. He'd had enough of Elizabeth anyway.

He bumped into Davies on his way back. "Haven't heard much about our bet," he said. "Why not try a quick snog in the corner before lunch?"

Despite all his previous resolutions, Davies was goaded to reply. "That's all you know."

"Oh yes? Where's your proof then?"

"Tomorrow," he said impetuously, "in the Greek lesson."

"Luncheon is served," announced the Italian butler. And they all had to file into the dining room.

"You've had three glasses already," said Digby sotto voce to Martin in passing. "And it's got to be the pretty one."

"Two affirmatives," said Martin.

The Dining Room was as impressive in its way, as the Drawing

Room. Lacking the green silk walls and the view of the river, it was more enclosed on itself, even to the point of being claustrophobic. The chandeliers bore down on one with a menacing glint, and the walls contained numerous portraits of previous headmasters. For the most part, they had a sardonic air, as if they enjoyed the discomfiture of the candidates. They would certainly have disapproved of Elizabeth, surreptitiously checking in her bag to see if she had any tampax, just in case.

The table, which normally stood highly polished and uncompromising in its splendour, was today covered in a white starched linen cloth. It contained a fair amount of silver, most of it having come from Digby's family. And Martin thought of Digby's illustrious ancestors, noblemen and squires, now retreating into the mists of antiquity. Perhaps this was from where he had got his looks and his easy air of authority. But his high connections were another of those things that Digby never mentioned, being modest in this respect, as he was in regard of his physique and, to be fair, his success. It was only, he reflected, in regard to sex, that Digby lost his way.

When they were all placed around the table, Elizabeth felt sure she could feel a familiar tug in her lower abdomen, and she started to move towards the door.

"We're just going to have grace," hissed Martin.

"Oh," said Elizabeth coming back. How everyone stared at her! Diggy said a long, boring grace all in Latin or Greek or something, and then they all sat down.

"I could send you my paper on Theocritus," said the Beard to Avenmore..

The prawn cocktail appeared.

"I hardly think that will be necessary," said Avonmore, tucking in. He was enjoying himself.

"It has appeared in *Greece and Rome*," said the Beard, not particularly liking Avonmore's tone, but mindful of the need to be polite to him. "Do you contribute?"

"My last contribution was made some thirty years ago."

"Quite right," said the large red woman. "Too much stuff written nowadays."

"Surely you can't be serious?" asked Digby. He had discounted her along with the Beard. He couldn't understand how the elderly man had got on the shortlist; he seemed to be totally uninterested in anything but the food.

"I am afraid I can't remember the name of your present school," he said, determined to give him a fair trial somehow.

"Yes," said the Elderly man. "I enjoy seafood". Then it dawned on Digby: there had been two men called Jones; Felicity must have sent the letter to the wrong one, because the other man had sounded quite promising. She really wasn't much good. He'd have to do something about her.

"I am so glad you like it," said Digby. He turned to talk to the pretty one. He'd bet Avonmore wouldn't want her. He'd want the man with the beard and the migraine.

"How's Ronnie?" asked Martin.

"He's all right," said Elizabeth. It was typical that she had to sit next to Martin. She could tell he was secretly criticising her and comparing her to the precious Belinda. Anyway, what business was Ronnie of his? She was fed up with the subject. Digby had made them all have supper together last week, Marie-Louise, Ronnie, her and himself. He went on and on discussing Ronnie's progress with Marie-Louise, and then they both ended up talking French, and she couldn't understand a word.

And then he kept saying she ought to do more with Ronnie, not realising how difficult he was with her, just because Ronnie was all right for him. And now it looked like she had to talk about it all over again with Martin.

"Do you have a child?" bellowed the red woman, leaning over.

"A delightful little boy," said Martin. All right, she could answer for herself.

"How old?" asked the Red. "What age?"

"Three," said Elizabeth.

"I thought he was still two," said Martin. "Have I missed his birthday?"

"I meant two," said Elizabeth crossly, "he's nearly three."

"Do you teach?" asked the Red. "Vegetables, please."

"No."

"Well, what do you do then?"

"Well, I ..."

"She helps her husband," said Martin, "at occasions like these." Couldn't he let her answer for herself?

"Excuse me," she said, "I just have to go to the loo." Once again, she found them all staring at her when she came back, and her period hadn't started after all.

"Did you go to the Classical Conference in Rome last Spring?" asked the Red of Avonmore.

"I never go to conferences." Spinach! Ah, he hadn't had that in six months, and fresh too, by the taste of it, none of your frozen stuff.

"I like to keep abreast of the latest developments," she said fiercely.

"I wasn't aware," said Avonmore, that Classics had changed significantly over the last two thousand years." He turned his back. He was going to talk to that little girl with the glossy black hair. Nice tight little figure. He would say something appropriate to her young years.

"Do you also prefer modern text books like the *Cambridge Latin Course*, or more traditional methods?"

"I'm happy with either," replied Yvonne, "but of course, if I was teaching here, I should have to be guided by your preferences."

"Ah," said Harold.

"I bet you didn't," said Stewart to Davies.

Digby gestured to the butler. "Has the vegetarian dish arrived yet, for the boy with the turban?" he asked. Poor Gowinder; he looked very lost. God, he wished Elizabeth would go to the lavatory before these lunches, and not disappear off there in the middle of a meal, like a child. How amusing that Avonmore was chatting up the pretty one! Of course, he should have remembered, he wouldn't necessarily be against a woman; he'd seen him eyeing up Elizabeth before now. And hadn't he been married once? Perhaps he wouldn't have too much trouble winning him over to his point of view, after all.

"I was five hours on the train," said the bearded man to Elizabeth, as she returned to the table.

"Oh, were you?" She really couldn't see why they were all making so much fuss of that dark girl; her suit was really old-fashioned and frumpy.

"I utilised the time studying. I am writing a paper on Theocritus."

"Who?" said Elizabeth. St John hadn't looked at her once – and she might be pregnant ... with his child.

"Have you come from a far distance, Sir?" asked Singh of the elderly man. He was still waiting for his vegetarian dish.

"I don't hear well," he replied, "and I can't get foreign accents at all. Pass the potatoes up, lad."

"Gowinder?" asked Digby. "How are things in the village?"

Singh's face lit up. "Thank you, Sir. We have a well now; a plough and six buffalo. It is all thanks to your appeal, Sir." He wanted to tell him that his photo was on the place of honour above the statue of the goddess Khali, but he considered it not suitable at this time. He hoped that one of these two women would not be appointed.

He would not like to receive his instruction from a female teacher. "Thank you," he said as the vegetarian dish arrived at last. It was quiche and salad, most of which he would be unable to eat as it contained egg, and a surprising amount of onion. He was, however, used to such privations and took a fork to the lettuce.

""I was on the train for five hours." Martin heard a voice close to him. He reached out his hand for the wine bottle, but catching Digby's eye, offered it to the Beard.

"I was able to utilise the time in writing my paper on Theocritus," he said, shaking his head at the wine.

"Really?" said Martin. Digby or no Digby, he was going to have another glass.

"It would be terrible to do all that work and leave the papers on the train," said Yvonne.

"I disagree," said Avonmore. "When I am caught short on British Rail, I can seldom find a sufficiency."

Chapter 16

"And now for my first exhibit…" said St John Davies as he, Stewart and Singh were waiting for the Latin lesson. Perhaps he was being stupid, but he simply couldn't keep quiet after Stewart had said Elizabeth hadn't seemed very interested in him at the lunch thing, and besides, it seemed that everything he did went right nowadays. And what a star he'd been at that lunch handing stuff round to everyone, just as if he'd been hosting it all! Watch out, Diggy!

Gowinder looked at his watch and noticed Mr Avonmore was five minutes late. It seemed that he was less punctual recently. He opened his text and tried to ignore Davies.

"You will be interested in these, Singh," said Davies, fingering his case and enjoying a sense of theatre."

"I, Davies?"

"Yes, you, Singh-a-ling, "and do you know why?" Gowinder made no reply. He had been subject to Davies' insults for three years. It was best to ignore them.

"I'll tell you why, because …" and Davies opened the case with panache, "because they're … black!" And with a flourish he drew out a pair of lace knickers.

"How about these, eh? Shall I tell you something?"

Stewart gaped.

"I've been inside what has been inside them! They're Elizabeth's."

"Liar," said Stewart promptly. He didn't know what to think. Gowinder, on the other hand, turned away in disgust. He wouldn't let his mind dwell on Davies' foul insinuations.

Davies turned to Stewart. "I did it, mate. And let me tell you .."

"They could be anyone's." Stewart played for time. Maybe Davies *had*, after all?

"They could be, but they're not. They're Elizabeth's. Now, let me take you through it, blow by blow. And I mean blow by blow."

"'Course you didn't."

Singh looked at the Latin verse and tried not to listen.

"Oh, before I elaborate, and don't you pretend, Singh, that you're not interested….we all know what Indians are like. I've got a little bill to settle with you, Stewart, apropos of a small bet we made." He drew out a sheet of paper, but before he could go on, the door opened and Avonmore came in. He was not alone. He was accompanied by the brunette woman from the lunch thing. Stewart appraised her, really not bad considering she must be about thirty. Gowinder sighed, he wished there were not suddenly so many ladies at Mowberry, for what did they bring, but trouble? Davies stuffed the knickers and the note into the desk.

"Salvete, iuvenes," said Avonmore.

"Salve, magister," replied Singh. Stewart made an inarticulate sound.

"Stewart!"

"Salvete, Magister."

"Stewart, I am not plural. 'Salvete' is the plural form of the imperative. Davies?"

Davies turned his attention to the brunette. He smiled winningly at her.

"Salvete Magister et Magistra."

"Hah!" replied Avonmore. "This is Miss Bonnington. She may

well be assisting me next term, prior to my ... ah ... departure."

Yvonne smiled. 'I am looking forward to getting to know you all," she said, "and Mr Avonmore has kindly allowed me to look in on this lesson for a few minutes. May I sit here?"

She took herself to the back; Davies wished she hadn't chosen to sit directly behind him and the desk with the knickers in.

Stewart felt a moment of great happiness. Hazzer was actually going! He would be taught by someone else! Marvellous! Elizabeth's knickers? No way!

Stewart's happiness was matched by Avonmore's. Lovely little woman sitting at the back there! And *she* could teach Stewart the difference between singulars and plurals.

"Perhaps you would care to tell Miss Bonnington, Stewart, what we are presently studying in the Catullus."

"Yes, Sir ... but I was in the San while you were doing it."

"Singh?"

"The Lesbia poems, Sir. We are about to start 'nullis se dicit'."

"You will enjoy teaching Singh, Miss Bonnington. He has the makings of a scholar about him."

"I'm sure I shall." Yvonne smiled at Singh; she supposed he would dislike being taught by a woman. Never mind, it would all work out all right when he had got over the first few lessons.

"Davies, have the goodness to give us the benefit of your erudition and construe the first two lines."

"Sir." Davies cast his eyes along at Singh's notes. "She says .. um ... my woman ... says that she prefers to marry no one, not even if Juppiter himself were to ask her."

"Hmm. Not bad. How many 'p's' in Juppiter, Stewart.

"One, Sir."

"Two, Stewart, two.

"I thought, Sir ..."

"Ah, you have that capacity, Stewart? Splendid! Now, Singh, pray continue."

"So she says," Gowinder continued, "but what a lady says to her ... er ... eager lover ..." Why were there all these ladies? "...ought to be written in wind and in ... um ... fast water ... rushing water."

"Very good, very good. 'Rapida aqua', a good description of the River Mow as it goes through our grounds. Stewart, repeat!"

"I wonder," said Yvonne, when Stewart had eventually finished, "if I might ask the boys a question, Mr Avonmore?"

"Hrmmm."

"Do you think," said Yvonne (and three pairs of eyes turned to stare at her), "that Catullus is being very unfair to us poor women? Some of us mean what we say."

Stewart smiled. "My girlfriend, Melissa ..." he said, and Miss Bonnington nodded encouragingly. But Davies interrupted to say that all women could be every bit as bad as Catullus suggested, and Singh said that he had no experience of such matters. Harold, on the other hand, simply smiled in a superior fashion; he was beginning to look forward to the time when he might become the cupidus amans of Miss Bonnington.

When they had finished the poem, Miss Bonnington said she was very sorry but she had been asked to return to the Staff Room at half past, for a further tour of the school. Would Mr Avonmore think her awfully rude ...?"

Actually, Mr Avonmore was rather relieved; as nice as it was having Miss Bonnington's soft green sweater to look at, he wasn't sure he wanted to hear any more of her polite little interjections. After all, a text was for translating, not for putting new-fangled ideas into.

"Davies."

"Sir."

"Conduct Miss Bonnington to the Staff Room."

"Sir." Typical, wasn't it. Normally it would be a dream to get out of Latin, but now he wasn't so sure. The knickers and note were there in the desk, all unattended. He wasn't happy; still, there was no escape. Forget it. Chat up this Classics bit.

He took Yvonne out of the Classics Room and prepared to turn on the charm. "I do hope you're going to be teaching us, Miss Bonnington. It will be so nice to have somebody young." Well, not so very young.

They left the Classics block and began to cross The Green Sward, Davies smiling his seducer's smile – after all, it had worked with Elizabeth, hadn't it?

"I don't know if you have been told about the mulberry tree over there, Miss Bonnington."

"I don't think I have, Davies. You must tell me."

"They say it's nearly a thousand years old." He thought he would test her. "A bit like Mr Avonmore, really."

"I don't think that's particularly amusing, Davies, do you?" was her short reply. "Mr Avonmore is a remarkable man. You are fortunate to have had the benefit of his teaching." Davies would not find it so easy to get round her, if she got the job; nor, she smiled to herself, would Mr Avonmore.

"Of course, Miss Bonnington. I was only joking. They say the mulberry was planted by William the Conqueror." He reflected that the glossy-haired Classics teacher would not be such a push-over, as he'd hoped.

They went up the steps to the Staff Room and Davies knocked politely. "Here we are, Miss Bonnington, I hope you enjoy the rest of your visit."

"Oh, I am sure I shall, Davies. Oh, and Davies, do brush up on your Catullus, won't you?"

Coles, the rugby coach came to the door.

"Great to see you, Miss Bonnington, come on in." Great tits, he'd have a go if she got the job. A good substitute for old Harold!

As he hurried back, St John heard the bell go. Shit! He'd have to get the note and the knickers and God only knew what he would do with them.

Back in the classroom Stewart had considered the knicker question while Avonmore held forth, and it was in his mind to take the note and the knickers at the end of the lesson. To be fair, he hadn't decided on what to do with them. Probably just make Davies sweat a bit and then hand them back. But the opportunity was not afforded to him.

"You will accompany me to the Staff Room, Stewart, and carry the *Liddell and Scott*. I shall enquire into your knowledge of the imperative *in itinere*."

So the business was left to Gowinder. He was not a vindictive boy, but he had his own sense of justice. Lifting up the knickers with his ruler so as not to be sullied by contact with them, he packed the items carefully into his case along with the piece of paper – he needed some time to consider carefully what best to do with them.

As he left the Classics block he was almost knocked over by Davies who appeared in a great hurry.

"God, you're always in my way, Singh," he complained. "Why don't you blacks know your place?" Gowinder's mind composed itself into resolution. He would rise early the following morning.

"Shit!" muttered St John again to himself when he opened the desk lid and found the knickers and the paper missing. Oh, no big deal, Stewart must have taken them He'd better get them back, though. Shouldn't be too much of a problem; after all, things usually worked out. The Gods had a habit of being on his side.

"Of course, it's your decision entirely," said Digby when the applicants had made their departure. ("Five hours back on the train" was the Beard's parting shot.)

Avonmore was sitting in the elegant chintz arm chair in Digby's drawing room. In fact, the very armchair he had sat in some three weeks since, when he had been given the fateful news. But this was a very different state of affairs; before he had been the minion, fit only to be dismissed, sent away at the whim of one man, but now this same man was humbly seeking his advice, begging him to talk of staff appointments at Mowberry. He crossed his legs and then uncrossed them again. The trousers were rather tight about the crotch.

"Quite, Headmaster." He wouldn't have him castrated now, and he no longer wanted to dally with Elizabeth on the purple couch. He would dally with Yvonne instead.

"I quite appreciate," Digby was saying, "that you may regard a female Classics teacher as inappropriate. We have shown ourselves to be politically correct, by interviewing two women and you must have no compunction about discounting them." Digby smiled benignly. "I expect you favour the man with the beard, whose name escapes me. He seemed a man of great erudition." It was all too easy really.

"Hah!" Avonmore held up his hand. "You must pardon me, Headmaster, if I interrupt you, but I fear you misunderstand the situation." Avonmore smiled quite as benignly at Digby.

"I am most interested," said Digby, leaning forward attentively.

"I fear you are sadly mistaken concerning the bearded individual."

"Really?"

"Yes; he was a man of much pretension and of little intellect." This sounded well. He would render it into Greek when he returned to the flat, using the style of Demosthenes.

"Ah, well, you know about these things, Harold."

This comment was a little ambiguous, so Harold hastened to continue. "We have never been backward looking at Mowberry, and no one has been more in the forefront of progress than I, although retaining the best of the traditional mores."

"Quite." Digby reflected that it was going to be a tedious quarter of an hour.

"And I see here, Headmaster, an opportunity, a fine opportunity of combining these two virtues."

"Please do explain, Harold."

"Yvonne," said Harold more abruptly than he had intended. "Yvonne Bonnington. She's the perfect exponent of these very qualities."

"What would you say are her particular assets?"

"Hah!" A nice firm little sit-you-on, little round breasts like tennis balls, and a desire to do whatever he advised. "A combination, I would say, of scholarship and diligence."

"Well ..." Digby sounded doubtful, "....what about the other woman, the one in red?"

"A monstrous woman!"

"Really? And the elderly gentleman, Mr Jones? He didn't have a great amount to say, but perhaps there were hidden depths?"

"Senile!" said Avonmore. "No, Headmaster. There is absolutely no doubt in my mind." He leant back triumphantly. It was amazing how far his trousers seemed to shoot up his legs. He leaned forward again.

Digby kept him waiting. "Well, Harold," he said at last. "I must bow to your superior judgement in this matter."

Harold smiled; he wouldn't even have Sherwood chained to the triumphal car now. He could stand in the crowd and watch as a member of the *vulgus popularis*.

"You'll be writing straight away, I trust. We shouldn't wish to lose this candidate through dilatoriness."

"I shall write later this afternoon and catch the evening post. Now what about some tea? I'm afraid we don't have biscuits from Dumfries, but the shortbread is very acceptable."

Chapter 17

When she woke up, she could hear Diggy downstairs talking to Marie-Louise – something about eyes... oh yes, she was going to take Ronnie for an eye test. She had said she would take them herself in the XJ6, but Marie-Louise preferred to walk with the push-chair. Elizabeth knew that it was because Marie Louise wanted to go on her own, though she said the fresh air was good for Ronnie. Yes, there was the door going. How early she set off, she herself could never get going until nine or ten. And then it struck her!

Something wonderful, something unbelievably wonderful! So wonderful she dared not believe it! She withdrew her hand from the bed. It was covered in blood! It had come! It had come! She wasn't pregnant after all. Oh, how fantastic! How silly she'd been to be worried! How stupid! Now she could get on and enjoy life again. She might even take a walk around school just to see if she bumped into St John. She could ask him to coffee or something. Oh how wonderful! She would never worry about anything ever again. It was almost worth pretending it hadn't come just to find out again that it had.

She hadn't heard Diggy leave, but she would put a CD on, something raunchy. He was really stuffy about pop music, just because he liked all that classical stuff. Then she would have a shower, get dressed, go into town, maybe buy some clothes. No, she'd take a walk round the school and just see if St John was about.

While she was drying herself after the shower she heard her music switched off. Surely it couldn't be Diggy? He would have gone by now. She came out wrapped in a towel, her hair hanging wet down her back. Oh, it was Diggy.

"What are you ...?" There was something very odd about the way he looked. Silently he held a piece of paper out to her.

"What's that?" she asked smiling. She was really, really, happy today. But Diggy said absolutely nothing, just handed her the piece of paper. She sat down on the floor to read it, all wrapped round with her green towel.

"The Big F" it was headed. "SJ.D's invoice to S.S. in regard to the bet in connection with the shagging... of E.S." She read on, not understanding. There was a list. It read:-

Kiss: £5
Snog: £10
Tits: £15
Cunt: £25
The Works: £50

By each line there was a tick. "Therefore," it concluded, "SJ.D. Is owed fifty pounds on the successful completion of the above objectives, (evidence appended)."

"What does it mean?" she asked, puzzled. Her husband drew a pair of knickers out of a brown envelope and held them out at arm's length. He did not look at her at all.

"Are these yours?" he asked.

Why did was his voice so strange? "Oh yes!" said Elizabeth. She looked at him puzzled. "I got them from Dorothy Perkins". Oh no ... Oh, Jesus!

She went on sitting on the floor with her green towel slipping down, as the full implications of what had happened began slowly to dawn on her: somehow Diggy had found out, and he had got the knickers that ...

"You let him fuck you?" he said very quietly. "St John Davies?"

"Well, not really. I mean ... I didn't mean ... It was only once and very quick." She thought she would smile at him. In the early days he said she had a smile like a Flemish Madonna. She hadn't known what he meant, but it sounded nice.

What frightened her most was the fact that he had gone into his dressing room and brought back a packet of cigarettes. Diggy, who never smoked and who had insisted she was not to smoke in the bedroom, now lay on the bed, a lighted cigarette between his lips. Why was he doing this and being so silent? She thought of something to cheer him up.

"It was only once, Diggy and I'm not pregnant or anything." He turned his head.

He seemed to think about something, but only for a moment. "So that's why you've been so quiet these last few days. You thought you were pregnant." He spoke slowly and deliberately. "And if you had been, and I had not had a vasectomy, you would have passed it off as mine. Perhaps you did that with Ronnie."

"No, I swear, I swear, Diggy. I only ever did it with St John, and only that once. Please ..."

"Where did you do it?"

At first she was tempted to lie, but she knew she was not clever enough to invent a cover story. She knew, although she didn't understand exactly why, that Diggy would be more angry about this than almost anything else. She wrapped the towel round her, it was wet and she was cold.

"Well?"

For the last twenty years of his life, as Housemaster and then as

Headmaster, Digby had been involved in interrogating boys over misdemeanours, some small, some less small, and some for which expulsion would be the only answer. Many boys had cause to fear that "well?"

"Here, Diggy. I ... we had to do it here, there wasn't anywhere ..."

He got up so suddenly and moved so fast that she thought he was coming for her and she shrank away. But he went instead to the lavatory that adjoined the bedroom.

The walls were very thin because the large bedroom had been partitioned off into dressing room, bathroom, and lavatory. He had wanted her to design it, but her taste was so poor he had ended up designing it himself; the walls of the lavatory were only plasterboard.

She got off the floors and sat on the edge of the bed. Her hair was all soaking wet and made her feel cold. She would have liked to put on a sweater but she was fearful of moving. She listened to him. He groaned a bit and she could tell he was having diarrhoea. And this was frightening too, for Diggy never got tummy things; she could only remember once in Greece, and that was soon over. Now she could hear the lavatory paper roll, on and on. But he didn't come out.

While she was wondering what she should do, he emerged, and it struck her as odd that he had not pulled the chain, he was fastidious and had been angry with her on the occasions she had forgotten to do so.

"Go into the lavatory Elizabeth." he said. He was so cold, almost polite.

"I ... don't want to."

"Do as I say, please." And she knew there was no alternative.

He shut the door behind them both, it smelt horrible. There was a pile of paper on the floor where he had wiped himself.

"Kneel down," he said, "and put your face into the bowl."

109

"No! No, Diggy."

"Do as I say, Elizabeth." And again, there was no alternative. And slowly, very slowly he pushed her head with her hair hanging wet down her back, down, inch by inch, and she could not call out for fear of the horrible stuff touching her lips. She shut her eyes.

And suddenly he released her head and pulled the chain. Some of it spattered at her; she did not know whether she was touched by it or not.

She hugged her arms to her and her hands moved convulsively over her shoulders; drops of water fell from her hair and dropped down her back. She began to shiver. "Oh, that was horrible, horrible."

He leant against the door, "yes," he said, "very horrible, but I have been more merciful to you than you to me. I merely showed you my shit, but you plastered me with yours.

"I ... I don't ..."

"You have plastered my hands that I place on small boys shoulders to guide them; you have plastered my feet with which I walk round to see that all is well; you have plastered my ears that hear boys' problems; you have plastered my eyes that looked with delight at what I saw. There is no part of my body upon which you have not defecated."

He had finished. He walked into the bathroom, washed and was gone.

*****

"Felicity! Will you get me Martin, please."

Felicity was relieved. She thought he was all set to lecture him about that letter being sent to the wrong Mr Jones, and that old twerp turning up instead, but he obviously wasn't. Something was up. He looked dreadful.

"I'm afraid Mr Wood is in a meeting, Headmaster. He has the Bursar and the Finance Committee. It's ..."

"I want to see him. Get him on his mobile. Immediately." He turned on his heel.

"Where shall I tell him to meet you?"

Digby went out without replying. Martin would know.

*****

"But Felicity, it's very difficult." Martin could hear her voice scratchily down the phone.

"He said 'immediately', I told him you were with the Finance, but he said ... and he looked very odd. I don't think he's well."

"OK. Can you organise some coffee for the committee and make a new date."

"He didn't say where you had to go, and now he's gone."

"All right, Felicity."

"I'm so sorry, gentlemen," said Martin, standing up and gathering papers. "I'm afraid something of an urgent nature has come up, and I shall have to leave you. Felicity will see to coffee, which is the least we can do. I am so sorry."

Old Colonel Haslett, who never understood what was going on and usually slept through meetings, was beginning to protest. "I say! Wood ..." But Martin had already fled.

*****

His head was resting on his arm on the desk, his other hand held a cigarette. He looked up without moving his head and said heavily, unemotionally, "I'm finished, Martin."

For a moment Martin was afraid Digby would bury his head in

his arms again and refuse to speak. "Don't fuck me about, Digby," said Martin, using the violence of language that might provoke some reaction, for he was shocked at the sight of Digby. He knew he must force him to unburden himself and not allow him to give way to any sort of despair, for that, indeed, would be the end.

"Don't give me shit, Digby, just talk to me." He must will Digby to raise his head by the force of his love for the man. He must mentally drag him, from whatever horror this was, into speech. He held him with his eyes, fierce and insistent. He, too, had been a housemaster and knew how to make the unwilling speak. He dropped his voice and spoke very softly.

"Tell me, Digby."

And Digby told him everything, including what he had done to Elizabeth. He spoke clearly and unemotionally, as if he was presenting a report to the governors. And as he listened, Martin could see that the worst thing for Digby was not the threatened loss of job, reputation, damage to the school, everything that he had laboured tirelessly for all his life, but the fact that he felt he had degraded himself by his behaviour to his wife.

"How could I do that?" he asked. "How can I have done that – and live with myself?" He did not raise his eyes to Martin.

"Well," said Martin, brusquely, getting the brandy and glasses out. "It was simply an object lesson." But he had to ask one thing. "Did you push her face right into it?"

Digby shook his head and Martin felt enormous relief. But what Digby said next was odd, sounding old-fashioned, stilted, even.

"I'm a man of no honour, Martin, no decent man could ever have behaved as I did. You, for example, you could not have done it."

And then Martin made a decision, a decision to disregard the wishes of his dying wife, and tell Digby what he had always known; and that if anyone was an honourable man, it was Digby.

"If I have not ever acted as you have done this morning, it is because I have not been tested." He took one of Digby's cigarettes and lit up. He had not smoked for ten years. "You see, Digby. My wife was not unfaithful to me, but she wanted to be. God, how she wanted to be! But the man she wanted was an honourable man, Digby, a man of impeccable decency." He sat back and began to talk.

Belinda had been in hospital, having given birth to Richenda just the previous night, and Martin and Jean had two year old Dolores to stay with them so that Digby could go to and from the hospital without bothering with baby-sitters, he had enough to do as it was, with running the House without coping with the demands of a two-year old. He had popped over to Martin's house to say goodnight to Dolores and, perhaps more importantly, to take Martin out for a quick pint, having forgotten that Martin was out at his evening course. Computers were just becoming important and Martin wanted to be in at the ground level. So Digby had a g. and t. with Jean instead, and they sat in her rather dowdy drawing room and talked babies and holidays and school gossip. After a while he felt a constraint in Jean's conversation and, guessing that he had overstayed his welcome, he got up to go.

"Digby," said Jean suddenly, "you must know I'm absolutely crazy about you." Digby stood still and looked at her, he was still holding a present covered in wrapping paper that someone had given him for the baby. He'd promised Belinda he'd take it home.

"No, Jean," he said quietly, "I didn't know." He felt exhausted and the direct nature of her comment stunned him. As he looked at her he saw that she had dressed herself up for this. She was wearing the black dress she usually wore for parent suppers and she had make-up on, too, something unusual for her; her cheeks were pink, and there was blue around her eyes.

When Martin had first introduced Jean to Digby, he had not thought that she was an attractive woman. He considered her pleasant and intelligent, but not particularly pretty. Nor was she a good dresser, and in those days, as now, Digby had liked that in a woman. But as the friendship grew between the two families, he revised his opinion. She had black curly hair which she wore very short, and unusual, slanty almond-shaped eyes. She must have had chicken pox as a child for there were some marks on her cheeks, but this did not make her unattractive, it gave her an almost racy air. She had a good figure too, very slight and boyish, which combined with her unfussy way of walking, irresistibly reminded him of some Shakespearean heroine dressed as a boy, Rosamund or Viola, perhaps. She was fun to be with.

"I've wanted you," she said, "ever since we met five years ago. Digby make love to me, make love to me tonight."

He saw her standing by the bar of the electric fire, her black dress a little dusty from cigarette ash, her cheeks flushed and her pupils dilated with desire for him. Momentarily he was tempted, sorely tempted. He even let his imagination give rein to the possibility – but only momentarily.

"You and I," she was saying, "we're two of a kind. Martin and Belinda are dear, sweet people, but they don't know anything about desire, do they? If you and I made love it would be something wonderful, something earth-shaking." He let her go on talking. She had lighted a cigarette and was taking great drags at it, "but I'm not greedy, Digby, I don't want to hurt people, break up marriages. I just want one night with you. Just one glorious, unforgettable night to remember until I die. Who will it hurt? No one will ever know."

He put the present down and spoke gently to her. "Sex doesn't work like that, Jean," he said. "If you and I made love, I have no doubt it would be, as you say, wonderful, quite wonderful for us both, but we would develop a hunger for it ... and then everything would come tumbling down."

She was going to interrupt him, but he continued. "But that is not why I say no, Jean, not for that, but for something else."

"What? You don't find me attractive?"

"No! It's not that, certainly. Not that. Come here. And she went there and he stood facing her with his hands lightly on her shoulders, and she could feel him hard against her stomach.

"Ah," she breathed, "you do, do you?" And she moved her mouth towards his, but he stepped back from her.

"So you see," he said, sitting down across the arm of a chair, "so you see, I do."

"Well then," she cried, "yes!"

"No," he said. "I wouldn't mind ..." he spoke quite unemotionally, "I wouldn't mind betraying Belinda – for, make no bones about it, betrayal it would be, and I don't mind betraying myself, but what I do mind and what I will never do, is betray Martin."

She was angry, stubbing out her cigarette and immediately lighting another. "What is it between you two? Are *you* lovers?"

"No," said Digby. "You know I like women, you know I like you, but there is something much more important than that."

"What? This awful male-bonding thing?"

"If you like, yes."

"But you'd like it!" She wanted to hurt him. "You'd like it, wouldn't you, you and Martin."

"Now come, Jean," said Digby laughing. "Can you imagine it? I'd be half way up Martin and his glasses would fall off and he'd say, "Oh Digs. I've just thought of a new page for the lizard book."

Rejected as she was, Jean smiled reluctantly, and admitted defeat.

Digby left soon after. Just before he reached the door he turned. "Don't ever tell Martin, Jean. Never." And he was gone.

115

But she had told Martin, and Digby had never, until this moment when he sat in total despair, known that Martin knew.

"So do not," said Martin, "ever speak to me of a lack of decency. Never tell me you are not an upright man."

"When did she tell you, Martin?"

" She never actually told me." Martin stubbed out his cigarette. He did not want it now. "She kept a diary, you know, and when she was dying, she asked me to destroy it. Of course, I couldn't – perhaps she knew that, perhaps she even wanted me to know exactly how it was."

"Oh, Martin."

"But I think I really always knew, probably before either of you did. It was just little things ... you know how we all gave each other birthday presents. Well, when it was your birthday Jean used to get so excited about giving you a present, just like she used to get when it was Richard or Duncan's birthday. I remember seeing her watching you opening your present – some book, I think. I forget what – an edition of Donne, perhaps. And her hands were all clenched up, and when you opened it and smiled she did a little dance on the spot; she was so happy that you liked it." Martin took off his glasses and wiped them with his handkerchief. "Of course, I knew it was always you she thought of when I made love to her."

"How you must have hated me."

"No, that's where you're wrong. I honoured you. I knew what it was like for you with Belinda – nice as she was, how you were often dull and empty-eyed because she gave you none of that sparkle that you needed, and I knew that Jean could have given you that, and that you knew Jean could, but that you would never take it. I could have given you Jean, Digby, and transformed your life, but you see, I loved Jean, too, and I couldn't do it."

"Why should you have given me what was yours?"

"Because it would have made you both radiantly happy."

Digby brought his fist down on the table. "You can't talk like that, Martin. It might not have been the case at all. And, anyway, Jean did love you."

"Yes, I think she did. And after that night, the night when Belinda was in hospital, I think she was happier because she knew she couldn't hope any more because you would never betray me, but that you were there, as a friend for us both. I think you gave her a kind of glow, just being there."

"Oh, Martin!" And Digby reached for the cigarettes. "Anyway," he held Martin's eyes for a minute to show him that the subject was closed, perhaps for ever. He must impose his will on Martin and end the subject; there was too much pain in it. Besides, the present pressed upon him with its own urgency. "What the hell am I going to do now? Should I resign?"

"Christ, no!" Martin was fiddling about with the paper knife and suddenly he threw it down so that it jumped off the table and embedded itself in one of the cushions.

"I suppose it's round the whole school now," said Digby. He played with the ash on the end of his cigarette so that the whole of the tip fell into the ash tray, and he had to light it all over again.

"That's just where you're wrong," said Martin, refilling the glasses so briskly that he seemed a different man from the one who had spoken earlier. "Think about it, Digby."

"You needn't worry about that," he said bitterly.

"No, listen. Suppose Davies goes round the school saying, 'I shagged Elizabeth!'" Digby winced but Martin repeated it deliberately. "'I shagged Elizabeth!' Well, who is to believe him? The smallest fourth-former, Graham Tully, for example, could make the same boast, but where is his evidence? You've got the knickers – not that they were evidence anyway, they could have been anyone's.

117

Who saw him go in or out of your house? Why should he not have been there? Boys often go to your house. No one suggests they go to shag your wife."

"The bit of paper. The bet?"

"Anyone can write something on a bit of paper. And I'll tell you another thing. Davies is a liar. I heard him telling that awful woman in red at the lunch yesterday that he lived in a castle in Northumberland. You know I said I'd run his details through the computer? Well, I happen to know for a fact that he lives in a semi in Saffron Walden! If he lies so glibly to her, he probably lies to everyone else. My bet is that he's known as a liar.

"So, what are you saying?"

"You'll have to brazen it out. You have to be seen a lot with Elizabeth around the school."

"Oh, Christ."

"With Elizabeth and Ronnie. You have to be seen as a happy family. People will have your evidence – their evidence before their eyes. What price Davies then?"

"Yes," said Digby slowly. "I see what you mean."

"By the way, who do you think sent the knickers and the paper. What was his motive?"

"Oh, that's easy. It was Gowinder. I'd recognise his writing anywhere. He must have filched it from Davies in a Greek lesson, probably." He closed his eyes. "Perhaps Stewart and Davies were discussing it."

"Singh didn't write anything?"

"No. But that piece of paper could have been all round the school."

"I don't think so," said Martin. "My bet is that Davies had just written it. Gowinder suspected something, and took it for you, because," he added deliberately, "because of the respect he has for you. No, Singh won't say anything."

"Maybe not," said Digby wearily.

"You're not going to like this, Digby." added Martin tentatively.

"Go on," said Digby. "I'm getting quite used to not liking things."

"St John Davies has to be the new Head Boy."

Digby got up. "No, Martin. No! Absolutely not."

"Yes," said Martin deliberately, refilling their glasses," for if there are rumours, everyone will be watching you. Are you likely to make Head Boy the pupil who has been to bed with your wife?"

"Oh God!"

"And Davies will be silenced for, make no mistake, he wants to be Head Boy above everything else. He will not be going around circulating rumours that jeopardise his chances."

"What about Stewart, and that awful, hideous bet?"

Martin smiled ruefully. "Stewart is a decent boy," he said. "He won't have said anything. He won't believe it, anyway, and if he does, he'll be scared. They'll both be scared. They've both got a lot to lose."

" 'Something rotten in the state of Denmark.' "

"Not necessarily. You can't have Singh as Head Boy. He doesn't drink, he can only eat vegetarian stuff, he doesn't make conversation – I was watching him yesterday and he hardly said a thing. He's not liked."

"I ..."

"Listen to me, Digs!" And it was a measure of Martin's increasing confidence that he had reverted to calling Digby by his more usual sobriquet. "I can't have Stewart because he's got no charisma. I could see that yesterday. Everyone likes him but nobody except me sees anything special in him and, after all, everyone wants Davies – his Housemaster, the cricketers, the other boys. He's personable, the boys think he's 'cool'. What is corrupt in that?"

"I have to work with this boy!"

"Yes, you do, Digby. It's the only way."

"The boy who came to my house and fucked my wife, in my own bed." The fact that it was in Digby's bed came as a shock to Martin, but he wasn't going to allow Digby to see this.

"I think you have to look on it as a schoolboy prank."

"Schoolboy prank? Martin!"

"No, listen. He probably thought of it as a laugh. He didn't expect to meet with any success, but an eighteen year old boy is easily aroused. I'm afraid the fault lies with Elizabeth, Digby, as much as with St John Davies."

And Martin, good though he was, could not repress a note of triumph as he said this. He had, after all, warned Digby about her before they married. "Don't do it, Digs," he had said, but Digby had taken no notice and married her all the same. He had always known what was best for Digby. Always. And he knew now.

"Yes," said Digby, bowing his head. "Yes, you're probably right, Martin."

And Martin's brief feeling of triumph passed from him and was replaced by a great surge of anger. How dare this girl, this chit, this ... what did the boys call them ... slag, do this to his friend, his friend who had given his wife back into his own safe-keeping, his friend who had given him the job, who was godfather to his son, the man with whom he had played cricket, taken God knows how many school-trips, and who had proved himself, again and again?. How could he be treated so? And then his feelings changed again and were replaced by fear.

"Elizabeth." he said. "Where is she?"

"I don't know."

"I am going to find her."

"Why?"

"To stop her talking to doctors, solicitors, whatever, to talk sense into her." He was already half way to the door.

'Do you mind, Martin?"

"No. But I think I should go now, just to be on the safe side."

"I think I'll stay here, Mart. Just lie down for a bit."

"Will you be all right?"

Digby laughed bitterly. "Oh yes. I'll be all right."

"Here," said Martin, going back to the desk and feeling inside the drawer. "Take a couple of these."

"What are they?"

"Never mind. They'll relax you."

"The story will be complete, won't it. 'Pervert Headmaster takes drugs after Head Boy bonks wife." He even smiled a little. Martin thought the comment was best ignored.

"I'm off then."

"Martin ..."

"Yes?" He paused at the door.

"You know ..." Digby looked at him.

"Yes. I know."

"Know what?"

"You ... I ... all of it."

"Yes, I know."

*****

"I don't know what it has to do with you. You're not my husband."

"You may not have a husband if you do not listen and do as you are told."

He had found Elizabeth at home; he could hear the television on as she came to the door and he felt relief. She had obviously done nothing.

"May I come in?" She shrugged, and he came in anyway. "Would you mind turning the television off?" he asked. He watched her while she obeyed him. That she had nice hair and a pretty face, even a very pretty face, was undeniable. But that was all, for it was a face without any vivacity. He supposed intelligence must play a large part in beauty. Jean had not been an obviously beautiful woman, she had marks on her face and her eyes were too narrow, but there was so much laughter, understanding and humanity there, that to his mind, there was no doubt as to which was the more beautiful woman. Oh, Digby, he thought. How could you? But if Achilles had had a heel, so did Digby.

"I think you know why I have come," he said.

"I didn't do anything so very bad," said Elizabeth defensively: Digby had been horrible to her, she wanted sympathy, not more nastiness. "Anyway, Digby was much worse than me. Do you know what he did this morning?" She looked at him defiantly; why should Martin come preaching at her, after what Digby had done? Anyway, she wouldn't offer him any coffee.

"Yes," said Martin, "but nobody else is going to know, Elizabeth. Be sure of that."

"I expect you're enjoying this. You've always had it in for me!" It was a relief to say it.

"Perhaps I was right. Now ..." He stood up to say what he wanted to say. "You have done something very terrible, Elizabeth. All his life Digby has worked towards something fine, something great. He's achieved miracles with this school, and he's done it through ability and hard work. He deserves every bit of the success he has got. And at one fell swoop you try to take it all away from him."

"I haven't ..."

He interrupted her. "The bottom line is, Elizabeth, if the scandal breaks and Digby has to resign ..."

"He can do something else."

It was all so unfair. She had been so happy when she had woken up and found she wasn't pregnant, and she had thought everything was going to be all right again, and she was going to have a really nice day. Then Digby being so disgusting - just think of pushing someone's head down into a loo! And now Martin had come to go on at her. Well, she would be glad to go somewhere else, somewhere away from this horrible place.

There was something about her total lack of understanding of the purpose of Digby's whole life that infuriated him. "Yes, certainly he can do something else. He can go and live in a semi in Saffron Walden ..." God, he must have Davies on the brain. "If he can afford a house, because there won't be any money coming in, no money for pretty clothes, or an au-pair for Ronnie ... nobody's going to employ an ageing, disgraced headmaster. And you can go on living with him, if he'll have you on no money, or you can get divorced and be a single mother on no money ..." He stared at her.

Elizabeth sighed. She really couldn't understand why everything should be so awful, but she would agree anyway, just to stop Martin going on at her. "All right." she said. "What do you want me to do, then?"

"You are going to behave impeccably." He looked at her and could see that she did not know what the word meant. She was playing with her hair, gathering it up into a bunch and letting it go again. "You will accompany your husband to all school functions – dressed properly. Put the teenage clothes away, Elizabeth." So he had noticed her after all; he probably fancied her like mad which was why he was always so nasty to her. Given half a chance he'd probably try it on like St John.

"Behave like a grown-up woman! Spend time with your son. Be seen doing so. Get involved with school life. Help with the Art or something. But, above all, see there are no rumours, no rumours about Davies, no rumours about ..." for a moment Martin wondered how to warn her off telling anyone about this morning ... "about anything that happened in the bedroom. You must make sure of this. If you don't, it's curtains, finito, not just for Digby, for you too. Remember Elizabeth, 'twenty-five pound cunt'. Don't ever let that get out."

Oh, so that was what it meant! Elizabeth was not quick on the uptake and she hadn't seen the relevance of St John's note. But now it began to dawn on her: he hadn't fancied her at all, he'd only done it for some silly bet. She had thought he really liked her, but all he had done, was to bring a lot of trouble. Before she had married Digby, everybody ran round after her, but since then nothing had gone right. Why was that? She didn't know, she had done her best, but it was never right. And now Martin was still droning on. Her head really ached.

"And you'll have to win Digby over; be very, very patient. He has an awful lot to forgive you for."

He was looking so stern and nasty. Thank God she could hear Marie-Louise and Ronnie coming back. He'd have to go now.

"I have your word, Elizabeth?"

Her word? What did he mean?

"To put these things behind you and not mention any of them to anyone?" She was watching the door because she knew her son would come bursting in. She hoped he wouldn't hit her as he often did, in front of Martin.

"Oh yes. Hello, Ronnie!" She had seldom been so pleased to see her son.

"Oh! I am sorry. Come with me, Ronnie," said Marie-Louise, seeing Martin and sensing an atmosphere. "Mummy has a visitor."

"It's all right," said Martin. "I'm just going." he turned to Ronnie and his face and voice underwent a sudden change. "I know a little boy," he said, "who's going to be three next week. Do you know him too?"

Ronnie, clutching his large purple rabbit in his hands, stopped and regarded Martin. "Me!" he said. And a huge smile spread over his face, so that Martin was reminded of Digby when he opened the birthday present that Jean had chosen for him with such care.

*****

When he returned to the den he found Digby fast asleep. Martin stood in the doorway looking at him. He was lying on his side rather in the attitude of the "Boy Chatterton", a copy of which hung on the wall above. The pills had relaxed him as Martin had said they would, and he lay among the cushions with one arm hanging down.

Martin shut the door and sat down in the chair opposite and regarded him. He thought of the times they had taken school parties out together, the time they had been to the Alps with five boys on a climbing exercise, and Digby had elected to be the one who stayed with an injured boy, even though it was desperately cold, and hours would pass before help came. He remembered the rollicking sailing holiday when everything went wrong, and he and Digby drank far too much, and Belinda had been so cross with them. He thought of the time after Jean's funeral when Digby had sat with him all night, and kept completely silent because he knew that was what Martin wanted. He thought of the many, many ways their lives had become entangled, and finally, he thought what a handsome man Digby was still, in spite of everything.

Martin knew himself to be plain. Twenty years or so ago, at least, he had had a good head of hair and had been quite fit, almost slim, but now he had developed a paunch because he drank too much, he was almost bald and had bags under his eyes from doing too much paperwork. He looked what he was, he supposed, an ageing school master. But Digby's hair, grey though it was, was thick and long and curly, his eyes, were he to open them, would be brilliant blue like his son's, and then he was so tall and slender, there was not an ounce of fat on him.

He was breathing evenly and smoothly and Martin could see the shape of his penis, a little hardness about it, outlined by the folds of his trousers and he remembered how, when they were younger men and had drunk a lot, he had twitted Digby about its size, and Digby had blushed, actually blushed. And as Martin went on sitting there and thinking about his friend, tired with the mental turmoil the morning had brought in its wake, he began to be conscious of a desire to take Digby's burden from him; the nature of his desire came at first as a shock to him, for he was not a man whom sex troubled greatly, but he was also a practical man, and he knew his desire derived as much from a sense of the pragmatic as from bodily urging. He wished that Digby would offer him this weight that troubled him so, this burning desire that Jean had known was his, this torment that had led him to marry Elizabeth. Martin's mobile phone rang; the noise seemed to crash through his thoughts. His first reaction was one of anger with the outside world for standing between him and this man, but he was conscious of a guilt that gave way to a sense of relief. It was as well perhaps that the call had come when it did.

It was Felicity asking was he going to go and teach the UIV biology or did he want cover?

The phone woke Digby, too. He muttered and stretched and for a moment and Martin could see that he had forgotten it all, but only for a moment, for his face clouded almost immediately, and he stood up.

"Martin!"

Martin smiled. "It's all right, Digs," he said, "everything is going to be all right."

Chapter 18

"…Thus freed from his most formidable foe, Timoleon soon drove Hiketas from Epipolae, and Syracuse was at length completely free. The Syracusans had found a deliverer who did not, like Dion seek to be their master …"

Always in the past Avonmore had prepared his Ancient History notes meticulously the night before, copying out previous notes, amending them, hi-lighting salient passages, interpolating items that had occurred to him in the interim, but now it seemed unnecessarily onerous; boys were not as they had been in '59, when he had the twelve Oxbridge candidates. He doubted they had the interest or ability nowadays. Just look at these three! Davies would be talking to Stewart as soon as his back was turned, and only Singh had any promise about him, but there, of course, you had the problem of a different culture … So he had decided to read straight out of the text book, known by its author's name, *Bury*. *Bury* had been good enough for him as a boy, and he dared say it would be good enough for this lot.

"'Whereupon,' he continued, 'the fortress of Dionysus was pulled down. This act of demolition …' Are you taking notes, Davies?"

"Sir"

" ' … seemed the seal and assurance of their deliverance. But the city ….'"

"Have you got the knickers?" wrote St John.

This came as a bit of a surprise to Stewart who had no notion what had happened to them, but as he was about to write "*NO,*" he thought again. It would do no harm to make Davies sweat a bit.

" Could have, on the other hand, I might have given them to the Headman."

"Balls you did" wrote St John. Stewart could bullshit him all he liked, but he could see through him, he'd obviously got them somewhere.

"And ..." continued Harold Avonmore, "it consisted of two hundred galleys and one thousand transport; there were ten thousand horses, and some four hundred war chariots, and the total number of infantry was said to be 70,000."

"Excuse me Sir," said Singh. "Would you mind repeating the number of the war chariots?"

"Certainly," said Avonmore, looking suspiciously in the direction of Stewart and Davies but, atypically, they were busy writing.

The door opened and Felicity put her head round. What did she want now? This was the second time she had disturbed his lessons, one disturbance after another.

"Excuse me, Mr Avonmore, the Headmaster would like to see St John Davies immediately."

Oh God! This was it. Stewart really had given the knickers to the Headman. But he wouldn't have ... couldn't have! Could he? Oh, the bastard ... The bastard. It was expulsion, he knew it was.

"Hurry up, Davies. ' Festina lente', as the poet has it."

"Sir." He began fiddling with his books.

"Hurry up, Davies," this from that bitch of a secretary this time. "The Headmaster is waiting."

Oh God, if only he could stay in the Classics room with Stewart – even with Singh. Even he was looking quite human for a change, almost smiling as if he were his friend. Oh God, why had he done it? He'd give anything not to have done it – even be friends with Singh.

The walk from the Classics Block to Digby's house seemed the longest he had ever taken, longer than that bloody CCF exercise when they had walked all night.

*****

"Come in, Davies," the Headman said. "Please sit down." And Davies went and sat in one of the leather arm chairs facing the heavy desk. Mr Wood was sitting in another. He could see expulsion written on their faces.

"Mr Wood and I have come to a decision," the Headman was saying. "And, I may say; a decision which is fully endorsed by your Housemaster, the Sixth form council and, of course….," Digby managed a smile, "most importantly by members of the first eleven."

What was going on? Was it …? Could it …? No, he mustn't hope.

"We have decided to ask you to be our next Head Boy."

For a moment St John Davies found himself incapable of speech, then, with an effort, he recovered his usual insouciance. "Gosh, Sir! I hadn't expected …"

"I hope …" said Mr Wood, "you will wish to accept?"

Words came. "Sir, I should be honoured, Head boy of Mowberry! I had no idea I was in the running."

"It is a wonderful position," said Sherwood ignoring this. "A position of great responsibility, and most of all, a position of trust." And for the first time the Headmaster looked straight at him. His eyes seemed to bore straight through him – Davies had never realised before how blue the Headman's eyes were. They were so blue, they seemed to dazzle almost as if sparks were flying off them, like the piece of metal he had worked at, for technology GCSE.

129

"I wonder if you understand the full implication of that trust?"

"No, Sir, but I am willing to learn, Sir." He couldn't believe it; well, yes, of course he could, but how stupid he'd been! Of course, Stewart wouldn't have given the Headmaster his wife's knickers back! What an idiot to think he might! He almost laughed. But he wouldn't refer to the knickers again, and if Stewart said anything, he'd just deny that they were Elizabeth's.

"You will have to put your duty to the school before your own wishes. Sometimes it will not be easy."

"No, Sir. I can appreciate that." He was going to be Head Boy! He was going to be Head Boy! He wasn't going to be expelled!

"As I say," the Headmaster's voice cut through his thoughts, "it will not always be easy. Sometimes you will be tempted to be less than perfect, for perfect you must be. There must be no falling off."

It was all a bit sombre really; you would think they could be a bit more jolly about it. Nettleship, the present Head Boy, had been offered champagne when he was told. It wasn't still possible, was it ...? No, she wouldn't have told him, and anyway, if she had, he certainly wouldn't be made Head Boy, he would have been expelled.

"You'd better cut along now, Davies," Old Woody was saying. "The bell went five minutes ago, and punctuality is one of the first things to remember in positions of authority."

"Sir," he said, and turning to the Headman, and made, he thought, quite a good little speech, seeing it was on the spur of the moment and he'd been pretty stressed out just now. "I would like to thank you, Sir, not just for making me Head Boy, but for all the things Mowberry has given me ..."

But all Mr Wood could say was, "cut along Davies." And the Headman made no reply at all.

It was a very different Davies who stalked back into the Greek lesson, none of the white-faced hesitation of only quarter of an hour ago. Could it only be quarter of an hour? But this jauntiness of the new, super-confident Davies was not missed by Gowinder, who noted it and wondered. For the first time he felt genuine admiration for Davies. Undoubtedly, the Headmaster had told him he must leave Mowberry School, but he did not quail beneath his punishment, in fact he displayed enormous bravery.

Could Avonmore still be going on? Oh, yes, it was a double period, but it seemed extraordinary to Davies that he had been through so many shocks and counter-shocks, and that all that time Avonmore had been warbling on about the Syracusians, quite unaware of it all.

"'....the field of battle which was now fought between the Greeks and Phoenicians on the banks of the Crimisus ...' I don't see you writing, Stewart."

"I was just wondering where the Crimisus is, Sir?" Davies was nudging him, trying to attract his attention.

"I don't think we need to worry about that now, do you, Stewart?"

"Oh, no, Sir," said Stewart and looked at the paper Davies was pushing his way.

"St John Davies: Head Boy!"

He wrote: "Congratulashuns!" He would really have liked to have been Head Boy. It would have made his mother really happy too. For a moment he toyed with the idea of telling someone about what Davies had said he had done to Elizabeth – Mr Wood, maybe, or even the Headman, but no! You simply didn't do things like that at a school like Mowberry; he would just have to put up with the situation. Well, now he'd have to turn his mind to things like Timoleon and Sicily, and try and get some decent A levels instead of being Head Boy.

After years of school-mastering, Avonmore could speak and read as if on auto pilot. As he read, "'Timolean had now delivered Sicily from both domestic despots and from foreign foes ...'", he thought of the latest edition to his scrap-book, a photocopy obtained from Felicity of Yvonne Bonnington's letter of acceptance. She had said she was looking forward to working very closely with Mr Avonmore. Working closely together, working closely with those little round breasts, those little tight buttocks!

"'He was lamented by all Greek Sicily, and at Syracuse his memory was preserved by a group of public buildings named after him." And then the thought struck him! Public buildings named after him! Hah! That should be his leaving present, his memorial. A public building named after him.

"Stewart! You're not listening to a word I'm saying." That was the trouble with young people nowadays, always off in some daydream or other.

At the end of the lesson Stewart walked out of the Classics Block with Singh, since Davies had uncharacteristically offered to carry Hazzer's books, creeping up already, now he was going to be Head Boy, Stewart supposed! Singh had little to say as usual, but as Stewart walked along, a thought struck him. Why *had* Davies asked him about the knickers? If he hadn't got them, where were they? After all, nobody but the three of them used the UVI Classics Room, and Singh was hardly likely to take them, was he? What *was* he going on about now?

"That was a very interesting lesson of Mr Avonmore's. But I, too, wondered where the River Crimisus was."

"Oh yes, did you?" Probably the cleaners had taken them. They were always nicking things. Oh no, he saw how it was: Davies had got them all the time, and wanted to wind him up, but that was before he'd been told about being Head Boy. Well, they wouldn't be hearing any more boasting about knickers now that he was so important in his new position; well, that was one relief, anyway.

"I will look up the geographical location of the river," said Singh.

"Oh, good, thanks." Davies was a jammy git all right.

They walked round the Green Sward in silence. Stewart felt depressed by the day's events, but Singh was pondering on the mixed nature of men: Mr Sherwood so noble and upright, yet married to that woman! St John Davies, foul in so many ways, yet now showing such bravery and bravado. But perhaps Davies had not seduced Elizabeth Sherwood, at all. It was all unclean talk! And he, Singh, had inflicted terrible suffering on Mr Sherwood and excited suspicion against his wife, quite wrongly.

"See you, Gowinder." Stewart was off back to the house.

So Mr Sherwood had sent for Davies and the matter had been cleared up. And Davies had returned so cheerful. How was that possible? What had taken place at the interview? Surely Mr Sherwood had been angry? Singh stopped to pick up an empty crisp packet and conveyed it to the waste-bin outside the School Hall. Perhaps Englishmen did not mind about such matters. Perhaps they had laughed together as he saw men here do. But no, Mr Sherwood would have found an excellent solution. He was a man of great ... inscrutability. It would be best to think of the subject no more. He would go and look up the whereabouts of the River Crimisus. He must devote himself to true learning and not allow himself to be deflected by foolish matters.

Chapter 19

It had not really been a successful day. The first eleven were playing against West Dean and Digby had wanted to be there. He went, firstly because he always went to first eleven matches on principle and, secondly, so that he could be seen with Elizabeth. Thirdly, he liked cricket. He had got a blue from Oxford.

It should have been an idyllic afternoon. The pitch was faultless, unfolding itself endlessly into woodland on one side, while the further edge stretched away down to the fast-moving river. To the side, the eighteenth century school buildings stood mellow in the sunshine, which beamed upon the rows of deck chairs and white-kitted figures. The school side was immaculately turned out, (for did not Singh see to the kit?) and the voices raised were well-sounding in their friendly emulation.

Tea had been spread out on white linen cloths upon the great trestle table, beneath the three horse chestnut trees. Colonel Haslett had already drawn up his deck chair to it and tucked into great chunks of heavy dark fruit cake, but Lady Jenkins who had also had designs on it, had rather lost out, as her attention had been deflected towards Elizabeth's tiny blue dress, and the Colonel had packed the remains into a bag brought specially for the purpose. Digby had eaten nothing.

"It is difficult for me, this cricket," said Marie-Louise. "I would like someone to explain, please."

"Oh, it's really boring," said Elizabeth. "I've never understood it." She yawned. It was a very long afternoon. And then, to make it worse, Martin had turned up and spent a long time explaining cricket to Marie-Louise. He tried talking in French and Marie-Louise laughed at him, but Martin didn't seem to mind, and they ended up laughing together.

Digby, who was teaching Ronnie to hit the ball with a tiny bat that Martin had given him for his third birthday, thought how odd it was that women always seemed to be able to relate to Martin, for in his tweed jacket and voluminous trousers, he was certainly not an object of desire.

And then, of course, St John Davies had come in to bat, and they all had to watch him make his century. St John looked well in his flannels. His hair was still uncut, but it was so glossy and golden that only Harold Avonmore could have objected to it. He was a good cricketer, too, but perhaps a selfish one, going for runs at the expense of the other batsman. And they all had to sit and watch him.

"He is a very beautiful boy," said Marie-Louise, "isn't he, Elizabeth? Do you think so too?"

Elizabeth pretended not to hear, so Marie-Louise said it all over again.

"I should say," said Martin, "that it's time he allowed himself to get out, and gave someone else a chance at batting."

"I don't see why he should", said Elizabeth.

"Mum, Mum, want a wee-wee!" said Ronnie, running up and pulling at her tiny, blue dress.

"Marie-Louise will take you," said Elizabeth. "Mummy's busy."

"You take him, Elizabeth," said Digby, coming over with the tiny bat in his hand. "Marie-Louise is learning about cricket. You don't even like it."

"I don't want to go with Mummy," said Ronnie. "I want Marie-Louise."

"I don't mind," said the au-pair.

But Elizabeth could feel Martin's and Digby's eyes on her. She knew that they thought she ought to take Ronnie. She really couldn't see why, after all Marie-Louise was paid to do that sort of thing. So why did Martin and Diggy have to look at her as if it was her job? What was so bloody fantastic about Marie-Louise? Martin trying to talk French to her and Digby thinking she wanted to know about cricket. Well, who would they like to go to bed with? Her or Marie Louise? She got up slowly. "Come on Ronnie." She yanked his hand. "Come on. Stop creating. I'll take you."

"I hate you!" said Ronnie, kicking at her. Digby picked him up.

"That is nasty, Ronnie," he said. "Say 'sorry, Mummy,' and you and I will go to the big men's lavatory together."

And St John went on hitting fours and sixes and they all had to sit and clap. Elizabeth yawned and Digby looked like the wrath of God. Eventually, however, the wickets fell and it was all over. "Now we can go and have a g. and t." said Elizabeth.

"Later," said Digby. "I have business to discuss with Martin." So Marie-Louise put Ronnie in the push-chair and Elizabeth dawdled along behind, just in case St John Davies should happen to come along. But he didn't, because he was drinking pints in the pavilion and telling the Captain of West Dean that his father had been a county player.

Digby and Martin, however, had lingered because the scene held magic for them both. "Come on, Martin," said Digby, at last, "let's walk back along the river."

Evening was coming on as they turned their backs on the wicket and headed towards the gate that led to the river path. It was unlocked and Digby carefully locked it behind them, mentally noting that he must remind the groundsman to keep it closed. Even groundsmen were subject to Digby's vigilant eyes. They continued on their way, following the path that ran alongside the river that would turn into the Thames some hundred miles on.

"I'm not happy about it," said Digby, "you know that." He had broken off a stick and was hitting at clumps of nettles and anything else really that stood in his way. Martin tried to turn it into a joke. "You're just miffed," he said, "because it's such a long time since you made your last century." But Digby ignored this.

"It's the whole moral thing," he said. "A boy does a bad thing, a bad thing in anyone's books, and he should be expelled. And what happens? He's made into Head Boy because I'm a moral coward. I am meant to be the arbiter of right and wrong and I confound them, basically, because I fear for my own little job." He lifted his arm and sent the stick whizzing over the hedge. "There is a lack on integrity, Martin. I felt I have betrayed, if not Stewart, certainly Singh. Poor Gowinder! What on earth does he think of it all?"

"I expects he finds it no more inexplicable than most of what goes on at Mowberry. Never mind Singh."

They continued in single file along the narrow river path, frequently stooping to avoid the overhanging branches of the willows.

"OK," continued Martin. "We do not emerge entirely unblemished from this; but on the other hand, what matters is, that it has been remarkably successful. I have kept my ear to the ground and my eyes open, and I've heard no breath of rumour, have you?" Digby shook his head impatiently.

"But I have acted wrongly, Martin." They walked idly now, for the path had come to an end, and eventually Digby sat down on the bank and listened to Martin.

"So," said Martin angrily, "let's look at the alternatives shall we? You could have gone to the governors and said, perhaps to old Colonel Haslett, if he happened to be awake, "Colonel. The boy I want to make Head Boy has been bonking my wife. What shall I do" "Hush it up, Sherwood. Hush it up!" Right?"

"I could have exposed it."

"Right. So you do the big moral thing. You resign from Mowberry and the tabloids have a field day. Parents take their kids away. The school reverts back to how it was before you came. Worse. I go because I am bound up with you. Your life's ruined, my life's ruined, Elizabeth's, Ronnie's, half the lives of the staff and the boys – all because you have made one big moral gesture. There's a kind of arrogance in that, far more reprehensible than anything else.

"I think you are being Jesuitical, Martin. You think exactly as I do. I should never have made Davies Head Boy."

"It was all part of the package," said Martin. "It was the only way. I think we should have heard plenty of that rumour by now, if Stewart or Singh had been appointed instead.

They sat side by side on the bank of the river and watched the sun sink in a mass of soft pink cloud behind the parkland.

"I've made an awful mess of things," said Digby slowly, his eye on a single moorhen paddling past, "ever since I left Belinda really. And then, Jean dying…it was when there were four of us, things were best. Good days, Martin."

"It's no use looking back," said Martin. He changed tack. "Anyway, they weren't so brilliant for you. You were never very happy with Belinda. She seemed right but she wasn't really. She was too like you in many ways, her upbringing, her attitudes, and so on, but not enough like you in others. She lacked your sensuality. And now there's Mowberry. That's a success."

"Perhaps."

"A flock of geese flew by in perfect v formation, cutting through the evening with their harsh cries. Both men stood and watched them pass by until they eventually disappeared over the woods.

"We've even started fucking, You can't call it making love. Yes, I've even fucked her again, Martin."

"Why shouldn't you? She's very attractive."

"I'd like a separate bed, but I can't because of the Housekeeper. It would be all over the school."

"I can see that."

Digby made no reply, for he was ashamed to tell Martin what it was really like. "Digby, please, you're hurting me," she had said, more than once, and he had taken no notice. If anything, her protests made his urge the stronger.

There were only a few pink streaks in the cloud now, and the oak trees on the far side of the park were dark against the sky. The river flowed silently past, broken now and then by a ripple or a bubble as a fish broke surface. Perhaps it was the extraordinary beauty of the evening, the clouds all tinged with pink, or perhaps it was the emotionally charged events of the last few days that caused Martin to feel a violent upsurge of feeling, so strong that he did not know if he could control it, yet he said nothing, and all his beseeching was done in silence. Struck by the silence, Digby turned to him and saw the stout, slightly ridiculous figure of Martin sitting on the river bank with his short, stumpy legs dangling. This was the figure he had known and loved for years, decades even. What he saw now, as he turned to him, he had never seen before, a frightening thing, this thing he had thought belonged to him alone.

"Digby," Martin burst out, "for God's sake." And Martin's face, Martin's familiar face was strange, for it was contorted with pain, and his arms, his short arms were reaching out, his hands searching for him, his breath coming in quick pants.

For a moment Digby was taken back twenty years to a time

when Jean had begged for him as desperately, and he had been sorely tempted, although he had not then fully understood why. But now as he looked at the squat distraught figure of Martin, he felt he finally understood the nature of this sexual need; perhaps Jean had understood a little. Elizabeth possessed no knowledge of his true nature, and it was his anger at her ignorance that perverted sexual love to lust and violence. But Martin understood, for he knew that Digby's passion was not only sexual, but moved in other directions too: in ambition, in his need for success, whether at Mowberry or in regard to the whole public school ethos, in which he was so entangled.

Digby stared at the balding figure of his friend and knew that it was not a question purely of sex that lay before them, of the shared pleasures of mutual masturbation and orgasm that would constitute such an act, but something altogether greater: an absolute affirmation of all they had believed in and worked for in their years together. Hitherto, he had blindly believed that it was the beauty of the female body that aroused him; now he saw that this was only, as it were, an optional side of this need, for a woman's understanding could be only partial, for the world in which he lived, he and Martin, was a masculine world and its ways were masculine ways. Only the male could truly understand the male. "Ah Martin," he said, "my friend and comrade," but he did not speak the words aloud, for he knew that this sweet thing, so clearly revealed to him, could not be, but, as he had once refused Jean, now he must refuse her husband, and the reasons were the same. He could betray his wife, betray himself, but Martin he could not betray. A sexual relationship with Martin would have to be concealed and clandestine; and while he, Digby, had done shameful things before now, he would not stoop to become an instrument that would bring shame upon his friend. For Martin was not a sensual man, he offered sex for Digby's sake, not from his own desire, and Digby must not take what Martin did not truly mean to give. A time would come when Martin would regret this act; perhaps he would feel he had cheated Jean, depriving her of Digby, and taking him for himself. Or perhaps he would simply feel disgust for Digby or, worse, for himself.

And Digby knew that he must be strong, stronger than before when he had rejected Jean, and that he must deprive himself of what might constitute his greatest happiness. But this time he would return, not to the cold sterility of Belinda, but to the miasma that was Elizabeth. When he had rejected Jean, he had been fearful of hurting her woman's pride and had been determined to show her he desired her, now he must treat Martin with equal courtesy, and assuage the pain that came from rejection; nor must he allow Martin to see the reason for this rejection, for if he was to show Martin for an instant that he desired this thing, perhaps even more than Martin, he would persist in offering it to him, and there might come a time when Digby was no longer strong enough to refuse.

Pushing Martin away he stood up.

"You offer me an inestimable gift, Martin," he said, "but I cannot take it." He gazed down at Martin who sat ungainly, glasses askew on the bank of a river where the waters ran softly.

"Jean knew the value of silence. She kept her secret to the end. Are you equally strong, Martin? Can you repay this debt to Jean?"

And as Martin continued to sit, not looking at him, Digby reached out a hand and the passive man allowed himself to be pulled to his feet.

Digby knew he must drive himself, exert the discipline on himself that he expected from others, and that now he must change the tempo.

"Anyway," he grinned at Martin, and his jaw ached with the grinning, "you have always been deeply offensive about my cock."

And as Martin stood there uncertain, bemused, Digby gave him a friendly push. "Come on," he said, "I'll race you back. You were never a patch on me at the hundred metres."

And Digby set off at a slow jog, and Martin stared at the tall, slim figure of Digby, who ran so much more slowly than he was capable of running, so that he, Martin, should catch him up and overtake him, so that he should not feel hurt by rejection, but elated by success.

"Come on, Mart," shouted Digby, running on even more slowly than before. Martin hesitated a moment while he untrammelled his mind from its turmoil, and then he too, started off.

"Pathetic," he shouted as he came panting up, "you wouldn't stand a chance in the mother's egg and spoon race!"

Singh, who was tidying up the cricket pavilion, saw them as they jogged companionably along the banks of the river. He liked looking after the pavilion, even though no one particularly wanted him to. Indeed, the groundsman, regarded it as an intrusion on his territory, but, nevertheless, Singh continued to be i/c Cricket Pavilion. He liked it for several reasons: firstly, because he was a very good cricketer, a much better cricketer than Davies, who had run him out earlier this afternoon. Secondly, he liked making order out of muddle, and it was a relaxation from work, on which he spent most of the rest of his time. But, mainly, he liked it because he could be on his own, away from the other boys.

When he had arrived first from Pakistan, with very little English, he had had a certain novelty value and, furthermore, the Headmaster's vigilant eye was there to see that nobody did him wrong. He was naturally reticent and hard-working and eventually boys lost interest in him. Nobody (except perhaps Davies) made any racist comments, but nobody bothered about him either. There was no fault to be found in him and yet he sensed that he was not liked.

Even Mr Yates, the Housemaster, seemed to avoid him. Gowinder made an orderly pile of cricket pads, ready for whitening. He would have liked to have made friends in order to join more fully into the life of this excellent school, but too many things stood in his way; his race, his religion, his abhorrence of alcohol. Nor did he think it right to join in the bawdy talk in which so much of the boys' time was spent, in the house.

There were many things that he did not understand about Mowberry: Davies, for example, had not been punished for his shameful boasting, and even though Mr Sherwood knew of it, he had made him Head Boy, over them all. "Well now, Singh-o," Davies had greeted him this afternoon. "Have you nothing to say to the new Head Boy?"

It was hard to understand such things, but now as he saw Mr Sherwood and Mr Wood running back to school together, he could see how decent and honourable they were. He should not be standing there idly questioning those in authority. It showed a lack respect.

Stewart and Davies who were hanging out of one of the windows of Stanley House suffered no such qualms, and gave Martin and Digby a cheer as they came panting into the school grounds.

"He's all right, Sherwood," said Davies, withdrawing his head from the window. He could not resist throwing out a quick remark about his new status. "Of course, I'll be working pretty closely with him now."

"Comparing notes?"

"What?"

"About Elizabeth."

"Don't know what you mean." Davies slammed the window shut.

"You were full of it a while back, showing those knickers before Hazzer arrived."

"What knickers?"

"Elizabeth's knickers – or so you said."

"Don't know what you're talking about."

"Did you get them back from that desk in the Classics Room?"

"Oh, those knickers!" Davies picked up Stewart's cricket bat and played an imaginary defensive stroke. If Stewart thought he was going to beg for them back along with the paper containing the bet details, he was wrong; after all, what could he do with them? "Actually," he said, "they were your girlfriend, Melissa's." Then he fled before Stewart could take any kind of revenge.

But Stewart regarded Davies' feeble shot with complacence. Poor Davies, always bragging about something or other, probably got them off his sister. Well, that's what you had to do, when you couldn't get a bird. He'd get Melissa to send some more photos. A bikini shot would be good.

Chapter 20

School terms for Elizabeth always went slowly, but no term had ever gone as slowly as this one, and it wouldn't end until 12th July. Here they were, only at the end of June, and day followed day in dreary sequence. Diggy had now drawn up a schedule: in the mornings she had to speak French with Marie-Louise, after which she had to go and help with Fourth Form Art. This was horrible too, because Miss Swithens, the art teacher, did not like her, and resented her being there. She made life as difficult as possible for her: "Oh, Mrs Sherwood, we don't use the charcoal....Mrs Sherwood, would you mind not leaning on the plaster board." The fourth-formers too, being at an age when they were becoming sexually aware, were by turns tongue-tied or silly. She hated it. And then, unless there were visitors, in which case she had to accompany her husband, she had to have lunch with Marie-Louise and Ronnie. And at lunch Marie-Louise told her all the things that needed doing, like getting the push-chair repaired, or making appointments for Ronnie's injections. And then in the afternoon she had to do what Diggy called 'an activity' with Ronnie, making something, or taking him for a walk. And then, if Diggy could get away, they all had an early supper with Ronnie, after which he played with him for an hour and put him to bed (telling him he was not allowed to get up again, an injunction which Ronnie unfailingly obeyed, which was unfair, because when she put him to bed he was running around half the night). Then, if there was a school concert or something, they had to trundle off to that, and sit through some great long orchestra thing. Or, if there were no school functions, Diggy would go off to his office and work and work, and she wouldn't see him again until he came to bed about two. She would awake to feel his weight on top of her, but even this wasn't nice like it used to be, but rather horrible. Although he was making love to her, she felt he no longer cared about her, and every thrust was like an act of hate. And Diggy, who had always been such fun to be in bed with, and very sophisticated, was like a different man. In the early days he had said nice, sexy things to her, and made it really good for her, but now he didn't care whether she came or not.

"This won't take long," he would say, or "you can go back to sleep in a couple of minutes." And when he came it sounded as if was going to die or something. Then when she woke up in the morning he was gone and another day began. He was never rude to her, nor referred to the St John business (which was a relief), but he seldom spoke more than a few words to her, unless they were with Ronnie or in company. She was beginning to put on weight too, eating all the horrible stews and stuff they had to have with Ronnie. St John Davies never took any notice of her either, even though she often passed him on the way to the Art Centre, which was right next to the Classics room where he did all that Greek and stuff. In fact, he seemed to go rushing off as if she were a leper or something.

Sometimes she felt like running away, but where would she go? Her sister was in Australia with her new boyfriend, and anyway they had never got on; there was her mother, but she lived in Spain with her new husband, and Elizabeth knew she would not be welcome there for long. Anyway, she could hardly go off to Spain, she didn't have any money – apart from Diggy's – and if she ran away, he would be sure to cut it off. And there was Ronnie, too, people would expect her to take him with her. There seemed no answer to it. If only there was someone to talk to, but there wasn't. Diggy never asked friends round now, only Martin, and she wouldn't give him the satisfaction of knowing anything was wrong.

Martin, however, knew anyway and had determined to do something about it. "Isn't it time," he asked, "that you stopped punishing Elizabeth?"

He and Digby were looking through the new building plans that would constitute the Avonmore Theatre on Harold's retirement. It had seemed to be what he wanted. Digby looked up from a roll of plans and said nothing, although there was a furrow between his brows.

"It's not like you, Digs, to be unkind." Still Digby said nothing, but he stopped unfolding the plans.

"You know I have never been a great supporter of your wife, Digby, but I do think, from the look of her, that she has suffered enough."

"And what about me?" cried Digby, "don't you agree that I have suffered? Don't you think I still suffer?" And he thought of the terrible thing that Elizabeth had done, and the revulsion it had caused him, which had, in turn, made him act in such a shameful manner.

"It is all finished," said Martin gently, "your wife, no doubt, regrets her peccadillo, and St John is preparing to be an excellent Head Boy. You must put it behind you and move on. Look at Avonmore! He's forgotten he never wanted to retire and he's .. well, look at all this!" For Avonmore had been allowed to obtain the architect's plans. He had, in fact, obtained the services of five different architects.

"You're right, Martin." Digby started rolling up the plans and stashing them methodically. "I am behaving like a bastard. Every night, you know how busy I've been with the new curriculum and the GMC and, well, I go to bed, and I want to sleep, but I can feel her there. I can feel her body and I don't want to, Martin, I don't want to, but it becomes unbearable. So, I have her and then I can sleep."

"I know," said Martin. But it need not have been like that. Digby could have had peace; he need not have done this. But he must accept Digby's decision – for whatever reason it had been made, and try and cobble things up for him if only to stop the degradation, and prevent him bringing misery upon both himself and his wife. Not that Martin had much sympathy for Elizabeth, but she was Digby's wife and Digby must look on her in that light, or he would lose his dignity. If he could show some, perhaps 'respect' was too much to ask, some affection perhaps – for he must have once had that for her – then something might be salvaged, some little spark of happiness might be kindled.

"What do you suggest?" asked Digby coldly, writing in felt-tip on the largest of the plans.

"Be kind," said Martin with feeling, "kind, as only you know how."

And he walked off briskly down thorough the school grounds to 'The Sportsman's Arms', for he did not wish to think in detail of the ways Digby might be kind to Elizabeth.

And as Digby worked on the paper he was engaged on in connection with the Avonmore Theatre, which he must present to the governors the following day, he knew that Martin was right, and that he must rethink his attitude towards Elizabeth.

Chapter 21

"How would you like to go dancing?" asked Digby.

Elizabeth turned the television off quickly; she had been catching up on *Neighbours* and what Digby called 'mindless programmes', and he did not like her watching TV during the day. When she had seen him appear in the living room doorway, she had assumed that he would be cross with her about it. And it was so long since they had done anything nice together, she could not believe her ears, and thought she must have misheard.

"What?" she asked dully.

Digby regarded her as she stood guiltily by the television, and thought how miserable she looked. He had not behaved justly or, rather, he had behaved justly, but not generously. He was much to blame.

"How would you like to go dancing?" he repeated.

Elizabeth ran her hand through her hair so it fell all golden round her face. "Dancing?" she asked. Her brain could not associate a Digby who spoke of dancing with the stern and frightening Digby of the last few weeks.

"Mmm," he said smiling at her, "because I've booked a table at *Serendipity* for us. Would you like that?" And he went on smiling at her and, as she saw him standing there, so tall and dashing and lovely, she remembered the Digby who had married her, the Digby who used to be sweet to her, and she smiled shyly back at him, even now hardly daring to hope.

"Would you like that?" he asked again, and he rubbed the back of his neck

"Oh yes! But what about Ronnie?" For they were all supposed to be having their meal together.

"Ronnie will have to manage without us tonight," he said lightly, "I am taking my wife out on the town."

And oh, it would be so lovely because he wasn't talking about Ronnie and didn't want Marie-Louise to come and speak French, and they could dance and enjoy themselves – and not have to go to school plays or Speech and Drama things, or meet new teachers and boring old parents. They could have fun!

"And you are to wear that very pale pink dress you used to wear on our honeymoon," he added, "the one with the big rose."

"Oh!" Her happiness was a little dimmed. "It's all old-fashioned, nobody wears dresses like that any more."

"Well," he said pleasantly, "I liked it, but you wear what you like, Liz." And he called her Liz, which he hadn't done since that awful morning. Another slight hitch, however, occurred to her.

"Do I have to drive because ...?"

"Taxi. Then we can both drink lots and lots." She smiled, although she knew he never drank very much.

Then he gave Ronnie his supper and bathed him and put him to bed, so that Marie-Louise shouldn't have any trouble with him while they were out.

*****

They had a really lovely time, and Diggy looked gorgeous in his jeans and his denim shirt with the buttons undone so you could see the hair on his chest. She loved it when he wore his jeans because she could pretend he was almost her age, and not all old and stuffy like he was when he wore his suits. And she looked really great! She was glad she had not worn the dingy old pink dress; anyway, it had a great mark on it. She had worn her slinky black, and she could tell how stunning she looked from the way men kept eyeing her. And they'd danced – not as much as she would have liked, and it was a pity they had to go at twelve, but the evening wasn't over, for when they got back, instead of disappearing off to his office like she'd been afraid he would, he came straight into the bedroom and began kissing her in the way he used to. And then he undressed her very gently, kissing her tits very carefully; and when she lay down on the bed, he kissed her all over, and then moved down and tongued her like she really liked; and just when she was about to come he moved back up and fucked her really smoothly, so she came with a big o.

And afterwards, instead of turning over and ignoring her, he began talking and saying how he hadn't been very nice to her, and how he was going to be much nicer now. And she wondered if she could ask him if she could stop learning French and doing the Art, and taking Ronnie out in the afternoon, but thought it might be better to wait a bit. Then he said, "are you enjoying doing the Art Classes?"

"Oh yes," she said.

"And the French? I know it's hard, but do you feel you are making some progress?"

"Oh yes," she said.

"And Ronnie? Is he getting any easier to manage?"

"Oh yes." Perhaps they could make love again soon.

But he went on talking, this time about the summer holidays and the house in France. He thought it might be fun to have a big family party. She could ask her sister and her sister's boyfriend, and her mother could come over from Spain with her new husband, and maybe Richenda and Dolores would come, and, of course they mustn't forget his elderly mother, although she might be too frail for the journey, and there was Martin.

"That would be lovely, Diggy," she said and before he could make any more horrible suggestions, she reached out and stroked it, and met with the required reaction. "Diggy," she whispered, "let's make love again."

And, afterwards, when she had fallen asleep, he lay and thought about it all, about Belinda and Elizabeth, Jean and Martin, and what a mess it all was.

He pulled the duvet back to gaze at his wife as she lay with her full breasts and pink nipples, her flat stomach and her cunt covered in soft golden, downy hair, like the petals of a rose. Her eyes fast closed, showed her long blonde lashes shadowing her pinkish cheeks, and the long, long, straight blond hair fell down her back and strayed over the warm full breasts. She sighed a little in her sleep: perhaps she was dreaming of some new, incomprehensible task that he would impose upon her. And as he went on gazing at her, he was reminded of his daughters, Dolores and Richenda, when he used to put them to bed as children, so many years ago. And then, in her sleep she moved her hand gently up to cover her cheek, and for some inexplicable reason this moved him, more than anything else. And he thought how sweet she was, and how he had made impossible demands on her, and recently, how he had used her body to satisfy himself, like some dirty old man with a prostitute, and how she had never complained, but looked puzzled, as if it was all too much for her. He thought too, how she had not understood how heinously she had betrayed him with St John Davies, but had responded only to the urges of her body which he had not bothered to satisfy. She had been uncomprehending of the reason for his anger, and felt nothing but dismay when he had acted as he had to her; yet she had never even reproached him. She had been, he thought, ignorant, silent, and yet trusting. He reproached himself bitterly. He would strive to behave better.

In the morning he woke refreshed; he had slept well and it seemed to him that a great burden had fallen from his shoulders. He remembered the tender nature of their love-making on the previous night, and he felt he was rid of the terrible, destructive urges that had recently possessed him. Something was settled too, for the Summer holidays: they would spend almost a month in France; it would do them both good to get away from Mowberry.

He got out of bed and stood looking down at her, what was it she reminded him of? A picture by Waterhouse; he could see it now, Hylas looking down, and the water nymph gazing up at him, pleading with him to be kind to her. He bent down and kissed her lightly, "my water nymph," he said softly, "my little water nymph."

He covered her over with the duvet and left the room. He had six meetings ahead of him.

Chapter 22

She had had such a nice night last night with Diggy, just like it used to be, and everyone looking at her in the night club. And then they had come back and Diggy had licked her and fucked her, and it had been really lovely. And then she'd woken up and found Diggy gone although she had hoped he'd make love to her again in the morning, now that he was all back to normal. But instead of Diggy, Ronnie had come in, jumping all over her stomach and pushing that stupid rabbit in her face, making her feel sick, because she was a bit hung over after all the wine last night.

"Get off, Ronnie," she had said, and she had not meant to hit him, but he got hurt anyway, and started bawling. And Marie Louise had come and said it was ten o'clock and time for their French lesson, and was she going to do anything about the brake on the push-chair, because it ought to go to Simpsons in Hopton.

The morning seemed to drift away, but when the time came for her to go and help with the Art Class, she was still not dressed. And when she saw Martin walk past the window and knock at the door, she knew he was coming to ask why she was late, so she hid in the kitchen until he had gone.

She had disliked Martin even before she had met him. Digby had said, "You'll like Martin, I don't know what I'd do without him. He's like the other half of myself." And Elizabeth had known fear, for if

Martin was the other half of Digby, where did that leave her? Oh yes, Martin always pretended to include her in the conversation: "what do *you* think, Elizabeth?" he would say, but he was only patronising her, and then they always seemed to go back to talking about the old days. What would it have been like if she had met Digby when he was young and he had married her instead of boring old Belinda? Perhaps it wouldn't have been any good because he wasn't a headmaster then, only an ordinary teacher, and she would have had to have done even more unpleasant school things, than she did now.

At one o'clock they had a lunch of braised beef which Marie-Louise cooked according to Digby's orders. He liked Ronnie to have a proper cooked lunch. Elizabeth hated braised beef; she could never face anything at lunchtime, and she left it on the table, and as soon as Marie-Louise had gone off for her free time, Ronnie grabbed hold of it and threw it on the floor, and she had to clean it all up. He was meant to have a rest after lunch, and she really had tried to settle him and even started reading him a story, but he wouldn't listen and so she decided to take him down to the village shop. "I'll buy you some sweeties," she said. Digby had told her not to let him eat between meals, but he hadn't eaten much lunch, so he must be hungry, and she couldn't think of any other way to keep him quiet.

As she trundled the pushchair down to the shop (and of course he fell asleep straight away, so she needn't have bothered), she wondered what her mother had done with her when she was little. Probably nothing, she had never been very interested in children.

She bought some sweets even though Ronnie was still asleep, and pushed the chair slowly back towards the school. As she came back along the river path, she looked up towards the school, she felt a familiar sense of oppression, everything looked so sensible and ordered: the cricket-pitches and the great stone buildings probably disapproved of her, as much as Martin did.

Would it have been better if she had not married Digby? She thought of her old boyfriends – there was one who had gone into television, and that could have been fun. She could have been a chat-show hostess or something. But then, she hadn't liked him all that much because he'd been mean. And she did like Diggy, well, not *like* him, but she did love him, especially when they were in bed together and it was like last night. Why couldn't it always be like that?

She looked at her watch and wondered what on earth to do for the rest of the afternoon. And then Ronnie woke up and she gave him the sweets.

"Don't like them," he complained. "I want goo-goos."

"Well, I'm not going all the way down to the shop again," she said crossly, and she thought perhaps she was still a bit hung-over, because she could feel her head starting to ache. "What do you want to do?"

"Quack-quack," he shouted, "feed quack-quack." And she remembered Marie-Louise had said she would leave some bread in a bag, because Ronnie liked feeding the ducks. Why hadn't she thought of it before? She'd just run back to the house and get it. If she parked Ronnie here, he'd be quite safe for a few minutes.

When she came out of the back door with the bag of bread, she thought for a moment, that she saw the push-chair moving, which was silly because it couldn't be, because she must have put the brake on. And, anyway, things always looked wonky if you had a hang-over.

But as she got nearer, she began to be sure that it was moving, and she started to run, because it was going in the direction of the river, but even then she wasn't really worried because it was going so very, very slowly.

Then it happened. Whether the push-chair struck a willow tree root or some bump in the ground, or whether Ronnie, whose legs and arms were flailing around, threw his weight forward, no one subsequently was able to discover, but the chair gathered momentum, and Elizabeth began to run, screaming, as fast as she could after it. She reached the bank just as the chair was going over the edge; she grabbed for it, but then, she too, was dragged down under the weight of the push-chair and the screaming, struggling Ronnie.

Digby had insisted on buying the most expensive push-chair. It was very heavy, and it must have borne down upon Elizabeth in the water, or perhaps, she received a blow to the head from a rock embedded in the riverbed before they were both sucked down into one of the deep pot holes that made the river so dangerous, and out of bounds for the boys. And Elizabeth, who had looked so beautiful in a bikini, was a very poor swimmer; it was one of those things that she had lacked the determination to master late in life, since her mother had not bothered to teach her as a child. And perhaps, her long, lovely hair got caught up in the mechanism of the brake, or the reeds, entangling in it, dragged her down. It was never established.

Singh and Stewart heard the screams from the cricket nets, where they were making the most of a free period. "That sounds like Mrs Sherwood," said Singh, stopping short in his run up.

"Yes, she's down by the river with the baby," agreed Stewart. "I saw her just now when I went for that six." Then there was a short pause as they looked out from the nets, towards the river.

"Oh, Christ!"

Immediately they broke into a run, but the gate to the river path was locked, the groundsman had, for once, had been all too conscientious. "We'll have to go round by the road," shouted Stewart. "Fast!"

They came through the school gates, Stewart yelling as they ran towards the river. But, reaching the bank, all they could see was Ronnie's toy rabbit caught up in an overhanging branch. For a moment they stared in bewilderment, and then the terrible truth dawned.

"Oh God, oh God!" Stewart began tearing at the straps of his cricket pads, Singh had already removed his sweater and was hauling off his boots. He dived first and Stewart followed. Together they struggled to dislodge the pushchair, but it was wedged among the roots of the willow. Diving and resurfacing and diving again, Singh brought out the small body of Ronnie, limp and lifeless, water streaming from his mouth. He laid his headmaster's son reverently on the bank and returned to the water. Stewart was struggling with the dead weight of Elizabeth. Her mouth hung open, and her sodden clothes clung to the outline of her slim body. There was no life in her. Stewart flung himself down over her and tried to give the kiss of life, while Singh gently stroked the little boy. There was nothing to be done. "I will go for Mr Sherwood," he said.

Singh ran for the Headmaster, but there was no need. He was coming, anyway, for his observant eyes had caught sight of some sort of disturbance down by the river as he left for his three o'clock meeting. The boys were generally good about keeping away from the water, and his safety measures were strict. So why ...?

It did not take him long.

At a glance he knew there was no hope for Ronnie, and he turned to his wife. He gave a cry as he pushed Stewart away, and to the boy the cry seemed more frightening than anything else. Digby fell down by his wife's side and tried his own kiss of life. And all the kisses he had ever given her were nothing compared to this. Stewart began to cry in a high-pitched voice. "I tried, Sir," he cried, "I tried, Mr Sherwood, I tried." Singh turned away; he could not understand the ways of god or man in this English world. He fixed his eyes on the cricket bat lying on the river bank; it seemed the one thing that made any sense in the whole of his life at Mowberry School.

Eventually Digby gave up, and laid his head on his wife's breast. Then he looked at the boys as if he did not see then.

"My water nymph," he said. And her long, straight, fair hair lay out on the grass all covered with green weed.

"Go for Mr Wood, Gowinder," said Stewart.

Chapter 23

Naturally, it all fell to Martin: the police, the newspapers, the Common Room, the boys, the phone-calls, the parents, the letters, everything, and, of course, the ordinary day-to-day running of the school; and, on top of everything else, the school examinations were still going on.

The only good thing, if anything could be said to be good at this juncture, was the fact that Digby was being kept drugged up in Hopton General. Martin had driven Stamford, the school doctor, to the hospital, put a bottle of port in his pocket and told him to check on Digby every hour. And Stamford, whom everyone called the 'horse doctor' because of his unfeeling methods of ripping off bandages, kept Digby in hospital. Martin wanted to get everything sorted out and Digby kept out of the way, until the day of the inquest was settled, and a date set for the funeral.

He was concerned for Stewart and Singh, but they eschewed outside help, and seemed to find most comfort in each other's company, although he could not imagine what that might be.

Each housemaster spoke to his own boys at Call Over that night, and Martin addressed the whole school at Chapel the next morning. Several of the smaller fourth form boys who had been in Elizabeth's art class cried. Martin was cynical about bereavement counselling, but he made arrangements for it to be available for anyone who wanted it, aware that many of the parents would expect something of this kind, and that it would no the school no harm to be seen taking a lead in this direction. The press were enjoying it all greatly; it had all the elements of a great story: death, a beautiful woman, a small child and a major public school. They were having a field day.

They knocked continually at the Headmaster's house, the boarding houses and the main school buildings. One reporter even insinuated himself into the School Assembly. Some were gleefully hostile, anxious to report on the evils of the public school system, others wanted to produce sentimentally pictures of tragedy in an idyllic Olde Englande setting.

The tabloids featured smiling pictures of Elizabeth, generally in unsuitable clothes, and much was made of the child bride angle. Others featured Digby in his gown, looking the picture of a Headmaster. The Sun demanded a public enquiry into the safety of push-chairs, demanding: "Must our children go on dying?" Some camera men wanted pastoral photos of Mowberry as the ideal public school, others hunted for the seedy story that might lurk below the surface. All this Martin must monitor. Then there was the question of Elizabeth's mother and sister; fortunately, at least, as far as Martin was concerned, the sister had gone on holiday to Australia with her boyfriend, and her mother and husband, or lover, or whatever he was, had gone out to see them; and none of them, when finally located, seemed inclined hurry back.

Then there were the statements and the rumours surrounding the inquest. He spoke sternly in the Common Room, forbidding any unwarranted speculation or leaks to the press.

There was the constant phoning and writing of parents, demanding new safety procedures in regard to access of the river. There were the inevitable withdrawals from the list of next year's entry from parents who now regarded the school as unlucky or too dangerous.

Martin also spoke at length on the phone to Dolores, Digby's elder daughter. She and Richenda wanted to come down, but Martin knew Digby could not stand that yet. He told them to wait a while and, because it was Uncle Martin, they did as they were told.

"Poor, poor Daddy," she said, and Martin remembered what a sweet girl she was. "We'll go and see Granny, Richenda and me," she said, "but I don't think she'll be capable of understanding; she's very confused now, you know; anyway, leave it to us, Uncle Mart."

And then he went to Digby's house with a number of cardboard boxes and filled them with Ronnie's toys and clothes and took them off and put them in the loft of his house, until he should know what to do with them. He emptied the whole of Ronnie's room, even the duvet cover and pillow case. He left only the Thomas the Tank Engine curtains at the window.

He arranged with the police for Marie-Louise to be allowed to return to her parents and excused the ordeal of the inquest.

"I tell 'er about the brake," said the au pair tearfully, as Martin was waiting with her for the taxi. It seemed to him that she had told him little else over the past few days.

"Yes, I know." Martin could see the taxi advancing up the drive.

"The brake needed mending. She had only to take it to the shop."

"Thank you, Marie-Louise. We know." He hoped Digby would not need to know this, but he supposed everything would come out in the end.

And all the time, Digby lay in the hospital somewhere between sleep and awakening.

Once he mistook the nurse for Elizabeth, but she smiled and shook her head and he could see that she wasn't Elizabeth, because she wasn't nearly pretty enough. Furthermore, she had no green weed in her hair. He asked her where Ronnie was and she sat on the bed next to him and held his hand, and told him that Ronnie had gone with his mother to heaven, and Digby asked where that was, and the nurse got up and came back with a glass and some pills, and he went to sleep again.

Martin popped in several times and, even though he was the one who had demanded Digby be kept drugged, he was still appalled that his friend stared at him so unknowingly.

Sometimes, when the haziness passed away, Digby knew he had lost his wife and child. And yet the idea was strange to him; he could not accept it, for it seemed to him that it was only this person lying in the hospital bed to whom this terrible thing had happened, but if only he could get back to Mowberry, then this person would disappear, and he would meet his wife and son again, and yet, he knew it was not so.

Once he dreamed he was in a court of law, standing trial for the murder of his wife and son. Singh was foreman of the jury. "We bring in a verdict of guilty," he said, and Digby could see Stewart was there, as well, and he was holding up a pair of black lace knickers. "Here is the evidence," he said. And then he was dancing with St John Davies in the very night-club he had visited with Elizabeth, and Martin was there, saying, "dance with me instead, Digs."

Richenda, Digby's younger daughter came and sat by him, although he did not wake. The nurse was afraid of her, for she wore her hair closely shaved and stared at her, full of hate, blaming everyone for her father's suffering. But, eventually, she too, went away.

At last Digby's head cleared and he knew what had happened. He knew he must not think of it all at once, but only approach, a little at a time, because if he took on the whole thing, it would fall on him like a great lump of iron, and he would be utterly crushed. He would move stealthily about it, now advancing, now retreating when the horror grew too great. He asked for some of the newspapers, but he found them uninteresting; he did not feel they related to him, or Elizabeth, or Ronnie. He had a great urge to read Donne's love poetry, but the nurse didn't understand what he meant. He remembered that Jean had once given him a copy.

It was odd that of all people, it should have been Avonmore who spoke to Digby first in hospital. Avonmore who, oblivious of visiting hours or security staff, walked down the corridors with a measured tread in his extraordinarily short suit trousers, with the flies held together with the safety pin, and let himself into Digby's private room.

Digby, who was working at his policy of facing small portions of horror, and then retreating from them, was now imagining Ronnie's terror as he felt the push-chair running, rushing, and finally hurling itself into the cold, reed-ridden water.

"Good afternoon to you, Headmaster," said Avonmore cheerfully. Digby could not bring himself back into the present very easily, and he stared vacantly at the large figure who was seating himself in the visitor's chair.

"Who are you?" he asked, although he realised immediately who Avonmore was and could not understand why he had asked. Perhaps he had meant to ask why he was here.

"I am Harold Avonmore, presently Senior Classics master at Mowberry School," he replied with a certain amount of satisfaction.

Digby said nothing; he could think of nothing to say. Harold said nothing either, continuing to gaze at Digby. He was impressed by Digby's striped pyjamas and he thought he might buy a similar pair for himself. Digby closed his eyes. He thought he should now imagine Elizabeth's horror instead of Ronnie's.

At last Harold cleared his throat. "I, too, have suffered tragedy," he said, "we have much in common." Digby said nothing. He could see the reeds closing round Elizabeth's throat.

"I was married too," said Harold, and his voice lacked much of its usual satisfaction. "She was beautiful, too. She died giving birth to my daughter. The child was still-born." He looked beyond Digby at the curtains.

"I'm sorry," said Digby automatically, but he could not take on board someone else's sufferings.

"I thought I would never get over it," said Harold, and his voice resumed some of its usual complacency. "But I did. You do in the end, you know. "Ho chronos iatros," he brought out triumphantly. "Time is the Doctor."

A nurse entered, the one whom Digby had mistaken for Elizabeth. "You have a visitor!" she said, "How nice! Would you like some tea?"

"Yes, indeed," said Harold. "That would be most acceptable." He had not yet finished what he had intended to say. Sherwood had inflicted a great blow on him, but since that time, Nemesis had taken charge and Digby had been brought low; it was a perfect example of Aristotelian tragedy: 'a great figure brought down by an error of judgement' It seemed to Harold that the Headmaster's error of judgement had lain, not in his marriage to Elizabeth, but in the dismissal of himself. But now he was minded to ease Digby's burden, for had not Sophocles allowed Oedipus to be freed from his suffering at Colonus? Now he, Harold Avonmore would grant Sherwood similar relief. Like the gods, he would make a divine intervention.

"Now you must sit up, Mr Sherwood, and have your tea," said the pretty nurse, returning with the tray, "and keep your visitor company."

"Yes," said Digby, but he left the tea untouched. Harold didn't though. He drank his lustily and took the plate of biscuits on to his lap. "Ah," he said. "Jammy Dodgers. I wonder how they might be rendered into Latin."

"I killed them both," said Digby suddenly.

"No, no," said Harold, his mouth full of biscuit. "You cannot think like that. I thought that once: if I had not impregnated my wife, she would not have died, but then, if her father (a very disagreeable man), had not impregnated her mother, she would not have lived at all."

"I should never have married Elizabeth. I should have left her like a flower in the garden," pursued Digby with no interest in Avonmore's words.

"Rubbish, Headmaster! Are you sure you won't have a Dodger? They are most acceptable ... someone else would have picked her or trampled her down, you're your son would have had no life at all. I wonder if there is more tea in the pot?"

"I never made her happy, Harold." Digby found that he could at last communicate.

"I don't agree. A very happy lady. She came into a lesson of mine once, laughing and smiling. It made a great impression on me. Ah!" Harold remembered the form the impression had taken.

"I have come for a purpose. I have come to offer you a ... ah ... great sacrifice."

As Digby said nothing, Harold continued. "I have, you may recall, been very busy obtaining architects' plans for the Avonmore Theatre, and a decision has, I believe you told me yourself, been taken upon its format. It will be a mighty edifice, a veritable aedificium mirabile ..."

Yes, Digby could remember something about a theatre, a theatre whose purpose was to right another wrong he had done.

"And I have decided to ... ah ... abrogate my rights. Its nomenclature shall be the Elizabeth Sherwood Theatre, in memory of your wife. That is my great gift, my mega doron."

And for the first time Digby smiled a little. Why, he hardly knew.

Chapter 24

"I'm glad Grandma didn't come," said Richenda in her angry way.

"Yes," said her sister. They had driven up to fetch her from the Retirement Home in Dorset, but she had been too frail for the journey.

"I don't think she really understood who Elizabeth was, anyway."

"But you'd think she'd remember Ronnie. I mean, with him being called after Grandpa."

"I'm glad," said Richenda, "that she didn't."

They were sitting together in a pub, breaking their journey back home. It was early evening and they could have sat outside, but found the drab interior more in keeping with their mood. Perhaps they sought some form of privacy, for both girls might well attract attention, Dolores for her mass of curly blonde hair and sweetness of face, Richenda for her striking appearance, with her shaved head, which showed her fierce face in its naked beauty.

Richenda, the younger of the two spoke with the cruelty of youth. "She was an awful woman, anyway. I mean all that crap in the service about her giving her life for Ronnie. If she'd put the push-chair brake on properly, he wouldn't have died."

"Oh Rich," said Dolores, "you don't know that."

"All this having to speak well of people just because they're dead. Do you want another drink?"

"Just an orange juice."

Dolores watched her sister thoughtfully as she went for the drinks. From her two years greater experience of life, or perhaps because she was of a gentler nature, she was prepared to forgive Elizabeth.

"Did you see Mummy's wreath?" she asked. "I thought it was nice of her, didn't you?"

"She wrote a letter too," said Richenda, who was spending the long vacation at home, "she showed it to me and asked me if I thought it was all right."

"And was it?"

"Oh yes!" said Richenda bitterly. "It was a good letter."

"Do you think, Richenda ... do you think there's any chance ...?"

"What? Of Mummy and Daddy getting back together? No! Nor should they."

"I never really understood why they divorced anyway," said Dolores, brushing off drops of beer which her sister had spilt on her skirt. "They always seemed a good team to me."

"Sex," said Richenda. "She wouldn't give him enough, so he went and got it somewhere else. In retrospect, I don't blame him." She glanced round the pub at the far tables, where a group of teenagers were making a lot of noise, banging glasses down and laughing.

"Yes," said Dolores. "I thought it might be something like that. Want a ciggy?"

Richenda shook her head. "I'm going to tell you something that I've not really thought about for years."

"Trust you!" said Dolores, "to keep things to yourself. I always have to tell everybody everything."

"Well, you haven't told me yet that Duncan asked you out across the funeral baked meats."

"I'm not a teenager," said Dolores, her pretty face dimpling at the memory. "He simply asked me to go to the theatre with him next week – just for old time's sake, you understand."

"So you can finish off what you started in the stables ...?"

"Shut up, Rich, and tell me what you were going to say."

"I'll need another pint."

"I don't know how you can drink all that beer."

"You're just jealous because you're driving!"

"I don't like beer anyway. Go on, get your drink and tell."

"Well," said Richenda, on her return from the bar, "I suppose I was about seven or eight, and we'd both been given money by Granny for some reason, and Mummy made us put most of it in the bank, but we were allowed to go the toy shop and buy something with the rest. You must remember. You probably bought something worthy and educational, knowing you, but what I wanted, Dol, I can see it now – was a huge purple rabbit.

"Yuck!"

"Exactly! But at the time I thought it the most wonderful and desirable thing in the world."

It was odd, thought Dolores, seeing Richenda with her austere hair-cut and long black dress, wanting anything as frivolous as a purple rabbit.

"It had great eyes and whiskers and it was incredibly glamorous and quite scary, and I wanted it. But Mummy said no, it was too expensive and it was vulgar and she pointed out a teddy bear, "he's nice, Richenda," she said, "a real friend. Why don't you have him, instead?" And I was angry – do you remember, Dol, how angry I always was.

"Oh yes!"

"And you were standing there looking all self-righteous with your book or whatever it was, and you said, "why don't you have the teddy?" So I took the teddy and threw it across the toy shop, and then I lay down on the floor and screamed. You must remember."

"Oh yes, I ..."

"Anyway, Mummy was very cross and I was made to stay in my room all afternoon, so I did what I always did when I was in disgrace, and fell asleep. And then later on I was all forgiven and everything, but because, I suppose, I had slept all afternoon, I woke up very wide-eyed in the middle of the night and thought I would go exploring."

"You were so much braver than me," said Dolores, looking regretfully into her empty glass. "I should never have dared. Stanstead was always scary at night."

"So I wandered about, and then I heard noises coming from Mummy and Daddy's room.

"Oh, Rich, you didn't?"

"No! Wait. I went and stood outside their door and Daddy was saying something like, 'Please, Belinda please. I want it so much,' and I remember thinking that Daddy was like me and that he wanted something like I'd wanted the purple rabbit, and I knew from his voice that he wanted it really badly, and that Mummy was doing what she'd done to me and stopping him from having it. And I was shocked, too, by Daddy's voice, because you know how sort of judicious he always was, and authoritative, and now it seemed as if that was all gone, lost, because of this thing he needed."

"I don't know that I want to hear ..."

"And he went on begging and pleading, and eventually she said something like, 'Oh all right but get it over with quickly,' and I could hear them, well, you know..., and then Daddy gave this groan – no, not what you think, really. Just a sort of cry – and it was a disappointed sort of cry, and I knew he had been fobbed off with something that just wasn't any good, just like I was fobbed off with the teddy bear. Mummy had been quite sensible and fair with us both, but it wasn't what we wanted. We wanted something extraordinary and exciting, and slightly dangerous. Do you see what I'm saying, Dol?"

"Yes, I do, but you have to remember that Mummy couldn't help it either. She gave you both what she could."

"But it wasn't enough!" Richenda leaned over in her eagerness to make Dolores understand, knocking her glass, in her excitement. She steadied it, and brushed at the spilt beer impatiently with her hand. "Daddy wanted fantastic sex, like I wanted the fantastic rabbit."

"Which is why he married Elizabeth."

"I don't blame him, at all," said Richenda.

"But it didn't work. And you said yourself she was an awful woman. And what will he do now?"

"Oh, I don't know," said Richenda, and the severity of her hair emphasised the dampening of her eyes as she sat there. "He looked so awful, didn't he, at the funeral? And then, so polite to everyone afterwards, so that they wouldn't offer him any sympathy. I couldn't bear it."

"Come on, Rich," said Dolores, who was of a more optimistic nature. "It may all come right in the end."

"Yes." said Richenda bitterly. "Daddy could marry Mummy again, and you could marry Duncan and have lots of babies to replace Ronnie."

"Of course I know life isn't like that," said Dolores. But all the same ...

Chapter 25

Every evening since Digby had been back home, Martin had asked if he would like him to come over and spend the night or, conversely, if Digby would like to stay at the bungalow, and every time Digby had firmly and politely refused. But tonight Martin was not offering him the choice; he arrived at nine with his overnight bag (actually the sports bag belonging to a boy who had been in his house fifteen years ago, and which Martin had made use of ever since).

Digby, of course, would have known that Martin must come on the night of the funeral, and he made no comment as he held the door open.

They went into the drawing room which the housekeeper must have tidied and from which the kitchen staff had removed the food; and all was so nearly back to normal that no one would have guessed that over a hundred people had been having tea there some hours before.

Martin announced that he would like a drink and Digby poured him a whisky, but took nothing himself, although Martin noticed that he was smoking heavily. They made a little desultory conversation.

"I thought Stewart read well," he said.

"Yes," said Digby. "He would have made a good Head Boy." And Martin cursed himself for tactlessness. As if to release Martin from any worries on that score, Digby said that he was glad that Singh and Colonel Haslett had got on so well together.

"Wasn't he out in the Punjab?"

"Yes," said Digby, "he was there at the time of Partition, he even knows Singh's village."

"That's splendid!" said Martin, and he was aware of sounding insincere, but the events of the previous fortnight had taken their toll on him, too, and he was conscious of great tiredness.

Digby said it was good of Martin's son, Duncan, to come, and Martin said how pretty Dolores had become, not of course that Richenda wasn't, as well – and perhaps when her hair had grown, she would even be prettier than Dolores. Digby said that yes, perhaps she would.

Martin attempted a little humour and said he had never seen anyone put away as much food as Avonmore, he had seen him eat at least three eclairs. Digby said he hoped he had enjoyed them, and that he had arranged for all left over food to be sent to the Fourth Form House, for the boys to have after prep. And Martin said what a good idea that was.

And then Digby got up abruptly, taking two packets of cigarettes and a lighter, and said if Martin would excuse him, he was going to bed. And after he had shut the door, he opened it again and said he was awfully sorry, he hadn't checked on sheets and things, but he thought there was a pile in the airing cupboard in the bathroom, also towels, and had Martin got everything he needed? And Martin said yes, thank you, Digby, he had.

After Martin had finished his second whisky he went up to bed himself, but he knew, tired as he was, he would not sleep. So he emptied out all the contents of the bag, most important among which was his own bottle of whisky, and went to bed. He also extracted a pile of Lower Fifth exercise books which he knew he would not mark. He even looked at some pages of Italian which he had printed off the internet from the Lizard man in Milan, but he didn't really bother about those, either. In fact, he let the biology books and the lizard papers slide off the bed and scatter themselves over the floor. Martin was unbothered, he was untidy at the best of times and now neatness did not seem to be of great importance.

He could hear nothing of Digby, through the wall and he wondered what he was doing exactly, but also decided that under no circumstances would he disturb him. Digby would know he was awake and, if he wanted to, he must come to Martin.

He cast his mind back over the days since Digby had been back; reflecting how immediately he had resumed school business and how extremely, almost excessively courteous he had been to everybody; but also how distant, as if to show the lines on which people might meet him, but also the space which they might not transverse.

The Inquest had been dreadful and Martin had wondered if he ought to have insisted on spending the night at Digby's house then.

It had been clear from the coroner's words that the push-chair's brake had not been put on correctly. A written statement taken before Marie-Louise had returned to France had stated that the au pair had several times observed Elizabeth leaving it off, and she had explained to her that it was not really stiff if you gave it an extra push with your foot. If she took it back to the man in the shop he would loosen it so it worked properly. She had apparently explained in English and French. Martin recalled the Coroner expressing the wish that mothers everywhere might learn a salutary lesson from this tragic accident.

He did not know, from Digby's point of view, whether the fact of the unsecured brake made the whole thing better or worse. It might be better in that Digby would feel himself less directly responsible for the deaths, but on the other hand, there was something particularly poignant about deaths that could so easily have been avoided, particularly the death of a small child. And there was the whole question of Ronnie. Martin knew that Digby had been nowhere near as fond of Ronnie as he was of his daughters. Again, did this make matters better or worse? The loss itself might be less, but set against that was the guilt Digby might bear in relation to his very lack of love. On the other hand, he had never failed in his duty to Ronnie and had initiated a strict regime for his welfare, although the very impersonality of such a regime might in its turn cause him to reproach himself for lack of spontaneous paternal feeling. The trouble was, thought Martin, that Digby was an intelligent man, a man to whom a brain was a thing of great value. He had been so absolutely delighted when both Dolores and Richenda made Oxford. Had he suspected that Ronnie was his mother's son, lacking any intellectual ability, and for that reason had entertained lesser affection for him?

To none of these questions did Martin know the answer as he lay in bed, in the beautifully appointed guest room. And yet he felt in his bones that Digby suffered more over Elizabeth's death than Ronnie's. Martin knew Digby would torment himself with guilt, guilt for marrying her and getting her pregnant, guilt for being unkind to her, guilt for all the times he had used her body, guilt for the time he had thrust her head into the lavatory bowl, guilt for taking her out the night before her death, for allowing her to drink too much, for making love to her, for just about everything. Martin sighed. Well, he would think of something else.

The funeral had been successful, if ever such a word could be applied to such an event. And so it should have been considering the number of hours they had all applied to it. Digby had left the organisation to him, merely asking to see the final programme. Only Elizabeth's mother and sister had Digby dealt with himself. Martin had guessed from early on, that Digby disliked and despised her, and he suspected she would now be intent on making capital out of the tragedy, and that her presence at the funeral would be nothing short of a disaster.

Martin gathered, moreover, although Digby had said little, that she, who had never been bothered with Elizabeth alive, was now back from Australia and constantly on the phone, making demands about travel arrangements, hotels and flowers. Elizabeth's sister had chosen to remain in Australia.

Eventually everything had been sorted out, but for once the gods had been on Digby's side. It would appear, or so Martin at any rate read it, that she had gone on a binge the night before her flight and had fallen and broken a leg. Perhaps, thought Martin, it was only an excuse, she could have come if she had wanted. Briefly, the dead Elizabeth had awakened an interest the mother had not experienced before, but only briefly. For whatever reason, she never came, either to see her daughter one last time, or to attend the funeral. And after all the arrangements that had been made! Martin had to smile; it would have been funny if it had not been so tragic.

The Director of Music wanted to compose a variation on the theme of a nursery rhyme for Ronnie, to be played and sung by the fourth form. So they had gone all through different rhymes, and each seemed more preposterous than the last: Humpty Dumpty had had a great fall, that obviously wouldn't do; Jack and Jill went up the hill and Jack came tumbling down. Worse still! The Grand old Duke of York, on the other hand, had all too much success with bringing his men up the hill and safely down again. Poor Ronnie! The idea was abandoned and some Mozart was settled for. The Head of English had his own ideas about suitable passages for readings, but the Chaplain did not get on with the Head of English, and refused to co-operate with him. Eddie, the handyman said they couldn't have any extra chairs for the chapel because they were all needed for the A Level examinations going on in the hall. Avonmore, too, had appointed himself as a sort of unofficial Master of Ceremonies, and was determined to read a long passage in Greek, about the sacrifice of Iphigenia, which Martin feared, Digby would be the only person to understand.

In the end the difficulties were more or less ironed out and the programmes actually at the printers when Martin remembered that St John Davies, as new Head Boy, was meant to be reading the lesson. He rang the printers and had the name altered to S. Stewart, and thereby incurred the wrath of the Drama Department. He had insisted on Singh reading something from Hindu. He hadn't a clue whether or not it was suitable, but figured that no one else would either.

Martin's worries were manifold. He had to fervently pray that the service would go off without a hitch, and keep an intent eye on proceedings, and at the same time keep an even stricter eye open for Digby.

But Digby did not flinch, not at the Mozart, nor at the speech about Elizabeth and the Art classes (written by the head of English), and delivered by two small fourth-formers. He showed no emotion as the coffin went on its way (there being only the one coffin for mother and son). Digby stood very upright and unmoving throughout, only occasionally moving his hand to the back of his neck as though it pained him.

Martin had been immensely thankful for the presence of his own son, Duncan, and for Richenda and Dolores. In a moment of abstraction he found himself wondering where Belinda and Jean were. Richenda held her father's hand throughout, looking fiercely ahead of her.

Everything went virtually without a hitch – old Colonel Haslett, original old boy and oldest governor as ninety-seven, was heard to ask loudly in the chapel who Elizabeth and Ronnie Sherwood were, but, apart from that, Martin was satisfied.

It was all right afterwards too, when they went back to Digby's house for tea. It was all most elegantly served in the dining room and drawing room. There had been trouble over who should be asked back. It was finally decided there should be members of the Senior Common Room, the prefects and a representative from each of the school houses. The governors were there in force, Richenda, Dolores, Duncan and quite a large number of former colleagues of Digby's and even a smattering of headmasters, including Graham Sutherland, to whom Digby had once introduced Elizabeth.

It had been immensely tiring and the stragglers had been difficult to get rid of, until Martin suggested to Avonmore that he speak with them, and then they all seemed to disappear in no time. Thank god it was all over.

And yet it wasn't all over. No one knew that as well as Martin, as he drank his whisky and listened for sounds from the next room.

Sounds of any kind would do; sounds of sobbing would be best because Digby must break out from the terrible carapace that he had formed of silence for himself, courtesy and concern, for others. And yet the carapace was poisoned too, for let no one who would remain unscathed, come close to it.

"I have been so upset for you, Headmaster," said Lady Jenkins, wife of the Chairman of the governors, "I have not been able to sleep." Stupid woman.

"I am sure," Digby had said, "Dr Canning will be able to prescribe something for you. Allow me to ask him."

If only Digby would cry. If he could allow his soul to seek release through tears but this too did not seem possible for him.

If Digby would shout and swear, rail against heaven and earth, blame anybody or everybody, and blame Elizabeth who, in his view, was entirely culpable for everything. But Digby did none of these things. He remained aloof and utterly silent. What was he doing in the next room? For a moment Martin was afraid he might have taken something, but only for a minute because he knew that Digby would scorn to act in self-pity.

Martin felt immensely tired. He had been through tiredness peaks throughout the day, once about ten when he was finally running through the service with Digby and the chaplain; once when he could legitimately rest his eyes during a prayer in the service, he found himself dozing off; and again, when he had returned to his house after the tea, he had nodded off for half an hour or so; and now he longed above everything to sleep; and yet, he had a feeling, perhaps only a superstitious idea, that if he slept, he would somehow or other have betrayed Digby. A phrase from the New Testament kept going through his mind. It was Christ saying to Peter, "What, could ye not watch with me one hour?" And yet, his baser self told him, 'Digby is asleep. He doesn't want anything'.

He had drunk half a bottle of his own whisky as well as a couple of glasses of Digby's earlier. He was weary of thinking over the inquest, the funeral, the deaths; he was almost bored of the whole thing, he was so tired. Why should he not knock on Digby's door; knock on the wall, shout out "are you all right, Digs?" But he must not do that. He must wait and, as he drifted off towards sleep, even then his brain forbade him the luxury of real slumber; it allowed him only a shallow loss of consciousness, so that he heard the movements almost as soon as Digby had made them; and yet they were so quiet that he was not sure even that it was Digby, or whether it was some sound produced in the tumult of his own brain. But now he became sure he could hear Digby walking, it must be to his door. The door opened and Digby's footsteps were outside his own. And then they

179

stopped; there was silence again, as if he did not know what to do, whether to come to Martin or to go back again to his bed, away from Martin, away from comfort. And Martin could all but hear his breathing outside, and still he must say nothing. And then such a long passage of time, or so it seemed, passed that Martin feared he had returned silently again to his own room and his solitude.

Suddenly his door was pushed open violently, so violently that Martin started, although it was the very thing he had been waiting for.

And Digby his friend, his dear beloved friend, came rushing, came tumbling towards him, calling out his name, repeating over and over again, "Martin, Martin, Martin." And it was a cry like that of a wounded bird as it wings its way homeward to the nest that it longs for so ardently, and then making one last effort with the weight of its body, it swoops tumbling down and down, to the secret place known only to the bird .

And Martin held out his arms like the branches of a tree, and it seemed to Digby as his friend murmured his name, the sound was like the rustling of leaves in the warm and pleasant summer breeze.

Chapter 26

Over the Summer holidays, Martin went to visit his son, Richard, who was spending a gap year in Australia. There was also a zoologist in Perth, whom Martin had hopes of meeting, as he was writing a new chapter of the lizard book. He hated leaving Digby and offered to cancel the trip, but Digby would not hear of it. He had made his own arrangements for the summer, it seemed. He was going to help with the Outward Bound Course that Alan Briggs, Head of Games, was running with Simon Barnett the Geography Master in North Wales for the lower fifth. And subsequently he would join Jim Elliot, Sergeant of the CCF and the sixth form cadets on their walking tour over the Andes. Each member of staff, truth to tell, was rather taken aback at the thought of having Digby with him. Briggs and Barnett intended to do a fair amount of drinking and feared this would be inhibited by the presence of the Headman and Elliot was legendary in his preference for running things single-handed. In the event, nobody's fears were realised. In fact, in both situations, Sherwood was a bonus. He had no objection to Briggs and Barnett boozing, and was happy to stay in the camp site or hostel with the boys while the masters went off to the pub, merely pointing out that a 6.30 start in the morning was easier without a hangover. Digby was happy, too, to take his orders from Elliot, who soon dispensed with the easier routes he had planned for Sherwood, as he could, in fact, out-walk any of them, but who was equally willing to stay behind with anyone who was unfit or unwell.

When the three of them discussed their Headmaster's abilities afterwards, they all admitted that he had, unobtrusively, been the lynch pin of the outings. They agreed that at no time had he complained, or as much as hinted at his recent tragedy. They all felt, actually, rather unnerved by him.

He spent six days in the house in France with Richenda and Dolores. He was quiet but quite willing to fall in with whatever plans they had for the day. He said he was pleased to hear Dolores was seeing Duncan. He hoped they would make a match of it.

Dolores told Richenda that she was sure he was over the worst now and Richenda made no reply. She had seen how often her father rubbed the back of his neck as if it pained him.

After the Andes tour, Digby came back to organise the school year and to urge on the builders who were to finish the Elizabeth Sherwood theatre by the end of term. The Classics Room and Book Store too, were being extended to form the Harold Avonmore Classical Library (a consolation prize for the sacrifice of the theatre). Martin need not have worried about Digby being left on his own: Harold appeared at his house most days with new sets of plans for the library. Digby was unfailingly co-operative and, if he had a free half hour or so, would invite him in for coffee and biscuits, even though he took none himself. And Avonmore spoke at length about himself and it was only when he began to speak of Elizabeth that the Headmaster remembered he had an appointment.

He thought a great deal about the two boys, Stewart and Singh. He had written and received a number of letters from Stewart's mother and, beneath the maternal fussing, his instinct told him that Stewart was all right. But Gowinder was a different matter, and Digby had no idea how the events might have affected him. As time went by he felt increasing anxiety since he received no replies to a number of his own letters. It was not until the end of the holiday that he finally received a letter.

Gowinder wrote to tell him that he would not be returning to Mowberry the following term, nor trying for Oxford, nor indeed returning to England at all. He explained:

"I hope you will not be thinking me ungrateful, Mr Sherwood; I gained an immeasurable amount from Mowberry School and I learned what an honourable and respected man was like; for you, Sir, were as fine and just a Headmaster as a boy could find. You will be remembering a parcel containing a piece of paper and a black female undergarment. I was thinking (for it was I who sent it) that you would be punishing the boy concerned for the insult to yourself; for I was not understanding your nature. Now I understand that you knew and understood what the boy had done, but would not allow this knowledge to cloud your judgement and deny the boy you thought most suitable, of his privileged position. I honour you, Sir. I could not have been so generous. Nevertheless, he is not a boy whom I admire and I should not wish to serve under him. It is possible that I am having feelings of jealously as I once believed I might hold that position. I am possibly deluded as I understood that Simon Stewart also believed that he might hold that post. He would, I believe, have been a worthy recipient. He is a boy I learned to admire only after the tragedy, Sir, but we enjoyed a brief friendship.

My true cause for not returning, however, is the village. I find that things have become very corrupt here in my absence, (you will not be understanding how a man may be less than honest, Sir. It would not be accessible to your nature). However, various evil men have encroached on our fields, and two of the buffalo have vanished we know not where. The well too is drying up. The villagers are ignorant men, Sir, and do not know how to deal with those in authority. But I am an educated man since my time at Mowberry, and I know how to address authority and how to make a speech, (you remember I made a short speech at the funeral of your wife and son). I believe I can do great things for my family, my village and perhaps my country. My place is here, Sir.

Thank you, Sir, for your example.

Yours with gratitude,

Gowinder Singh

Postscript: Please thank Mr Avonmore for his most excellent teaching.

Recovering from the death of Elizabeth and Ronnie, Digby had thought that nothing much would touch him again, but Singh's letter distressed him greatly, for it intensified his feelings of failure; worse, it brought home to him how his own morally dubious actions had spoiled the lives of others – those of his own wife and his son, and now, Gowinder. He must ensure that Martin's life at any rate, remained unscathed.

Digby thought for a long time and eventually wrote back to thank Singh for his letter, and to tell him that in his personal opinion, he was doing the right thing, although most people would not agree with him.

He asked Felicity to photocopy the postscript, for he knew Avonmore would wish to add it to his scrapbook, which he had been shown now on a number of occasions.

He wrote and asked Elizabeth's mother what she would like done with Elizabeth's effects, but receiving no reply, he took everything to the local Oxfam shop, including all the jewellery he had given her. It must have raised a great deal of money; he wondered if any of it would find its way to Singh's village.

He visited his own mother too, now in her ninety-second year.

She had no memory of Elizabeth or Ronnie, but asked him a great deal about Belinda, of whom she had been fond. Digby felt no compunction in telling her what she wished to hear.

And then, as August passed into September, everybody began to return for the Michaelmas Term. Martin was usually back well in advance of a new term, for as Second Master there was much for him to do. This year, however, because of the Australia trip, he was back only the night before the commencement of term. Nevertheless, he went round to Digby's house almost as soon as he returned, excited at the thought of seeing his friend again, and anxious to discover Digby's state of mind.

On the whole, he thought Digby looked well; he had always been keen on outdoor pursuits and the walking holidays had obviously suited him. Further than that he could not judge, for Digby, pleasant and courteous as ever, did not ask him in.

"I hope you have some photos for me to see, Martin," he said, holding the door, but not opening it fully.

"Now come on, Digs," Martin had said, attempting a joviality he did not altogether feel, "you know I take dreadful pictures." And immediately he regretted his remark, for he thought of all the photos he had taken of Digby, Belinda and Jean, and knew that Digby would think of them also. So he added hastily, "anyway, I take slides now; that way I can bore people for longer." He wondered whether to demand that Digby ask him in for a drink, but looked at the hand firmly grasping the side of the door and decided against it.

"You're all right, then, Digs?" he asked, and thought what a totally inadequate question this was, but Digby replied firmly in kind.

"Absolutely fine, Mart. Up to my eyes in work, of course."

It was, Martin saw, a tactful request for his departure. He could not refuse; he must play it as Digby wished, comply just as he had always complied in everything from the managing of the school to being run out by Digby in cricket, and, once he had complied in another greater, although unspoken imperative.

"Well, I'll be off then, Digs."

For a second Digby's hand faltered on the door, and his body moved in a way that would have been imperceptible to any but Martin; but then he regained his sangfroid, and said that a projector would be sent over to the Senior Common Room tomorrow so that anyone who might be interested could view the slides. From which Martin understood that he would not be invited into Digby's house. and that Digby was warning him off any à deux activities.

Chapter 27

At the beginning of a new school year, a major public school is a frenetically busy place. Not only are five hundred boys returning, most of them hell-bent on mischief, but apart from those, there are some hundred new boys who must be made to feel at home in their new school community, and their anxious parents reassured.

Then there are the meetings: curriculum council meetings, Heads of Department meetings, the Senior Master's Committees, the A Level Committee, the GCSE Studies Colloquium, the Housemasters' Confederation, the Science Staff Seminar, the Prefects and Staff Committees, and so on and so forth. It was rumoured too, that Digby had plans to set up a new appeal for Gowinder Singh's village in the Punjab.

Everyone, boys, masters, matrons, maintenance staff, kitchen staff, Uncle Tom Cobley and all, were immensely busy. Mowberry was in the thick of it. The events of the previous term were swallowed up in the general mass of activity. People no longer thought of Digby Sherwood as a man who had only recently suffered two terrible deaths; they saw only the man they needed Felicity to make appointments with ASAP to sort out their own particular problems.

In all this activity there was one person and probably only one person who was not busy, who had time to stroll in leisurely fashion about the school, giving a word of advice here, and a reprimand there. This was a happy man, and his name was Harold Avonmore.

He had been looking forward to the arrival of Yvonne Bonnington, the new Classics teacher, with eager anticipation, and in honour of which he had purchased a new suit, somewhat longer in the leg and fuller about the body than the previous one, which had, admittedly, served him well over the years. It had, indeed, featured in the photo of himself in '59, surrounded by his twelve Oxbridge candidates. The photo showed no obvious evidence of the safety pin, so that may have been adopted at some later date. He had also purchased a pair of striped pyjamas, not unlike the ones he had admired upon Sherwood in Hopton Hospital. These, however, were not for public display, although he could conceive of a time when other eyes than his own might gaze upon them, even when hands other than his own might find their way within the lower half.

Yvonne Bonnington liked being at Mowberry from her very first day when a fourth former, looking at her in astonishment, asked, "Were the Romans real people, then, Miss Bonnington?" She laughed. "As real as you and me, Carter," and she organised a special Roman day for the fourth form with a chariot race round the Green Sward and authentic food – stuffed dates and honey-soaked toast. She liked teaching and she was good at it. She expected the best from her pupils and didn't spare them, but neither did she spare herself. She helped Stewart with his dyslexia in her own time, while she accepted no excuses from Davies.

But if she was honest, she reflected as she laid down her pen one night, after correcting a pile of Lower V exercise books, there was another, rather unexpected, side of Mowberry that appealed to her. She found she liked the company of male colleagues; she liked the cut and thrust of their repartee and, more than that, she liked being a woman in a male stronghold.

She wasn't vain, but knew she was attractive and it was pleasant to be the object of male attention. But she had no wish to rush into an attachment; she looked, she smiled, and she bided her time. In her thirty-three years she had had two long-lasting relationships, both of which she had ended because the men had disappointed her. She wanted the next one to be right; in fact, this time she wanted marriage, and as she looked around the staffroom, her eye fell upon Martin. She had immediately warmed to his solid dependability, his sense of humour and his quiet efficiency. She wasn't worried by his plainness, but looked beneath the surface and saw kindness and understanding there. To be frank, she smiled to herself as she screwed the top on her pen, she would also like to go to bed with him.

In the eyes of the rest of the staff, Yvonne Bonnington was an immediate success. She was efficient but deferential, pleasant and attractive and, in a short while, she achieved that most difficult of accomplishments, to be liked by both the male and female members of staff. She was generally felt to be a great asset to the Common Room, and although various members of the younger staff had plans to ask her out, she was closely guarded by Avonmore, who regarded her success as an unqualified accolade to himself.

He was reassured to observe that Yvonne did not entangle herself with any of the 'young puppies', but disappointed that she seemed equally unwilling to form a relationship with himself outside the Classics Room. Still, it was early days. He had dreams and fantasies, he even had hopes. She had replaced Elizabeth in his imaginings, and was far superior since, being a Classicist, she might be viewed lying down most obediently next to the big Liddell and Scott Dictionary, reciting from Ovid's *Ars Amatoria*' as she parted her legs.

It was a shock to him to hear her name linked with Martin's as the term proceeded. He thought of the Emperor Claudius and how he had Gaius Siticus executed for stealing Messalina from him. Martin Wood was a good chap, but he needed to take care.

189

Chapter 28

Martin had gone for a walk along the river bank, in fact the same walk he had taken with Digby last summer, but this time Martin was on his own.

The river walk was very different now as Autumn had come early this year with rain and mist, and now, in mid-October, the trees were almost bare, and the haws in the hedgerow were turning black and unbeautiful.

Only the river was the same, moving more sluggishly here than it did in its passage through the school grounds, and yet it was these same waters that had sucked Elizabeth and Ronnie down, and taken them away from Digby forever.

The first thrust of the term was over and life was becoming less hectic – which was why Martin had allowed himself the luxury of a break from work, and to take an opportunity to think over those things which were foremost in his mind.

He was not therefore best pleased to come upon St John Davies and two of the less reputable members of 6A having an illicit cigarette in the coppice.

"Not," said Martin to Davies and the other two, who had jumped up guiltily on seeing him, "not what we expect from our Head Boy. I was with you, you may remember, last term when the Headmaster appointed you. I remember distinctly his words on trust, the importance of responsibility and," he added with emphasis, "not succumbing to peer pressure. It is a great pity your memory is not as retentive."

The other two said nothing, but St John Davies was all apology. "I'm so dreadfully sorry, Sir. I quite agree with everything you say, Sir. I have never done anything like this before or drunk alcohol, or anything, Sir. I think it must be all the pressure, Sir."

"What pressure?"

"Being Head Boy and ..."

"It seems to me, Davies, that the pressure may soon be removed from you."

"Sir! I hope you don't mean ..."

Martin noticed a watery sun trying to break through the clouds and was reminded of another day, a summer evening when geese were winging their way home through a sunset.

"I have no immediate plans for you demotion, if that's what you're worried about, although I cannot, of course, speak for the Headmaster."

"Oh Sir! Thank you, Sir. I think I'm still upset, Sir ..." St John, in keeping with his new Head Boy status had had his blonde locks trimmed and so could not shelter beneath them; he could, however, still open his eyes very wide, or furrow his brow in the most affecting way.

"Still upset, Sir, after the events of last term." But Martin had been a housemaster for fifteen years.

"I think that's a pretty cheap excuse, Davies, one which I would be happy to accept from Simon Stewart or Gowinder Singh, but not from you."

"No, Sir. Of course not." Just because he hadn't been there to run down to the river with Stewart and Singh.

"My advice to you, Davies, is to keep your nose clean."

"Sir."

"Hand over the cigarettes, all of you." Martin held his hands out for three packets of Marlboro Lights. "If there is any further infringement of rules, of any kind, you, Davies, will be immediately demoted and you, Hubbard and Sweeney, will be suspended. Do I make myself clear?

"Sir."

"Sir."

"Get back to school then. You, Davies, if you're doing Oxbridge, you should be working."

"Sir. Yes, Sir. Thank you, Sir."

Actually, Davies thought to himself as he sauntered back, being Head Boy wasn't all it was cracked up to be. If he had known how much hard work there was in it, he wouldn't have been so bloody keen to do it. He let the other two go on ahead and stood, skimming the odd stone into the river. Nothing was much cop nowadays; Bonnington kept him slaving away and always seemed to be praising Stewart – at least, that never happened in Hazzer's day. She threatened him, too, saying he would never make Oxford if he didn't do some more work. Actually, now he came to think of it, nothing was like it had been last term. It had all gone sour from the time Elizabeth had drowned. Well, no, from the time he had fucked her. But the drowning had altered things, turned his luck around. Everyone thought Stewart and Singh had been so bloody marvellous – and they hadn't even done any good. Stewart giving the kiss of life! He'd have done that if he'd been there. Ironic that would have been. And then Stewart and Singh had got so matey together. Sometimes he even wondered whether the two of them had got together and sent the knickers to Sherwood because the Headman was never very nice to him. Oh well, at least the nigger had gone. It was bad enough having to cope with everyone's Mr Favourite, Stewart.

Martin watched the boys until they were out of sight and pondered, not for the first time, the wisdom of their decision in appointing Davies Head Boy.

Walking further along by the river, he thought he would sit on the bank for a while, but when he had taken off his jacket to spread on the ground, for it was wet from recent rain, he found it was pretty much the spot he had occupied with Digby. He hesitated a moment and then sought out a different resting place.

Why was Digby doing it, keeping him at arm's length, freezing him with icy courtesy?

Whenever he went round to Digby's house, either there was no reply – well, that he could accept, for Digby was often out, visiting the different school houses for meals or to cast his eyes over activities or problems, or he might be at some school function – but even when he was there, he would have some excuse ready for not inviting him in. Nor did he ever ask Martin to meet him in the den, and meetings were either in his office or Martin's; after which he would thank his Second Master and leave abruptly.

Why was he doing it? Was Digby ashamed, and was he ashamed for Martin too? Was he even trying to pretend for both of them that it had never happened? Did Digby fear him, fear that he would make demands on him, seek to establish as accepted and ongoing what they both knew to be the singular outcome of an extraordinarily complex and emotional situation?

Would he be happy in such a relationship, Martin asked himself? Would he, all things being equal, want to continue in that sort of a relationship with Digby? Well, the answer was probably, yes. For it had, in very truth, been all that he had longed for consciously and unconsciously over the years that had passed since Jean had died.

When had he started wanting Digby? Years ago maybe? Perhaps unconsciously his desire had been awakened when he read Jean's diaries and saw Digby through her eyes, as a man of immense desirability. Was it after he had come to Mowberry and started working closely with Digby, and had his admiration for the man increased witnessing the way in which he doggedly overcame obstacles, and set about rebuilding the school with such determination? Or had his own feelings been stimulated by sexual jealously, seeing Digby with Elizabeth and imagining him in bed with her?

There came the crux, with St John's seduction of Elizabeth and Digby's dubious behaviour with her afterwards; and he remembered how he had gazed on Digby asleep on the couch in the den, and had for the first time openly admitted to himself that he did desire him.

And yet ... Martin felt in his trouser pocket and drew out one of the packets of cigarettes he had confiscated. He lit up. He seldom smoked, finding alcohol more to his taste. And yet ... as he had told Digby in a conversation early last term, he was not a man to whom sex meant a great deal. Sex with him was inextricably mixed up with love. Because he had loved Jean he had loved to satisfy her. And with Digby too, in spite of his intense sexuality, he had wanted more than anything, to give him solace and ease; sexual pleasure came a second to this.

Perhaps all these reasons played some part in his desires, as Martin watched the slow grey waters drifting past, yet he would want to remain in a sexual relationship with Digby, all things being equal? But all things were not equal. Was that what Digby was telling him?

Were the ramifications too great? Was the fear of disgrace and scandal, so narrowly averted last term, at the back of Digby's mind? Did he feel that Martin would not be strong enough to resist him if they spent time together alone, or did Digby himself fear he would be unable to resist Martin?

Perhaps Digby simply regretted what had happened, did he feel disgust for Martin, dislike, even? Was the knowledge of what had passed between them making it difficult for him to work with Martin? Did he fear Martin's love for him, attributing to Martin the sexuality that was his own, not understanding that Martin's was like the slow passage of the river before him, calm and unhurried while Digby's was turbulent and troubled like the fast-running waters of the river as it passed through the school grounds?

Martin stood up and threw the cigarette into the water. He would have to do something to reassure Digby. He picked up his coat and put it on and set off back to school. He had thirty-six biology books to mark before six o'clock.

Chapter 29

It was through the Italian evening classes that Martin and Yvonne became friendly. It was clear to Martin that he was not making much progress with Italian on his own with his tapes and grammar, so he had decided to go into Hopton on a Wednesday night and attend Italian classes, for he wished to be able to communicate with Signor Morelli, the Italian lizard man, on the internet. Yvonne, for her part, had spent a holiday in Florence and wanted to keep up her Italian and it was there, at the classes that they met. True, they came across one another in the Senior Common Room, but their friendship would never have got off the ground without the shared experience of the evening classes.

As two people will, who know each other slightly and are faced with a number of others whom they know not at all, they drew together and fell into the habit of taking their coffee together and sitting together. It made sense to take one car into Hopton and Martin drove Yvonne. The classes were not very good, and they tended, as teachers often are, to be difficult pupils and they sat at the back, asking awkward questions and laughing together. And, afterwards, they would go back to Martin's house, where Martin would drink beer and Yvonne coffee, for half an hour or so before Martin walked Yvonne back to Stanmore House where she was living as assistant tutor.

Martin liked Yvonne; he admired her quiet efficiency and the way she handled Avonmore. He also felt the sympathy a middle aged man feels for a younger, attractive woman. They also enjoyed the same sense of humour; he enjoyed Yvonne's company, but laughed when Stanley and Fawcett twitted him about the relationship. But it made him think, and it occurred to him, modest though he was in regard to his plain looks and unglamorous person, that Yvonne was quite keen on him. It struck him as odd that she should prefer him, an elderly widower, to the young and glamorous brigade of bachelor masters with whom the Common Room was thronged.

They had returned one Wednesday, to Martin's bungalow on the edge of the village, and were having their drinks in his extremely untidy kitchen which contained everything from dirty cups to exercise books, because he tended to live almost exclusively there, although the bungalow was, in fact, quite roomy.

"I hear," said Martin smiling at her over the kitchen table, "that you have rejected the advances of Roger Coles. Such failure is surely unknown to our all-England rugby star!

"Oh, not really," laughed Yvonne, her black glossy hair moving like a single curtain as she shook her head. "Well, I suppose ... I mean, yes." She sipped the coffee and looked at the pile of exercise books on top of the draining board.

"May one enquire why?" asked Martin, opening another can of beer and dashing to the sink as it overflowed. "Isn't he generally considered rather a catch?"

"Well, actually," said Yvonne, "I've made a conscious decision not to get involved with young men." Why should she not be honest about it?

"Good heavens!" said Martin. "That sounds a bit drastic."

"Well, you see...," she said, picking up her mug of coffee and putting it down again. "Actually, you see, I'd like to get married, and

197

I don't think he'd be a very good bet , do you?"

"Perhaps not!" said Martin thoughtfully. "Perhaps you should marry Avonmore," he continued grinning. "I'm sure he'd jump at the chance."

"Well, actually," said Yvonne. "He's already sort of hinted at it." She looked at Martin and laughed, "oh dear, can you imagine! I hope...," she added, "I can do a bit better than that."

"I'm sure you can!" was Martin's response. He avoided her glance.

A silence ensued and they both looked round the kitchen, and Martin thought what a desirable wife Yvonne would make, with her black glossy hair and pleasant ways. Yvonne, for her part, wondered why Martin had to have quite so many bottles around the place.

"Are you a good cook?" he asked suddenly, although he would not have been willing to analyse his reasons for asking.

"You can put me to the test, if you like!" she answered readily. "I'll come and cook you a meal. When shall it be?"

But before he could answer there was a ring at the bell. "Excuse me," said Martin, getting up to answer it.

"I'm sorry," she said, "were you expecting someone?"

"No," said Martin. "I'll go and see who on earth it is."

It was Digby, Digby who rarely came to his house nowadays, and certainly never in the evenings.

"May I come in?" he asked politely, as if Martin would be conferring an enormous favour on him by agreeing.

"Of course. Come on it. Yvonne's here," he added hastily. "We've just been to Italian classes."

"Oh!" Martin saw Digby hesitate, disconcerted. It had not occurred to him that Martin would have a woman in his house, especially not at ten o'clock at night. "It doesn't matter; it wasn't important. I'll come back another time."

And Martin could see that Digby was every bit as embarrassed as if he had found them in bed together. "Don't be silly!" he said. "Come on in. I'm afraid the kitchen is in its usual state."

By the time he had reached the kitchen, Digby had quite recovered himself.

"How nice to see you, Yvonne," he said. "Are you attempting to instil a little order into Martin's life?" For she was washing up, not just her own cup, but a pile of miscellaneous crockery.

"Oh I don't think that would be possible," said Yvonne smiling. "It seems to me that Martin is congenitally disorganised!"

She really didn't mind Martin's untidiness; it was an endearing trait, for Martin was only untidy where it concerned himself and his own inconvenience. He was meticulous enough with his teaching and his timetables. She could put up with his muddle if he asked her to marry him. There was something else, though, that she did not know if she could accept, and that was his drinking. In a sense it would be a lowering of her own standards to accept such a failing in a husband. Perhaps it was not excessive, merely the result of living on his own, of loneliness. Perhaps she could wean him off it. Anyway, she would just have to wait and see. She liked Martin, she liked him a great deal, but she was not madly in love with him. But, on balance, she thought it would work. Men with happy first marriages often had successful second ones; probably it was up to the individual. Success in marriage was like success in teaching; some natural ability and a great deal of intelligent hard work.

But her thoughts were interrupted as both Digby and Martin started speaking at once. Digby felt all the embarrassment and panic of the intruder, for he saw instantly how it was, and how it would be. He saw that Martin had, rightly, put last term's events behind him and was embarking on something good and wholesome, such as he had always envisaged for him, and which he had feared he had taken from him, by his act of despair after the funeral.

He had come intending to bare his soul to Martin and saw now that it was inappropriate to do so, would probably be inappropriate to do so, ever again. He thought of the love they had shared. Would that pass as his marriages had passed? Was it now his lot to accept and endure? He knew he should rejoice in Martin's happiness, but found he could not take the pleasure in it he would have wished. He must learn to brace himself again.

Martin in turn knew much of what was passing through Digby's mind, which was why he started speaking at the same time.

"What would you like to dri ..?"

"I mustn't keep you," said Digby.

"I ought to go," said Yvonne, chiming in.

"Oh no," said Digby and Martin together, although they would both have given a great deal for her to do so.

But it was Digby who, as always, imposed his will. "You really must excuse me," he said, "I only dropped by to remind Martin of the governors' meeting tomorrow at nine. I really must get back." The governor's meeting was the most important of the month; was it likely, thought Martin, that he would have forgotten? And Digby turned to go. Determined to avoid any awkwardness however, he paused in the doorway.

"Are you settling in all right, Yvonne? Although, if you're managing to sort out Martin's kitchen, you've got a better grip on things than the rest of us put together!" He smiled pleasantly. "Harold not causing you too much trouble? Jolly good. We must have a chat about the future of Classics. When you have a spare moment you might make an appointment with Felicity and we'll talk things through. I hear splendid reports of Roman cooking in the fourth form. Make sure you ask me along next time." And he was gone.

"He's very nice." said Yvonne.

"Yes."

"But he doesn't look happy. I suppose he hasn't got over ... I mean, I suppose you never do."

"Probably not," said Martin. Shortly afterwards he walked her back to Stanmore House.

Avonmore, looking out from his window, biscuit in hand, saw them walking together. From where he stood, although you could never tell (tenebris obscuris), he could have sworn they were holding hands. The Great King of Persia, Xerxes, had devised a splendid punishment for the hubristic Pytheas; he had taken his son and had him sliced in two and then led his whole army through the middle of the two halves, one placed on each side of the road. Well, Wood had a son, he'd seen him at the funeral. With the opening of the Avonmore Classical Library, he could have a bit of Martin's son placed under the map of Syracuse and a bit by the *Liddell and Scott*. It was strange, he reflected as he got into bed in his striped pyjamas, how the mental image of the great Greek lexicon, august and learned as it was, always opened the path nowadays for pleasant reflections, for, by the *Liddell and Scott* stood Yvonne. "I like your pyjamas, Harold," she said as she reached out her hand through the handy aperture the trousers contained, and he could feel the hand closing over his penis, and moving gently up and down, up and down.

Chapter 30

Half term came and went. Martin let one, then two weeks pass, and waited, as he always waited, for Digby to contact him again, but Digby made no move and Martin felt annoyed or, rather, he persuaded himself he felt annoyed because he was wondering whether he should marry Yvonne, and he would have liked Digby to state categorically that he didn't need him now. Martin told himself he couldn't spend all his life waiting for Digby not to say anything. It was obvious that a sexual relationship between them was no longer an option; Digby had made that clear with his coldness. Admittedly, he had come round that night when Yvonne was there, but he had said his intention had been merely to remind him of the governors' meeting. Only Martin knew that it wasn't that at all.

On the other hand, it seemed that he was no longer of any use to Digby; he could not be his lover and he would always be his friend, whether he married Yvonne or not.

He had thought a great deal about marrying Yvonne, weighing up the pros and cons. Being of a logical turn of mind, Martin sat down and listed all the pros, of which there were a vast number: she was nice, kind, pleasant, good natured, humorous, efficient, attractive, even a good cook, for she had made dinner for him on a number of occasions. She was bright, she had a good figure and he sensed she wanted to marry him. She would make him an excellent wife. He liked her very much and it would be good to have company in the evenings, to have someone to organise him; and although she was young, she was not silly. She had also admitted that she did not want children, which was another plus because he did not feel he could face a new family at his age; they had interests in common, they were eminently compatible; it would be good to feel her next to him in bed; it would be good, too, to satisfy her, for he suspected, even though he had done no more than hold her hand, she liked sex,

But, on the other hand, did he really want another wife? Was there disloyalty to Jean in this? Yes, he did think he wanted another wife and, no, Jean would have understood, even been happy for him.

Another slight worry was whether Yvonne wanted sex and marriage rather more than she wanted him, but then that was natural enough. There was nothing so very fascinating about his person; he should be very thankful that she did desire him as a husband and lover.

There was the question of booze too. Yvonne did not drink, whereas he drank rather a lot. Still, he could hold his alcohol and she need not know exactly how much he drank.

So it was only this nebulous question of Digby. Although, why on earth should he need Digby's blessing? After all, Digby had acted in direct opposition to his own warning. "Don't do it, Digby," he had said when Digby had told him about Elizabeth, but he had disregarded his advice, and gone off and married her.

He was under some pressure, too. Yvonne showed signs of impatience when he merely kissed her lightly on the cheek and said goodnight; he suspected she wanted a sexual relationship then and there, perhaps as much as she wanted marriage. Furthermore, she might think his lack of sexual ardour due to some other reason – such as a lack of interest in women; she might suspect him of homosexual tendencies and start thinking god knows what.

But the pros outweighed the cons, and as Martin made his decision he began to be sure it was the right one, and to feel great fondness, although possibly not love, for Yvonne. And yet he continued putting off asking her.

He was sitting in his office one Thursday after half-term, working out figures for Digby on numbers of teaching hours, when the phone went.

"Felicity here, Mr Wood. I have the Headmaster on the line for you."

"I wonder, Martin," Digby was saying, "whether you could spare me a few minutes, or if it would be a great bore?"

"Not at all, Headmaster," said Martin for Felicity's benefit. "I'll be with you straight away." He knew now where Digby would want to meet and suddenly he felt a sense of extraordinary joy; a joy, he thought, that Jean must have felt when Digby opened his birthday present. It had lain like Martin's own affection for him, closely wrapped, its effect yet untried, but now Digby had torn the paper and the gift was what he had wanted most of all. Fleetingly he thought of Yvonne but he did not think she needed such a present, and there were plenty of others to give her gifts. Only he knew Digby's needs.

They arrived at the den at the same time and Martin switched the lights on, as it was dark. Because they had not been alone in the den since last summer there was an awkwardness between them. Martin got out the glasses and poured the brandy, and then knocked the glass over, and had to soak up the liquid with some blotting paper, and Digby for his part talked very fast about a multiplicity of things, finally asking whether Martin knew that Davies had not got through the Oxford entrance exam, claiming that he had too much work to do as Head Boy?

"Too much drinking and smoking, I should think," said Martin and told Digby about the encounter on the river bank. There was nothing more to be said on that issue; they both knew he was a poor investment. Had Martin heard about his idea for supporting a boy from Gowinder Singh's village through school in the Punjab, not England? Digby wanted an underprivileged boy, a boy who was not academic; and Martin knew it was in some way a tribute to Ronnie, and could only nod his head. Did Martin know how successfully Stewart had acquitted himself in the Oxford exam? Digby had rung up his old tutor and found that Stewart had done amazingly well. It was probably thanks to Yvonne, for hadn't she taken on the Oxbridge work on top of everything else?

There did not seem much for Martin to say about that either. Did Martin know that Dolores and Duncan were going out, and did he think they would get married?

"And talking of marriage, Martin ..." said Digby at last, his face smiling and his hand rubbing the back of his neck, "I hear congratulations are in order. When is it to be? Have you popped the question yet? They're all taking bets in the Senior Common Room, you know. I bet the sixth form are running a tote on it, too." And he went on smiling and his hand worked away at the back of his neck.

"Oh, you mean Yvonne?" said Martin, feigning innocence.

"Well, unless you have any more women hidden away to surprise us with. What a dark horse you are, Martin!"

"Nothing's settled yet," said Martin. He was looking in the cupboard for another bottle.

"Well, you'd better hurry up," said Digby; he had stopped rubbing his neck and was feeling about for cigarettes. He lit up and smiled brightly at his friend. "Honestly Martin, I hear nothing but good of her from all directions – boys, staff, even the kitchen who always hate everyone, and I interviewed her myself the other day, did she tell you?"

"You interviewed her?"

"Yes, not about you, about Classics. I thought we might keep it on after all. I thought her intelligent, charming and thoughtful. I cannot see how you could find a better wife." He finished abruptly, as if he had conned the speech by heart, and looked directly at Martin, as if daring him to disagree.

And Martin made a lot of business over opening the new bottle, peeling off the foil and sniffing the contents, because he was trying to work out what hurt there was in all this for Digby. There was the whole question of marriage, marriage to a second young wife, the very thing that he himself had advised Digby against; then his advice had been ignored and, in the ignoring of it, Digby had brought untold misery on himself, and now the roles were reversed. Digby was saying in effect, 'I know that I am not a good person to offer advice on this subject, but because you are Martin, I am offering it anyway'. But he was saying much, much more than that; he was saying "you must not let the question of our relationship stand in your way; the fact that an act of love has passed between us, must not stop you marrying an eminently suitable woman." Martin was confused by the sheer number of nuances to every word that Digby uttered, for he was also admitting that Martin was discarding him for a young woman, thereby demonstrating that while he himself now had nothing, no Jean, no Elizabeth, no Ronnie, no Martin, Martin had everything before him. He found himself unable to cope with the sheer number of cruel blows that he was aiming directly at Digby. And so that he would not have to think through all the implications of his actions any more, he blurted out the first thing that came into his mind. "I don't sleep with her, you know," he said, as if in some measure this could be of comfort to Digby.

"Why on earth not?"

"Because, I suppose," said Martin, "that I don't particularly want to."

"Yes, I was afraid that might be the case."

They sat across a battered old desk at each other, fidgeting and fiddling with bottles, cigarettes, paper knives, anything to stop them looking at each other.

"What do you mean?" asked Martin at last.

"I cast a shadow, don't I?" said Digby, "across the sunlight of your bedchamber."

"No," said Martin slowly. "It isn't that, for I know that is all in the past, it is over and I accept that. I could see what you have been saying to me all this term. "Stand back, Martin," you have been saying. "I wish it had never happened." I have accepted that it should be so."

"No!" Digby brought his fist down on the table so that the bottle rattled and ash flew out of the ash tray. "It is not like that. How can you say so? How can you say so? Do you not remember what it was like?" And Digby's blue eyes blazed at Martin.

"Oh yes, Digby," said Martin. "I remember." And Martin could no longer avoid the piercing blue of Digby's eyes, he looked up and Digby grabbed both his hands across the table, and gripped them so tightly that Martin could feel the physical pain of it.

"Can you imagine, Martin, what it was like for me?"

"I don't know, Digs," said Martin. "I hoped it was something." And Digby released his fierce grip, but he would not allow Martin's hands to move.

"It was something magnificent," said Digby. And quite suddenly he let go of Martin's hands and began rubbing the back of his neck again and talking very fast. "I haven't known what to do, Martin and I couldn't think straight because of ... well, you know, and I didn't know what to do and I thought about it all the time, all the time I walked in North Wales, and all the time those two sat in the pub, and I thought of it all the time I walked across the Andes and all the time in France, and all the time I was here with Avonmore, even when I visited my mother in her home. I thought about Elizabeth and Ronnie and you. And perhaps of the three I thought of you most and I thought ..." Digby paused and continued deliberately. "I thought how much I loved you." He did not pause here for Martin's reaction, but continued, "I came to the conclusion that the best way for me to act was to release you. For what could we do? Sooner or later someone would find out, and this time there would be no shady dealings and cover ups with another St John Davies ..."

"I should never have gone to Australia," said Martin.

"No, no, you should. It was right, and it gave me time to think for both of us. And the more I thought about it, Martin, I came to the same conclusions that I had come to that day on the river bank when we were together. Do you remember?"

"Of course I do. What did you think?"

"That you didn't really want this thing any more than Jean did, really. That although you both thought you wanted it for yourself, you really wanted it for me, you wanted to give me yourselves, but really you wanted or, rather, needed, something less dangerous, more comfortable. Jean really wanted you, and now you really want Yvonne."

"I don't know that I do really want Yvonne."

"As St Paul says, Martin, better to marry than to burn."

"But I don't burn, Digby," and Martin thought of how he had compared Digby to the turbulent river that passed through the school grounds and himself as the sluggish river further on, but he knew such a simile could only be painful to Digby. So he repeated, "I don't burn, Digby. I just blazed a little, the once." And he smiled and took off his glasses and wiped them because they were a little bit tacky, and because it gave him something to do. Digby touched his fingers a little with the tips of his own fingers, and for a moment the two pairs of hands lay together on the table, Martin's rough and hairy with the nails cut square, and Digby's long-fingered, hairless with beautifully cut, tapering nails. The only thing common to each, was the wedding ring they wore on the fourth finger of the right hand.

"And I sought to freeze you out, Martin, freeze you away from me, so that you should not hanker after what was not good for you."

"Could I not have been the judge of that?"

"No. You would not have had the strength. And I succeeded, succeeded beyond my wildest dreams, for you have found what you really need." And Digby took away his hands and lit another cigarette.

"Then why did you come round that evening?"

"Oh, Martin. I was weak that night – I was worn down with the freezing. I came, Martin, for you to thaw me out, as it were. But the gods were with you, and Yvonne was there and I was able to go away again."

"Digby, I should have come after you."

"No. It was better as it was." And Digby began very slowly to rub the back of his neck again.

"And you, Digs, you say that I have found what I want, what then is there for you?" And Digby could see that Martin's eyes, without the barrier of his glasses, were infinitely kind.

"I think I must pay for my sins, Martin. I think that is what there is for me."

"I don't think your sins so very great. What did you do but marry a young and silly woman? You blame yourself for making her unhappy and causing her death. But I don't think she was unhappy. Of course, she was not happy all of the time, who is? But I think, in

209

her way, Elizabeth loved you. I should think she was a woman who was made happy by the act of love, and you must often have made her very happy indeed. No, don't argue, Digby. You forget I know what I am saying. And the death of Elizabeth and Ronnie - how could that be your fault? As you know, she failed to put the brake on the pushchair, but she died heroically. You must see it in that light, Digby. You have nothing to reproach yourself for.

"You are good and kind, Martin."

"What concerns me, Digby, what worries me ....."

"What?"

"You asked me once what I did, how I managed, and I told you sex was not a great problem to me, but it is for you, Digs."

For the first time Digby seemed impatient. "How prurient of you, Martin. What do you think I do? Watch sexploits on the internet, look at erotic magazines, send for sex toys? It's very simple: Doc Stamford gives me loads of bromide, if you want to know. It works a treat."

"Oh, Digby."

"Don't worry about me, Martin. As long as I have your friendship..."

"Friendship?"

"Friendship."

"And you have my love too, in whatever form you require it."

And Digby picked up Martin's hands, his heavy hands with the square-cut nails and brought the knuckles to his mouth and bit them gently. Then he got up.

"Oh Mart," he said, rubbing his neck. "I shall expect to be best man, you know."

And before Martin could answer, he was gone. Apparently he wanted to see how the Harold Avonmore Classics Library was progressing.

Chapter 31

He saw her waiting by the front door and was amazed at how beautiful she had become, and he was irresistibly reminded of the goddess Athene, for Richenda was bold, fierce, and virginal. Her hair, too, now, grown into a soft down in the months since the funeral, fitted her head like a helmet.

He was returning from the Sunday service at Chapel and feeling low. Even now he could not attend services in the chapel without being reminded of the funeral; he could always see the coffin containing his wife and son passing down the aisle.

"Richenda!" he said. "What a lovely surprise!"

Richenda apparently had been to a party the night before, some twenty miles or so away, and had decided to call in on her father.

"Daddy," she said. "How are you?" And her fierce, beautiful face scowled at him, because she could see his unhappiness.

"I'm fine," he said, "come on in."

He led her into the kitchen and she opened the fridge.

"There's not much to eat," she said. "What do you do for meals?"

"Well, I usually eat in the school canteen. Would you like to go over to lunch, Richenda?" Richenda tossed her helmeted head and said, "No, I should hate it, all those boys staring at me."

"Well, you couldn't blame them, darling. You look so beautiful."

Now Richenda had grown her hair, she was stunning. She had

her father's enormous blue eyes, a straight Roman nose, too, like Digby's and a very pale complexion, so white that her skin was almost luminous.

"Oh, looks," she said. "What do they matter?"

"Quite a lot, I think," said her father. "What shall we eat?"

"Nothing, just make some coffee, Daddy."

So he made coffee while they talked of this and that, and then he took her through into the drawing room. "God, I'd forgotten how posh it is," she said critically.

"Well, I am Headmaster of a major public school."

"No you're not," she said. "You're just you." Digby laughed.

"So tell me," he said. "Why you're really here."

"Perhaps you are a headmaster after all. You can certainly see what you're not meant to see." He took out a cigarette. "You shouldn't do that, Daddy, it's not good for you."

"No but, as you say, I am Headmaster, so I can do as I like." He looked at her questioningly, so Richenda told him.

"It's Dolores," she said. "She's got everything worked out. You're to come to us for Christmas ..." Digby raised his eyebrows. "And you're to bring Martin because she'll be bringing Duncan and ..."

"And what does Mummy say?"

"Oh, she's in on the plot too?"

"And you don't think this is a good idea?"

"No, I know it's not. You can't bring the past back. We shouldn't even try. And it wouldn't be right for you, Daddy. It's not for you. You must start again, go in another direction. You must strike out again. I know you must not slip back into the past. You and I both need a purple rabbit."

"A purple rabbit?"

And she told him the first part of the story of her longing for this toy, although she did not speak of the second part. "It's a sort of symbol, you see, of something out there, something challenging and dangerous. Expensive, but you must try for it. Keep trying for it. Do you see?"

"I think," said Digby, "that is what I tried to do in marrying Elizabeth, but the price was too high."

Richenda stood up and walked over to the bay windows, the beautiful windows that looked out and down towards the river.

"Oh, Daddy, how can you bear to look out on it every day?"

"I have become used to it," he said. There was silence for a moment and then he said,

"Wait there, Richenda. I have something to show you." And she heard him go upstairs. And she stood and gazed out at the river, full of anger for her father's sufferings.

"Look!" said Digby, returning. He was holding something wrapped in brown paper. "Open it." And from the parcel she drew out a child's soft toy, its fur all matted as if it had been soaked for a long time in water. It looked as if it might once have been blue, or mauve, even.

"What it is?" she asked, holding it awkwardly, and examining it.

"It was Ronnie's," said Digby. "He had it with him in the pushchair. He took it with him everywhere. The corner's office sent it back last week; they apologised for mislaying it." He watched her. "It's rather sad now, isn't it, Ricky?"

She put the rabbit down carefully on one of the priceless sofas. "Let's go and make some more coffee," she said, "and sit in the kitchen. I don't like it in here."

As he was making more coffee, the bell went.

"I'll go," said Richenda. It was Avonmore.

"Ah!" he said. "The Goddess Diana!" He thought of how even that chaste goddess had drawn Endymion down to her and kissed him secretly while he slept. Sherwood certainly knew how to surround himself with good-looking women. The other daughter was a looker, too; he remembered them both from the funeral; they had put him in mind of vestal virgins.

"What do you want?" said Richenda in her graceless way.

"A word with the Headmaster." He thought she could have acknowledged the compliment. Digby came to the door and his heart sunk at the sight of Harold.

"I have a ... ah transcript of my speech for the opening of the Harold Avonmore Classics Library. I thought we might run through it together."

"How extremely good of you, Harold," said Digby.

"It's Sunday," said Richenda. "And Daddy needs a rest from school stuff."

"Hush, Richenda," said her father in the stern voice that he had used to stop her childhood tantrums when nobody else could. "Harold, you and I really need to devote quite some time to this. I wonder whether you could spare some time tomorrow, in your busy day?"

Richenda stalked off to the kitchen from where she could hear her father being terribly nice to the frightful man. The door finally closed.

"I don't know how you can stand all these people." She poured him out some more coffee.

"It's my job. Anyway, he was very kind to me when I was in hospital."

"Oh? What did he do?"

"He told me of the death of his wife who died giving birth to his daughter."

"So he just wanted to talk about himself."

"And then he did an even bigger thing. He suggested calling the new theatre after Elizabeth and Ronnie instead of after himself, and that was a big sacrifice for him, Richenda."

214

"So what is it being called?"

"The Elizabeth Sherwood Theatre."

"What about Ronnie?" For although she admired her father's courage in reaching for the purple rabbit, she had disliked Elizabeth, whom she simply regarded as selfish and unworthy of him.

"I've set up a trust fund, darling, in Ronnie's memory. There will always be a boy from a village in the Punjab assured of a good education, not a clever boy, Ricky, because clever people are all right, but a boy who would otherwise miss out. Do you understand?"

And Richenda, who loved her father more than anyone else in the world, understood.

"Daddy," she said, flinging her arms round him. "You're so good."

"Oh no, Richenda. I'm not. It's like Hamlet. 'I myself am indifferent honest; but yet I could accuse me of such things that it were better my mother had not borne me ..' how does it go on? 'more offences at my beck and call ...'".

"Oh shut up, Daddy," said Richenda. "Look, I've got some photos to show you, they're mainly of Dol and me, but there's one or two of Mummy."

"I'll look at them in a minute. Are you sure you wouldn't like something to eat? I've got all sorts of secret supplies in case important people call unexpectedly – like yourself."

And they rummaged through the cupboards and found a bit tin of caviar, and Digby made some toast and they spread it on thickly so it all oozed over the top, and they devoured it ravenously. Then Digby looked at the photos.

"It's all right," he said, replacing them in the envelope, "I'm not coming back at Christmas. I wouldn't have done anyway – even without the photos – that was a little underhand of you, Ricky, not quite worthy of you." For he had seen, looking through the photos why Richenda had brought them. Belinda had become rather fat and, although she was the same age as Digby, she looked as though she was well into her fifties. Richenda acknowledged the rebuke with a shrug.

"How is Mummy, anyway?"

"Actually, she's on cracking form. She's on all sorts of committees and things, as well as being Head of Maths and, oh yes! I meant to tell you," said Richenda, rescuing a stray bit of caviar from the table, "she's been offered the job of deputy head at Sheldon."

"Will she take it?"

"Oh, I'm sure she will now," said Richenda.

"You mean, now I'm not coming for Christmas."

"Mmm."

"She doesn't need me?"

"No."

"Well, that's all right then", said Digby, lightly and firmly, although Richenda had to acknowledge to herself that she did not really know what lay in her father's mind. "Would you like to try the jar of peaches soaked in amaretto?"

"Oh yes!" And she smiled the dazzling smile that was Digby's, too, and which they both of them made so little use of.

Then Digby cut himself opening the jar, and Richenda made him hold his finger under the tap and searched and found some dreadful old sticking plaster, and bandaged it up very badly.

"I don't like to think of you all alone in this house, Daddy. Why don't you get Uncle Martin to move in with you?"

"I'm afraid people would gossip."

"Oh god! Not Uncle Martin, Daddy. Nobody could imagine a relationship between you two. I mean, Uncle Martin is hardly an Adonis, is he?" No, thought Digby, I was the Adonis.

"Anyway, he's got a girlfriend. She may even be his fiancée by now."

"Uncle Martin! What on earth is she like?"

"She's extraordinarily nice, intelligent, sympathetic and attractive. He couldn't find a better wife."

"But you don't like her?"

"Oh yes, I do. I'm not sure about these peaches, though, are you? They have rather a taste of paraffin."

"They're nice. I like them. So what about Martin's woman?"

"If I'm honest, Richenda, I suppose I'm jealous."

"Who of, him or her?"

"Perhaps both. Him because he will have a pretty young wife, and her because she has Martin. I'll never be so close to Martin again."

"He's the real thing, Uncle Martin, isn't he?"

"Absolutely."

A pause ensued which Digby sought to break because he and Richenda had always been frighteningly on the same wave length, and Richenda was bright.

"Tell me about you, Ricky. Lots of suitors for your hand?"

"No!" Richenda flung the word out as she flung a peach stone into the sink basket. "Once or twice I considered, but there's no one good enough."

Other men might have thought her arrogant, but Digby knew it was not that at all. By 'good enough' she did not mean in comparison with herself, but in a moral sense. Her man would have to be of high moral worth as, Digby thought sadly, she imagined him to be.

"You see," she said. "I still want something ... magnificent." And Digby remembered it was the very word he had used to Martin to describe their act of love.

"Well, Oxford's as good a place to find magnificence as anywhere." It gave him great pleasure to think of his daughter there in the same college he had been at himself.

"I may stay on and do research...," she said. And he imagined her meeting a fellow academic who would become a don or even a professor, and how such a one would be a worthy mate for his beautiful and clever daughter. "…while Dolores marries Duncan and has a hundred babies. Anyway," she added, "I must go. Mummy always worries when I'm driving."

"You can give her a ring if you like, I do have a telephone."

But Richenda wanted to be off.

"Wait a minute," said Digby and he returned with the rabbit. "I think you'd better have this," he said.

"Thank you, Daddy."

But after she had driven a few yards down the drive, she reversed back again, opened the window of the car and threw it back at her father who was standing looking after her.

"You need it more than me, Daddy," she shouted, and drove off, very fast, down the drive.

Chapter 32

"Cabbage soup," announced Harold Avonmore with aplomb, "home-made, ipse feci." He was carrying four enormous bowls of what looked like boiled cabbage on a tray which, Digby noted, looked far from clean.

"I think you'll find this not displeasing," he added, as he unloaded the bowls, splashing some of the contents at Yvonne. Digby saw her eyes meet Martin's in laughter. He told himself how right it was that this should be the case, and that Martin and she would soon inhabit a world of their own from which he would, rightly, be excluded.

"What a very unusual flavour," he said, as he forced down some cabbage water.

"I knew you would like it," said Harold. He was beginning to enjoy himself, although it was a very different evening from the one he had originally planned. He had been hearing rumours about Yvonne and Martin all term, but nothing seemed to come of it, so although he had not made enormous headway with Yvonne, he had thought it worth a final stab. Anyway, what had he to lose? He would be gone from Mowberry in a week. And who knew? He might take Yvonne with him. After all, she often deferred to him in matters of translation, and had frequently welcomed his advice in the matter of Greek prose. Why should not such a relationship be extended into another sphere? True, he had invited her to other evening entertainments and had found her always to be engaged. But there was something, ah, poignant about a leaving, a farewell. Why should not fond thoughts be stirred in her round little breasts at the idea of his own imminent departure? She had thanked him warmly for the invitation. Then she had asked if she might bring Martin. He had been disconcerted, even seriously displeased, but Harold's chagrins, bitter as they were, seldom lasted long. He cast about in his mind for a suitable punishment for Wood. He recalled how Nero had invented a novel game, he was released from a cage dressed in the skin of a wild animal and then he attacked the private parts of prisoners bound to stakes. After he had enjoyed watching Martin being lashed to the rugby posts and had deflowered Yvonne one more time by the *Liddell and Scott*, he felt no more animosity and thought it would be no bad idea to make a party of it, he would ask Sherwood to dinner as well. And Sherwood had looked at his diary and said, yes, Harold, he would be delighted, and was there anything he could bring? And Harold had waved his hands dismissively and said, "Nothing, Headmaster! Nothing." But the Headmaster had brought a bottle of brandy, nonetheless. It was good brandy too, none of your cheap stuff.

Martin was coping manfully with the soup, Digby noticed, but then, Martin had never much minded what he ate. Yvonne said it was absolutely delicious but she wanted to leave space for the next course. Digby took a little and left the rest. One of the virtues of being a headmaster was that you did not have to offer excuses. Nevertheless, he was conscious, as always, of the vulnerability of others and offered consolation. "Could we have a little foretaste of your speech for the library, Harold?" And Harold, who had stood up to take out the bowls, went and got out his speech instead.

Digby relaxed. While Harold read he was able to get used to the idea of Martin and Yvonne, for he could see that it would be Martin-

and-Yvonne. And, of course, it was right that it should be. It amused him to see, looking at her, how like Jean she was in many ways. She was attractive, but not a good dresser, nor would Martin ever take her in hand, for he had even less idea himself. And yet, in spite of a certain dowdiness, Digby suspected she would like sex. Martin had satisfied Jean; he would be able to cope with Yvonne.

As Digby looked round Harold's dingy flat, its brown leather armchairs and incongruous picture of what looked like the beach at Blackpool, he thought how Martin had been more successful than he with women; for all his own looks and passion, Jean had really loved Martin more than him, and now Martin had inspired love in another woman of character.

Finally, Avonmore concluded his speech and disappeared off into the kitchen for an immensely long time. Martin, who had brought two bottles with him was steadily drinking his way through them, for Yvonne drank nothing and Digby drank very little. When Martin got to the end of the second one Yvonne said, "you do drink a lot, don't you, Martin?" And it struck Digby how quickly he had looked up and replied, almost glibly for Martin, "not more than I can manage." And Yvonne had said nothing and played with her knife and fork, and Digby asked Martin if he had seen Duncan recently and Martin said he had phoned yesterday, and there was some talk of him and Dolores moving in together.

"I hope," said Martin, "you won't be as cross as you were before, Digs."

And, so that Yvonne should not feel left out, Digby explained to her about his finding Duncan and Dolores in a compromising position in the stables at Stanstead many years ago.

"Well!" said Yvonne, her face dimpling. And it occurred to Digby that it was a position that Yvonne would not mind occupying herself.

"Yes," said Martin and started opening one of Avonmore's bottles.

"I trust you like it rare," said Harold, returning at last with a piece of beef that looked totally raw. Even Martin looked surprised.

"With cabbage," he added. And they all suspected he had been taking the remains of the cabbage out of the soup bowls.

"The potatoes are a little charred, but none the worse for that."

And this time it was Digby's eyes that Martin sought and Digby's heart leapt, although he knew it shouldn't. And he resolved to make amends to Yvonne so he turned to her and said, "I hear you're a wonderful cook too, Yvonne."

"Oh no, not really," she replied. She was watching Martin emptying another glass.

"This looks jolly good," he was saying. "Roast beef of Olde England."

"Indeed," said Harold. The beef seemed to be extraordinarily difficult to cut. And Digby thought how nice things were now for Martin. And he tried to be glad that it was so. For it was good to be out of an evening, particularly if it was a bad evening and as you sat there, you thought that in one hour or two hours it would be over, and then you would be back home with the woman who sat across the table from you, and you would be drawn together by shared events so that there was the warmth of understanding between you, and you would immediately seek out each other's body and shortly there would be pleasure, and the great consummation of pleasure. And that was how it would be for Martin now and, although it had once been like that for him, it was no longer so, because his wife lay with his son in a coffin in the vault below the school chapel.

"I must ask you to excuse me from this course, as delicious as it looks," he said.

"Yes," said Yvonne. "The soup was a meal in itself."

"A feast for a king, eh, Wood?" said Avonmore, who had decided it was best to saw off chunks. "A veritable Cena Trimalchionis."

"I'll just take a little of this lovely cabbage," said Yvonne.

"Ah!" said Harold. He took a great piece of raw flesh on to his plate. "Butcher's meat!"

And as Martin sat sawing at great pieces of blood-streaked flesh, he thought, not at all of Yvonne, but of Digby, as he sat with an empty plate in front of him, and he felt the wine and indignation work within him. For he knew everything that his friend was thinking, how he would have imagined him in bed with Yvonne, and how bitterly, and yet how generously, he would have thought it out. Oh, Digby, Digby. Do you think I forget? Do you think I have forgotten what I called 'something' and you called 'magnificent'? He placed a great piece of black potato on his fork and raised it to his lips. Do you really think, Digs, that I would do that to you, flaunt a woman in front of you when you had none? Can you not remember how I never did as much as put an arm round Jean in your presence? Do you really think I shall take this woman, nice as she is, to my bed, when yours is empty, because you have decided I shall not enter it?"

"Do you mind, Harold," he asked, "if I open this other bottle?"

"No, no," said Harold, who was following Martin's example. "Let's crack it open, as Hecuba says, 'wine puts new heart into a man'". It was true, he did not know when he had felt so happy. Opposite him sat a beautiful woman who might well fall into his arms in this last week of term, next to him sat Digby Sherwood, Headmaster of Mowberry School, looking solemnly on at the proceedings, and opposite him, his good friend and companion, Martin Wood.

Yvonne watched Martin raise the glass to his lips and felt irritation. All evening, for hours and hours it seemed, he had done nothing but sit and drink. It was all very well to be good-natured and easy-going, but there was a thin line between that and downright self-indulgence. Look at the muddle in his kitchen! Why didn't he clear it up? And then there was that book he was meant to be writing. Ten years he said he had been doing it. Ten years! And why did he never kiss her? Would it take him ten years to get round to that?

"And you'll come back and see us, Harold?" Digby was saying. His eyes crinkled and Harold could see what a fine-looking man he was. "We shall miss you, you know."

Of course they would miss him, how could they not? Twelve scholars in 1959, and an Oxbridge entrant this year! They would miss him, oh yes, his teaching, his book-plates, no one would ever sort the lost property as he had done, even taking the laces out of the boots. And now his cooking, too! Look at Wood with great streams of meat juice dripping off his chin!

"I shouldn't drink any more, if I were you, Martin," said Yvonne.

"I may not return; I shall be rather busy with my telescope," said Harold in answer to Digby. He thought he wouldn't eat any more of the meat, he didn't have the stomach for it that Wood had.

Digby was remembering what a good cook Jean had been. "It's all wasted on Martin," she had laughed. "He would be happy with egg and chips every day. But you like it, don't you Digby?" And Digby had said yes, he liked it, although he knew Jean wasn't referring to cooking at all, and he had got up and left as soon as possible so he wouldn't be tempted in any way to betray his friend. And Elizabeth had not cooked at all, but she had fed his other appetite as Jean would have done, and Martin did once.

"Another course! You're spoiling us Harold!"

"Vanilla ice-cream," said Harold. "It's not everyday you'll have that, I'll be bound!"

"My favourite," said Yvonne. The wine, she noticed, was all gone. Martin must have drunk the best part of three bottles.

"I'm fine, thank you," said Digby, refusing the ice-cream.

And why, cried Martin's spirit, enlivened by the bottles of indifferent Beaujolais, why should you of all men, Digby, sit there with an empty plate? You of all men, whose passion blazes so that even dullards like me can be lit and flame from it? Why should you go home to an empty plate? But it wasn't until Harold had opened Digby's brandy that Martin saw what it was that he must do, although not exactly how he must do it.

"Well," he said finally. "I must see about getting you home, Yvonne." And Digby noticed that Yvonne's face did not light up at these words, as he had imagined it would. In fact, she did not ask Martin back to her flat, as Martin had feared she would, but she left him at the door with a brief goodnight.

After they had gone, Digby remained for a while, although he did not tell Harold of his decision to keep Classics on after all, under Yvonne, for his fondness for Harold was not so great that he would risk involvement in a law suit for wrongful dismissal. They drank his brandy for a while and Avonmore talked of himself, although he had never again mentioned the death of his wife and child, and Digby wondered if there was any truth in it, or if Avonmore had invented the parallel.

Under the melancholy influence of the brandy, it came to Digby that he too might become another Avonmore, wifeless, dwelling on past glories, real or imagined, an anachronism left behind as others got on with their lives.

"A delightful evening, Harold," he said, rising, "I hope we may make it an annual event." And although Harold smiled in acknowledgement, Digby could see that the suggestion was as still-born as Harold's child, as much dust and ashes as the bodies of his wife and son lying under the Chapel vaults.

Harold decided to leave the washing-up (although Yvonne had volunteered, he was gallant to the end, wouldn't hear of it) ,until the morning. Now he needed to get to bed and think over the splendours of the evening. He took a last glass of Sherwood's brandy and he stood it on '*Greek Erotica*'; there was a little flute girl on a fourth century red figure vase painting that reminded him of Yvonne. Naturally she had no clothes on and she was bending over to facilitate the advances of the reveller. Ah! The *Liddell and Scott* came to mind.

Chapter 33

It was the best day of his life, reflected Simon Stewart as he looked round the hall personally decorated by himself, for this fab end of term party. The music and DJ were great – and who had fixed all that? No one other than Simon Stewart; and there was everyone drinking and dancing, all down to him.

"A pint of best and a gin and tonic," he said to the barman. The gin and tonic was, of course, for Melissa, who was undoubtedly the fittest girl there in her black slinky dress, *his* girlfriend. And poor old St John! All that boasting about his fantastically amazing bird, and who does he bring? "Thank you," what a price drinks were, wow! Who does he bring, but his sister – and not much cop at that! And ... he let his mind dwell gloriously on this truly amazing fact, as he eased the froth off his pint ... his Oxford place confirmed today, Classics, of course, or, as he must now learn to call it, Greats! Poor old St John with his two offers from some second rate place or other! And all he, Simon, needed was three E grades in his A Levels, and he'd certainly get A's for Latin and Greek with that cracker Yvonne Bonnington teaching him, instead of boring old Hazzer. The Headman's old college, too! Probably put a word in for him somewhere along the line, that would be like him. His eye sought him out: oh, there he was, sitting where the lectern usually stood, poor bloke, he must find it lonely without Elizabeth! Poor Elizabeth! Funny how things could turn round in a year: that terrible day last term, when he and Singh had dragged her out, her and poor little Ronnie, and the Headman desperately pushing him aside and trying to give her the kiss of life. And then ...

"All right, Stevens! What? Melissa? Yes, she's fit, isn't she. What? Hey, keep it clean." What was he thinking of? Oh, yes. Him and Gowinder standing there, wondering what to do. He was all right, Singh. Shame he'd never come back. But if he had, he might have got the Oxford place instead, he was bloody hard working. And ... where was Melissa? She'd gone to the bog ages ago. And then not being made Head Boy and he knew Mr Wood wanted him to be, but again, perhaps if he had, he wouldn't have got into Oxford. Davies maintained it was all the hard work being Head Boy that had stopped his getting in. Mind you, that was probably crap, most of what he said was. Think of all that bullshit about Elizabeth. Funny business, though – he had got hold of those knickers – but they had probably belonged to his sister. And look at his parents! So much for the castle in Northumberland! Thank God for his own parents. His mother looked nice, he'd seen the headman giving her a look, poor sod. Hurry up, Melissa, this is a smoochy and I can have a bit of a grope. Pity we've got to go back with the parents. I might have made it with Mel tonight. Always very strict about sex, the Headman. Wonder how he manages now. Fancy old Avonmore congratulating him too, rabbiting on about twelve Oxbridge scholars in nineteen-something! There he was, all dressed up in his new suit, eyeing up the women. And, my God! He's dancing with Melissa. Hey, Hazzer, keep your hands to yourself. Old Woody over there with Miss Bonnington, he looks as if he'd had a few. People always said he drank. She looks nice, doesn't look any too pleased with Woody though.

"Another pint, please. Hey, it was only one-sixty last time."

Digby sat as far away from the disc jockey as he could and tried to collect his thoughts through the enormous roar of the music. He was pleased it was proving such a success – everybody was having a good time; look at old Harold dancing away with Stewart's pretty little girlfriend. It was good about Stewart. What a day it had been, though.

"No, I'm all right thank you, John. At least half a glass left. Enjoying yourself? Splendid!" It had been a long day. The opening of the Elizabeth Sherwood Theatre in the morning with old Colonel Haslett making that dreadful speech and calling it the Belinda Sherwood Theatre, and Martin prodding him and whispering and everyone sniggering. And then, while they had all been there, that new boy, Cockburn, whose parents could never make up their minds whether they liked Mowberry or not ... the boy had gone down to the village shop and stolen a Mars Bar, and the shop had been hell-bent on making a scandal out of it, although they made a fortune out of Mowberry boys. He and Martin had to sneak out of the governors' lunch afterwards to try and pacify the shop, get hold of the parents and talk to the boy. And all the rest of the school hyped up because it was the last day of term and Christmas coming.

Digby looked at the great Christmas tree in the corner of the hall, and thought of all the Christmases he had spent with Belinda and the girls, and sometimes with Martin and Jean, and how that time seemed a faraway golden age. There were, of course, the last two Christmases when they had gone to a hotel for lunch because Elizabeth didn't know how to cook turkey.

"Happy Christmas, Sir! Great party, Sir!"

"Wonderful news, Stewart. Very well done."

"Thank you, Sir. This is my girlfriend, sir. Melissa."

"Hallo Headmaster!" And Digby knew it all so well, through the music, the decorations and the booze; he knew it all, how Stewart

229

had drunk too much, and how Melissa would not be at all sorry to swap Stewart for himself. "You should be jolly proud of him, Melissa," he said with a smile. And Stewart, perhaps alerted by some sixth sense, or because the beer was beginning to take effect, said quite crossly, "Come *on* Melissa," and dragged her away.

And there was Coles, the rugby coach, dancing drunkenly with a dubious looking red-head, and Elliot too, with whom he had gone to the Andes, with his extraordinarily plain and unpleasant wife, and all sorts of parents, all of whom he had hopefully spoken to. And then they were doing the conga along across the stage and out into the night. How Elizabeth would have enjoyed this! There would have no one in the whole room as desirable as she. "Come on, Diggy," she would have said, "let's dance." And they would have stood up and danced together, and Elizabeth would have danced provocatively, and there would have been a hundred men to envy him, and he would have liked to think they knew that at the end of the night he would go back home and make love to her, once, twice, three times, maybe.

"No, no, I'm too old, Alan." It was Briggs gesturing him to join the line of conga dancers, "but thanks all the same." No more dancing for Elizabeth now, and no dancing ever for Ronnie. Ronnie had not danced at all, unless it be the times he had been chased into bed by his father.

"Ah, Headmaster, a splendid day, a splendid day! You will permit me to join you?" It was, of course, Avonmore, wearing his new suit and what looked exactly like his own striped pyjama top. How extraordinary!

"You see I have my party gear on, Sherwood."

"And very smart you look in it, Harold."

"You would never believe this, Headmaster..."

"No?" Perhaps, oddly, Avonmore would rescue him from his

despair as he had once before. "What wouldn't I believe, Harold?"

"You see this striped shirt of mine, reminiscent perhaps of a *toga praetexta*?"

"If you say so, Harold."

"It's really my pyjama top. There! That came as a surprise!" Avonmore looked at him triumphantly.

"Indeed it did!"

"And what a day, Sherwood! What a day! I think I acquitted myself non sine honore, with my oration!"

And Digby remembered how, after the theatre opening and the lunch and the stealing of the Mars Bar, they had trooped over to the new Classics Library; all the boys who did Classics, and Yvonne and Martin and even Colonel Haslett, who had drunk a bottle of wine at lunch and thought they were all off to a party. And Digby had stood up and made a great speech in praise of Harold, throwing in everything he could think of to feed his vanity, and even producing one of Avonmore's Oxbridge scholars from 1959.

Yvonne had made Stewart and Davies write an oration in Latin and Greek and deliver it, and some of the fourth form had enacted (very badly) a scene from Aristophanes. And Harold had nodded and smiled and even given himself a round of applause before standing up and making his speech. And the boys had all fidgeted and pushed each other and giggled, even the mildest yawning and falling off chairs, and doing the things boys generally did when they were bored. And Harold went on talking about himself for almost an hour, and Digby whispered to Martin and Martin whispered to Yvonne, and they might, Digby reflected, still be there now, if Colonel Haslett had not stood up and asked loudly where the lavatory was. But it was over and Avonmore had been given what he wanted.

"Yes, you were quite splendid," said Digby, smiling his warm and kindly smile.

"Lots of nice young misses here," commented Avonmore, looking round appreciatively. He had had a dance with one. She was the girlfriend of the stupid boy, Stewart. Couldn't think how he got into Oxford. Yes, nice young lady, she'd been, nice dress she'd had on too, clinging to the curves. He'd say he'd cut Stewart out there!

"Can I get you a drink?" asked Digby, although he suspected that Harold had drunk more than enough already.

"Oh no! I have my supplies over there. I'm sitting with the youngsters," and Harold gestured airily into the midst of Stewart and Melissa and all their cronies. "I only came to see how you were; you'll be missing your Elizabeth, I know."

How strange that out of the hundred or so people here, staff, wives, girlfriends, boyfriends, boys, parents, uncle Tom Cobley and all, only Avonmore spoke to him in his distress. No one else, not even Martin had said anything to him to acknowledge his loneliness and unhappiness. Only Avonmore had seen the sexiness of the evening: the women with their low-cut dresses and their short skirts, and boys in their tight jeans, and the drink flowing and the ash-trays full, and the thin veneer of civilised behaviour wearing away and revealing the raw desire within, as thigh touched thigh, and hands brushed against breasts, and mouths touched flesh. Avonmore had seen this and relished it; he had also seen that Digby was not part of it, that he alone did not sit inside this charmed circle.

Had he come, perhaps, to gloat? This, after all, was his last night, for had not Digby decreed last summer that he must go, had he come, then, to enjoy his revenge? Digby did not think so; he believed he had come out of kindness, as he had come to the hospital to offer what he could of the crumbs of the biscuits of kindness.

"Thank you, Harold," he said, "it is very good of you to think of me, especially as I have caused you so much heartache."

Harold was puzzled. "Heartache? What can you mean, Headmaster?"

"Your retirement. I ..."

"Oh that! Oh, I've had a wonderful time ever since I've known. I had, I admit, a night of distress, some physical sickness ..."

"I am so sorry."

"But, after that, right as a trivet. Little Yvonne doing my work and I still on full pay, mark you. And look at my Oxbridge success! Not like the twelve scholars I had in 1959, admittedly, but not bad, not bad. And a whole day of people making speeches ..." Digby smiled, Harold had obviously mentally added the opening of the theatre to the opening of the library. "And tonight! Lots of winsome young ladies. Cut Stewart out!"

"And where is it you are retiring to?"

"Blackpool."

"Oh, do you have relations there, perhaps?" For Digby remembered, all too well, that Harold had no children. A crafty look came into Avonmore's eyes.

"Oh no, I have something better than that. I have a little flat on the front and ..." Harold bent his mouth close to Digby's ear, "it's not everyone I would tell this to, mind ..."

"Yes?" said Digby.

"A telescope!"

"Oh!" said the naive Digby. "I didn't know you were an astronomer."

"Hah!" Avonmore laughed, appreciating the jest. "I shall be looking for my little stars on the beach!"

"Goodness me!" said Digby. He felt quite shocked.

"And now, Headmaster, our ways must part. Salve atque vale!" And off he went. Digby watched him weave an unsteady path across the floor, and experienced almost a feeling of regret for the departure

233

of the old rogue. And he wondered, not for the first time, if he too would in the end become another Avonmore.

Somebody burst a balloon next to him and some girl rushed past him, brushing him with her long hair. He saw her toss it away from her face, as if it were troublesome to her, as Elizabeth used to, but this girl's hair was not like hers, for Elizabeth's hair was longer and more golden, and made her look like a water nymph. Yes, once he had possessed a water nymph, but the waters had closed over and taken her from him.

"May I introduce my sister, Sir? Sally, this is the Headmaster."

"I hope you're enjoying yourself, Sally." said Digby.

"Oh yes," said Sally. Digby reflected, as they passed on their way, that St John had taken all the looks. Perhaps, thought Digby, the sister's ordinariness revealed Davies' own, what did he have but a veneer of good looks and a plausible manner developed from his time at Mowberry? For a few brief seconds he had enjoyed his wife and he, Digby, had made him Head Boy, but his hour had passed. He had been insignificant in office, had failed Oxbridge, and had not even had a girlfriend to bring to the party. He had adopted the Mowberry style, but not its true tenets; those had been understood by Singh and by Stewart, the two he had passed over. But perhaps they had not needed popular acclaim. They proved their worth without it. But once St John left Mowberry he would have nothing, because the world outside would have little interest in the facade. St John would have to develop a new persona. Well, perhaps he would.

"There you are," said a familiar voice, "hiding away in the corner. Yvonne and I have been looking for you all over the shop, haven't we?"

"Well, actually," said Yvonne, and there was a steely edge to her voice, "I would say you'd spent most of the time retracing your steps to the bar."

"Come and sit down," said Digby, "both of you. Did you know," he smiled, "that Harold has bought a telescope especially to look at women on the beach?"

"Good heavens!" said Yvonne, but she did not seem particularly interested.

"I think I'll just get another drink," said Martin, putting a supporting hand on the table.

"Oh, for God's sake!"

"No, for mine," said Martin and he burst out laughing.

"Don't be hard on him, Yvonne," said Digby as they watched Martin weave his way towards the bar. "He very seldom gets drunk, actually."

"I'm not hard on him," said Yvonne. She looked across at Digby and felt instinctively that this was a man to whom you told the truth. She had spoken to no one of Martin and bottled things up for too long. Almost involuntarily she added, "I just don't want to marry him, that's all." And she didn't. She watched him as he stood at the bar, glass in hand, and she knew she neither desired him nor wanted to marry him. This man was not the kind and efficient Second Master of Mowberry she had admired, but a man with little control over himself. But even as she thought this, she knew that Martin's drunken appearance was only part of the story, and that she was inventing a cover for her own disappointment, for she had come to realise that Martin did not want to marry her. A week or so back she had believed he did, had been sure he did, but there had come a change over Martin. She could almost pinpoint the time. It had been after that awful meal at Harold's. Why he had changed, she didn't know. Perhaps her cold goodnight had discouraged him. Perhaps he thought she had wanted to snub him. But somehow she didn't think so. Martin was not the sort of man to lose interest in a woman because she did not ask him back to her flat. He was too much of a gentleman. More likely it was the drink. He had seen her disapproval and judged that he must choose between her and his habit – and had not thought her worth the sacrifice. Or perhaps it was not as crude a choice as that. He had seen his freedom to drink as he liked as the freedom of the unmarried state; he had grown used to it and he liked it. Even her attractiveness was not sufficient inducement. Sex was obviously not high on Martin's list of priorities. After all, he had never even kissed her. Well, then, it was not such a tragedy. There were plenty of other unmarried men in the world. One was sitting opposite her now.

"Well, hello again," said Martin, plonking a pint down, so it swished over the table. "What were you saying about Harold?"

"He's bought a telescope to look at what he calls 'little stars' on the beach at Blackpool," said Digby. And they all laughed, and it seemed for a moment that the laughter had united them and Yvonne's disappointment, Martin's drunkenness and perhaps even Digby's sadness could be dispelled by it. But only for a moment, because Martin leaned forward, putting a hand in the ash-tray and overturning it.

"Purvis told me a funny joke," he said, "I must tell you." And Digby remembered that Martin had a quite uncharacteristic liking for dirty jokes, perhaps that was why he had laughed when Digby had been so furious about Dolores and Duncan in the stables.

"There's this elephant, you see. Well, two elephants ..."

"I do hope, Martin ..." began Digby.

"Shut up, Digs. Now one of these elephants has got the most enormous ..."

"I think," said Digby, glancing at Yvonne, "amusing as, no doubt, this joke is, it lacks a little of your usual subtlety, Martin."

"The fact is," said Yvonne, "you're disgustingly drunk."

"Drunk!"

"Yes," she said decisively. "And I'm glad I've found this out now. I think you know what I mean, Martin."

"Yes, well," said Martin, suddenly quiet. "It's just one of those things, isn't it?" He got up unsteadily, finished off the pint and smiled, and both Digby and Yvonne thought what a nice smile it was, even for a drunken man. "No hard feelings, Yvonne?"

"No," she said, "none." And this time it was she who smiled, and both Digby and Martin thought what a nice smile it was, even for a disappointed woman.

"I think," said Digby, "if Yvonne will excuse me, I'll take you home, Mart."

"No you bloody won't" said Martin. "I can find my own way home, thank you." And he wasn't smiling now.

"Very well," said Digby. In all the years he had known Martin, he had never seen him like this. He was trying to understand it. Was he upset because Yvonne wouldn't marry him, or what? Digby did not know.

"Night," said Martin and they watched him turn round and swing uncertainly through the crowd to the door.

"Old Woody's pretty gone," Digby heard St John Davies say to the plain sister.

"If you'll excuse me," said Digby to Yvonne, and he made his way to the door, but by a circuitous route, round tables and behind couples, so that no one should guess he had gone after Martin.

But when he got to the door he saw Martin walking jauntily down the lighted school drive, nor was he in any way swaying or lurching, but moving in an extremely brisk and purposeful manner, even stopping to pick up some pieces of litter and place them in the litter bin. Now he was heading for his bungalow in the village, nor was there any uncertainty of purpose, and his gait was the gait of a sober man. Digby understood: Martin had set him up.

Chapter 34

Martin had planned it all, thought Digby – as meticulously as he planned the school time-table. And he did not know whether he felt shocked, horrified, amused or overcome by emotion by what his friend had done. The only way he could not treat it was the way in which Martin had intended that he should. For Martin had planned to give him a gift, as he had done, or not done before. Martin had wished to give him Jean but he could not bring himself to do so, and many years after, late at night after a funeral, Martin had indeed given him an even greater gift. And now he intended the greatest gift of all.

As Digby stood in the winter night outside the School Hall, he could hear the rhythmic thump of the music within punctuated by the odd burst of laughter or sound of voices raised in glee. He felt in his pockets and drew out a packet of cigarettes; he was aware that he was doing a politically incorrect thing, and Headmasters were meant to have no vices, but if license could be afforded to the Upper VI tonight, it could certainly be extended to him, who had so much more to bear than any of them.

It was a chilly night, with stars bright in the sky, but Digby did not think of the cold as he stood outside the Hall. Occasionally he moved a little, as the night air struck him.

Had Martin set it up by himself, or had they been in it together? How would it have gone?

"You don't really want to marry me, do you Martin?" She might have said.

"No, Yvonne, but you don't really want to marry me either, you just want to be married. Well, I have a solution."

"What?"

"Yes. You can marry Digby. He's a much better catch than me, anyway. He's got position, money, and he's good-looking, or so I'm told. Wouldn't know about that."

"That's a monstrous thing to suggest; handing me over like a used parcel."

"But you're not a used parcel, I've never touched you. And where is the immorality? You want to be married, and Digby needs a wife. I believe you would suit each other very well. It would be a happy solution for the three of us, don't you think so?" And would he even have brought himself to say it? "I should think that Digby would be a wonderful lover." And Yvonne would have been very angry, but because she was a sensible woman, she would have considered Martin's suggestion, not immediately perhaps, but over hours or days.

"But how could I ... I mean, I hardly know him."

"Leave that to me," Martin would have said.

But no! Digby folded his arms into himself, it was getting cold and the hand that had held the cigarette was numb. Martin would not have plotted with anyone else, the scheme was entirely his, for he alone knew what Digby needed. He had been moved to action by pity for him, and he had known he must make the biggest sacrifice of all.

It was as if, thought Digby, Yvonne was a boat, a boat belonging to Martin and he and Digby had to get to the other side of a turbulent river – always the river – and Martin knew that Digby could not swim, and there was only room in the boat for one. "You take the boat, Digs," he had said, "I may not be a good swimmer, but I shall get across somehow." Oh Martin! And Digby stamped his feet with the cold and the need to kick away the weight of his feeling.

And what about Yvonne in this? She was not an object, she was a woman of character and dignity. What a cynical act of Martin's to think that she could cast off one man and exchange him for another! How humiliating for her to be thought of in those terms! But no, not really. Yvonne was not a naive, impressionable woman like Elizabeth. Martin had merely freed her. She could make up her own mind.

But then, what was it that Martin would want him to do? Would it bring him happiness to have offered him the woman he wanted for himself and who would finally take Digby from him? Would the greatest sacrifice give him the greatest satisfaction, knowing that he, and he alone, had given Digby the only chance of happiness? Would Digby's acceptance be the final consummation of their love? Or would Martin ultimately grow to regret it, to resent it? He didn't know. And, God, he was tired! He threw away the cigarette and returned to the warmth of the hall.

The sudden heat hit him so it hurt, the noise of the music deafened him and the flashing of the lights dazzled him. Perhaps Yvonne would be gone; he had been outside a long time, or so it seemed. Perhaps it was actually only a few minutes. Perhaps she had joined another group, for she would not remain long on her own with her glossy black hair and her attractive ways. And he hoped she would not be there, for then he would not have to accept, or refuse Martin's gift.

"Mr Sherwood! We have been looking for you everywhere."

"Mrs Stewart, how nice to see you again. Mr Stewart, how are you?"

"We just want to say a big thank you for Simon's success." Mrs

Stewart smiled seductively at him. What a good-looking man he was! She expected he would be getting married again soon.

"Yes indeed," said her husband. "We never expected it, you know."

"I did," said the proud mother. "I knew Simon had it in him."

"He's come on splendidly," said Digby. "We're all very proud of him." He thought of Stewart trying to give the kiss of life to Elizabeth.

"And how are you, Mr Sherwood.... such a terrible thing."

"Thank you, I am quite well." There was a pause and the husband cleared his throat and said, "we'd like to thank the new Classics teacher, Miss ... Miss?"

"Bonnington," said Digby.

"We've been looking for her but we don't know who she is!"

"You must let me introduce you," said Digby. "She's just over there." And he led them towards Yvonne, who was still sitting by herself. Her dress, he noticed, fitted her very well. Had Martin chosen it for her – or him?

"Miss Bonnington," said Digby. "May I introduce Mr and Mrs Stewart?" A couple were dancing next to them, and the girl was pulling the boy greedily to her.

"You've done a wonderful job," said Mr Stewart, "Simon was getting nowhere last year. I think he found Mr Avonmore rather intimidating."

"Well, we all have our different methods," said Yvonne, smiling diplomatically.

"Oh, I don't think it was that," said the affronted mother. "It's no good speaking crossly to Simon. Do you know, he even called Simon 'stupid'?" And she brought out the offending word with horrified indignation.

"I saw the chap in a pyjama top just now," added the father.

"Well," said Digby, smiling pleasantly, "Simon gave him a splendid oration this afternoon at the opening of the Classics Library. What a pity you weren't able to be there."

"And how beautifully he has decorated the Hall," added Yvonne. "It was all his own work, you know." And they all looked at Simon's Christmas decorations, or what was left of them, for the Upper VI had now bedecked themselves with most of the tinsel. Avonmore too, Digby noticed, was adorned, wearing the tinsel on his head, rather in the manner of a victorious Olympic athlete.

"Yes, he's very artistic," said the mother, looking around with satisfaction, and Digby knew that, in the mother's eyes, the decorating of the Hall was a much greater feat than the Oxford place.

"Well, we must see about getting him home," said the father, "him and young Melissa. We don't want any shenanigans there!" And he looked with satisfaction towards his son, who was dancing cheek to cheek with his girlfriend, and Digby felt that the father placed a much greater value on his son's sexual prowess than on his Oxford place.

"We just wanted to say thank you," said his mother, the insults to her son assuaged.

"Oh, it was nothing," said Yvonne. "Simon did it all himself really. I just gave him a push in the right direction."

"Well done!" said Digby, as he and Yvonne watched the retreating figures of the Stewarts. "You said all the right things." He wondered how he could part company from her, as she stood pleasantly smiling, at his side. But his natural courtesy forbade any abrupt dismissal of the woman whom his friend had so patently rejected.

"May I get you a drink?" he asked, as St John bopped past them with his plain sister. "Although in view of recent events, it's perhaps not a very tactful request."

"Oh, you mean Martin?" said Yvonne. "I don't really mind. I think it was probably a lucky escape for both of us."

"Yes?" said Digby.

"But I would like to dance," said Yvonne, smiling warmly at him.

"Oh," said Digby, taken aback. "I am afraid I haven't danced since my wife died." And he thought of the night they had spent at Serendipity, that last night, and how pretty she had looked then – and how terribly different she had looked after she had been brought out of the river.

"Oh, of course!" said Yvonne, instantly remorseful. "How stupid and tactless of me! I'm so sorry." And Digby, looking at her, felt remorse too, for had not this woman once already tonight been rejected?

"No," he said, "I was most ungracious. I should love to dance, Yvonne." And as she stood looking doubtful, he added, "please," and he guided her with his arm behind her back to protect her from the wild dancers, and also from the hurt of his own words.

But when they reached the dance floor, the tempo changed and the music became soft and sensual, such was appropriate at that late hour of the night. And Yvonne smiled at him so radiantly that he wondered for a moment if she had instigated Martin's plot, after all. He clasped her lightly, but firmly, in his arms and guided her in amongst the other closely entwined couples.

As Digby held Yvonne, a woman not unlike Jean, and, as they swayed together to the crude and evocative sound of the cheap music, avoiding other couples clinched together more closely than they, he turned many things over in his mind and, as the lights changed from dazzle to darkness, and from darkness to dazzle, he became bemused and a sense of unreality came upon him, and he felt he held now Elizabeth, now Jean, now Martin in his arms, and it seemed to him that Yvonne had become an amalgam of all these different people.

He became aware of the closeness of Yvonne's body; he could even feel her breasts pressing against him. And Digby, who had not held a woman in his arms for six months, felt the immensity of desire upon him, as Martin had, not doubt, known that he would.

"Digby," said Yvonne. And although they both knew that she should have addressed him as headmaster, he merely murmured, "yes?"

"I like this," she said softly, but whether she was responding to the hardness of Digby's body against her, or whether she was referring only to the act of dancing, Digby neither knew nor cared.

Chapter 35

When Martin returned home, he went into the lavatory and relieved himself copiously, for he had drunk his last pint in considerable haste. Then he went into his chaotic kitchen (for Yvonne was no longer there to create order out of chaos). He switched on his computer which he had recently moved in there, to join the majority of his treasured possessions.

He stared at the screen for a while, but its brightness hurt his eyes, so he switched it off and took down the bottle of whisky which stood on the top of the fridge. He removed an unwashed glass from the draining board and poured himself a hefty amount, and sat down at the kitchen table to think.

He thought of the time he and Digby had batted together in the Staff v 1st XI cricket match at Stanstead, and how Digby had shouted 'yes!' at Martin for impossible runs, and yet how they had notched up fifty three together before Digby had run him out. He thought of the time when Duncan's dog had been run over and Digby conducted a funeral service for him in the garden, with Belinda and Jean and the children, and they had buried him under the cherry tree, and how Belinda had made a great tea afterwards, and they had all sat in the garden, his boys playing with Dolores, who ordered them about; but Richenda had sat on her father's lap, scowling at them until Digby had told her all about the special heaven that dogs went to.

There were the nights they sat doing the school timetable together, he drinking beer and Digby some coffee, which Jean brought for him, freshly brewed, for he could not drink instant coffee.

Once they had gone on a walking holiday together and the landlady at the bed and breakfast place had thought they were brothers, and Digby had laughed and Martin had felt affronted, for why should they not be brothers?

They had re-housed the whole school library one Summer holiday, and Digby had been indefatigable, continuing long after Martin had grown tired.

And more recently, they had striven and laboured together to build up Mowberry, walking along by the river arguing and discussing the best course of action for raising money or dealing with an expulsion.

There were the blessed times they had spent sitting in the den together, with so much unspoken between them. And finally Martin thought of the night of the funeral, of the love that had passed between them, and how Digby had found comfort and peace in his arms.

Martin sighed and went off to the lavatory again, and with the flushing of the chain it seemed to him that the past too was being flushed away. For, always before, the past had been part of the present. Elizabeth had not been able to stand between them, nor had Jean, but Yvonne would, because Digby must start a new life, unencumbered by these memories, and then they would belong to Martin alone.

Martin poured out some more whisky and, seeing there was not much left in the bottle, added the rest, and resumed his place at the table, now resting his head on its sticky surface, raising it from time to time, for the glass. From now on he must dispense with the past and face the present.

Digby would not have been able to resist taking Yvonne back

to his house. Then he would have made her coffee in the cafetière and they would talk, the two of them, of this and that, Avonmore, Stewart, perhaps even of himself. And then when the conversation ebbed, would Digby say to Yvonne, with his exquisite politeness, "would you allow me to make love to you, Yvonne?" He would he make any crude move towards her, but would wait for the woman herself to come to him. And Yvonne, seeing Digby so tall and handsome, would assent wordlessly. And they would climb the stairs, were perhaps climbing the stairs at this very moment. And he would take her to his bed … no, he would not take her to the bed where he had lain with Elizabeth, for he had not taken him there, but he would take her to one of the beautiful guest rooms, perhaps the very room in which they had lain together on the night of the funeral. And they would undress quietly, for Digby was in some ways a modest man and shy of his beautiful body. And Yvonne would look at him from the nakedness that Martin could so well imagine, her small round breasts and her cunt covered in the same glossy black hair that lay so smoothly on her head. And he would stand with his magnificent jutting cock, but it would be she who would make the first move towards him, would draw him down onto and into herself, a woman who would not be afraid to welcome him with cries of desire. And Digby, as he thrust, as he thrust the past from him, would be mindful of her pleasure, even as Martin would have been and, at last, when Digby had cried out his very soul with the relief of deliverance, there would be a quietness.

Martin raised his head from the table and removed his glasses because they were all blurred with crying, and a harder thought was still to come: he must imagine Digby asleep afterwards in a sort of innocence, for the disruptive thing would now have passed from him, and now he could lie sweet and vulnerable, as Richard or Duncan had lain, as children or young boys.

And would she guard Digby as he had done through the dark watches of the night lest his sleep be troubled, or the chill air strike him? He thought she would not, for she was a woman and women slept soundly, folded into themselves once their bodies had been satisfied.

Well, that was the way he had known it must be.

Martin replaced his glasses and reached for his Italian lizard notes. It seemed to him a proper thing to look through them now, even though he would have a great deal of empty time, even the rest of his life, to devote to his book about reptiles.

Lightning Source UK Ltd.
Milton Keynes UK
UKOW04f2206211113

221582UK00009B/371/P